SECRETS

Recent Titles by Jane Adams from Severn House

The Naomi Blake Mysteries

MOURNING THE LITTLE DEAD
TOUCHING THE DARK
HEATWAVE
KILLING A STRANGER
LEGACY OF LIES
SECRETS

The Rina Martin Mysteries

A REASON TO KILL
FRAGILE LIVES
THE POWER OF ONE
RESOLUTIONS
THE DEAD OF WINTER
CAUSE OF DEATH

SECRETS

A Naomi Blake Novel

Jane A. Adams

severn
House

This first world edition published 2013
in Great Britain and the USA by
SEVERN HOUSE PUBLISHERS LTD of
19 Cedar Road, Sutton, Surrey, England, SM2 5DA.

British Library Cataloguing in Publication Data

Adams, Jane, 1960-
  Secrets. – (A Naomi Blake mystery ; 8)
  1. Blake, Naomi (Fictitious character)–Fiction.
  2. Ex-police officers–Fiction. 3. Blind women–Fiction.
  4. Detective and mystery stories.
  I. Title II. Series
  823.9'2-dc23

ISBN-13: 978-0-7278-8290-5 (cased)

All Severn House titles are printed on acid-free paper.

Severn House Publishers support The Forest Stewardship Council [FSC],
the leading international forest certification organisation. All our titles that
are printed on Greenpeace-approved FSC-certified paper carry the FSC logo.

MIX
Paper from
responsible sources
FSC® C013056

Typeset by Palimpsest Book Production Ltd.,
Falkirk, Stirlingshire, Scotland.
Printed and bound in Great Britain by
TJ International Ltd, Padstow, Cornwall

PROLOGUE

'There's a man with a gun standing in my garden. I want something done about it.'

A beat of shocked silence met this pronouncement and Molly sighed in exasperation. 'Did you hear me? I said there's a man in my garden—'

'Yes, madam, I did hear. Can you give me your address, please and we'll get someone right there.'

'Beldon Avenue, number twelve. Not that it is an avenue, you understand, it's a cul-de-sac. I'm right at the end. The big house with the high hedges, right at the end. And my name is Mrs Chambers.'

Molly could hear the sound of a keyboard rattling and a woman's voice checking details.

'Madam, are you sure he has a gun?'

'Oh, for goodness sake,' Molly exploded. 'Young woman I have lived long enough and seen enough to know a gun when one is waved in my direction.'

This was a slight exaggeration. So far the young man in the garden had simply stood uncertainly, with the weapon slightly raised. Molly cursed the dusk and her own failing sight; had either been clearer she could have issued a more exact description.

'At you? He's pointing the gun at you?' That last seemed to have got the call handler's attention, Molly noted with a degree of satisfaction. Sometimes one just had to overstate the case. It was the only way to get attention in these desperately hyperbolic times.

'Madam, do you believe yourself to be in immediate danger?'

'Young woman, I consider that to be a very stupid question. In my experience, and contrary to what so many idiots tend to believe, guns do not equal security.'

'Please madam, if you could just—'

Molly sighed. 'My dear young lady, I've already made certain I'm not in his sight line. I'm upstairs in the front, that is the master bedroom. I have a clear view of him, but he not of me.'

'And are the doors and windows locked? Madam, there are officers on their way as we speak. They are just minutes away.'

'My dear,' Molly said with heavy irony. 'Unless one lives in some kind of bunker, then the act of closing windows or locking doors will do little to stop a bullet.'

During the conversation she had moved back from the window and no longer had the young man in her view. She returned, now, swearing softly to herself in Swahili, a language she had always considered very suited to such a purpose.

'Madam? Mrs Chambers? Are you all right?'

'He's gone,' Molly said sharply. 'He must have gone round to the back of the house while I was talking to you.'

'Officers will be with you very shortly,' the call handler said, though Molly could hear the tension in her voice. That and a little bit of doubt.

She thinks I'm off my rocker, Molly thought. She thinks I imagined the whole thing.

Had she locked her back door?

True, as she had told the young woman, if someone with a gun wanted to shoot off the lock, then there was little she could do to stop them, but if she'd been so forgetful as to leave the door undone and thereby made it easy for him, well then she really would feel foolish.

'I can hear the sirens,' she said.

'Good, that's good, Mrs Chambers. Just hang in there for a couple of minutes more. Officers will be with you in no time at all.'

She could hear something else, Molly thought as she turned from the window to face the bedroom door. The sirens were louder now, blanketing that smaller but unmistakable sound of footsteps on the stairs.

Molly straightened, squared her shoulders and lowered the phone. Dimly, she could hear the young woman on the end of the line calling her name.

Slowly, the bedroom door opened and Molly gazed upon the apparition that stood there. For a moment she was more puzzled than afraid, her senses telling her something impossible was happening.

'Oh,' Molly said. 'It's you.'

Sirens so close now as the cars sped into the cul-de-sac. The sound of the young woman calling out her name. Then everything overwhelmed by the blast of the gunshot as the noise echoed and resounded through the house.

ONE

Molly Chambers sat on one side of the kitchen table and regarded her honorary nephew with some small disdain. 'I'm fine,' she said. 'I don't want anyone fussing over me and I certainly don't need your advice, Alec.'

'I'm not offering advice. I just came to make sure you were OK. That's all.'

'Because your mother was making a fuss.'

'Because, odd as it may sound, we actually care about you, Molly. Mum just thought you might want to go and stay for a few days.'

Molly harrumphed, but she seemed to accept that with reasonable grace. 'I understand you've resigned from your job,' she said. 'What do you plan to do now?'

Alec managed to hide the smile. Molly did so disapprove of people not *doing*. 'I've resigned, yes. I've not decided what is next.'

'You'll need to earn a living.'

'I've money in the bank. I've got time to make some decisions. First thing is to get the house sold. We don't feel we can live there any longer.'

'Why?'

'Because finding a dead body in your kitchen sort of ruins the atmosphere,' Alec told her.

'I had a man shoot himself on my landing,' Molly pointed out. 'Brains all over my stair carpet. You don't find me running away. This is my home and I'm not letting an incident like that drive me out of it. Neither should you.'

'It's not a competition, Aunt Molly. It isn't a case of who's had the worst case of violent death happen in their living room. It's a matter of, well it's a matter of it being time to move on.'

'Have you *tried* to get bloodstains out of an oak floor? I got some specialist in, someone the crime scene person recommended. Even *they* couldn't get all the bloodstains out.'

Alec said nothing. He saw her purse her lips and twitch her shoulders, squaring them ready for battle again. Molly had lived an eventful life, he knew. A girl in Kenya during the Mau Mau uprising and then the wife of a diplomat who seemed to specialize in setting up shop in whatever happened to be the fashionable theatre of war for that year, Molly had led a nomadic and edgy existence. This house was the first really settled spot. Now death had come calling even here.

'Show me,' he said. 'I might be able to suggest something.'

Molly shrugged. 'Oh, I've got a man coming to fit a new stair carpet,' she said. 'I've said he can do the landing and the spare bedroom while he's about it. And I've scrubbed the walls. I'll get the decorators in. I'd do it myself, but I think I'm getting a bit too old to be climbing ladders.

Alec could feel a hint behind the words, but Molly was far too direct to merely hint.

'Of course, you could always come and do it for me now you're not at work.'

'I could,' Alec agreed. 'If you want a bad job doing and gloss from here to Christmas. You'd be better asking Naomi. She may not be able to *see* the wall but she'd make a far better job of putting paint on it.'

Molly harrumphed again. Alec knew she was never quite sure how to deal with what she saw as his wife's disability. Molly would say things like 'I think she copes wonderfully' and 'She's quite remarkable, considering' but she found it very hard to comprehend just how independent Naomi really was. She also found it distasteful for Alec to make what she saw as a joke about another's misfortune.

He had expected a rejoinder, but for the moment, it seemed, she would let it pass. Molly led the way up the stairs and Alec followed.

'I've had to get rid of the carpet on the top flight,' she told him, pointing at the bare treads and the naked boards on the landing. 'I borrowed one of those retractable knives from Mr Johnson, next door, and cut the carpet away. I didn't make the best job, though. Carpet fibres are tougher than you might think.'

Alec nodded, looking at the rather uneven edge that Molly's efforts had left. 'I think I can at least manage to tidy that up,' he offered. 'Do you still have the knife?'

Molly snorted. 'Of course not,' she said. 'I took it straight back once I'd finished with it. But he's a decent sort, Mr Johnson. He'll probably lend it to you if you ask.' She sighed, then, 'Just look at the state of these floorboards.'

Alec looked. Old boards, wide and long as reflected the age of the house. Someone had taken a sander to sections of them in an effort to remove the stains that had been absorbed into the grain of the wood. Frankly, Alec thought, it would have been better with a good scrub and a pot of wood stain. 'I think covering them over is your only option,' he agreed. 'It's a bit of a mess, isn't it? Who sanded them? Surely not the person the CSI suggested?'

'Oh, that was me,' Molly admitted. 'I borrowed a little sander thing from Mr Johnson. He had a bigger one, but didn't think I'd be able to handle it. Of course, being a gentleman, he offered to come in and give it a go himself, but I wasn't having any of that. I've always shifted for myself and I'm not going to start accepting charity now.'

Alec was amused. 'Unless it's from me and it's painting your walls?'

'Oh,' Molly waved a dismissive hand. 'That's different. You're practically family and anyway, Mr Johnson goes to work all week, I'm not going to interrupt his weekends.'

Alec let that pass. His gaze travelled from floor to walls – she'd had a good go at those too, scrubbing away at the wallpaper until the stripes had all but disappeared. 'You must have been scared,' he said thoughtfully, expecting some smart rejoinder. Instead, Molly met his gaze, the blue eyes steely and amused, but the little twitch at the corner of her mouth told him that she had, indeed, been scared and the memory of her own fear disturbed her far more than the strange death on her landing.

Molly didn't *do* scared. Never had. It had come as a shock to her, Alec realized, that she was even capable of such an emotion.

'Let's go down,' Alec said.

They settled once more at the kitchen table and Molly fetched two glasses and a bottle of brandy from the kitchen drawer. Alec smiled. She'd always kept two glasses and a bottle in her kitchen drawer, whatever house she'd lived in. He remembered as a little boy he'd been allowed to keep his own little brandy bottle, filled with pop, beside her alcoholic beverage and the second glass had temporarily become his.

Molly set the glasses down and splashed rather too generous measures of spirits into them.

'I'm driving,' Alec reminded her.

'You can at least make a pretence,' she said. 'Take a sip or two and make an old woman feel she's not drinking alone.'

'You aren't old, Molly.'

'Damned fool. Of course I am. Getting older by the day and resenting it more by the hour.' She lifted her glass. 'To the lost ones,' she said. As she always had, even in the days when Alec toasted in bright red pop. She waited, expectantly.

'May they find their way home,' Alec completed. He sipped at his drink, letting it evaporate on his tongue, watching as Molly gulped half of hers down. He had asked only once who the lost ones were. Molly had not replied, but there had been something in her eyes, some pain that even a small boy was capable of understanding and which prevented him from asking ever again. He thought about it now; decided against.

'You're right,' Molly said. 'I was scared. When we moved here I thought we'd left those days behind us. I'd seen a lifetime's worth of killing even before I was twenty-five and married Edward. I saw several lifetimes more in the years we had together. I never thought it would come to find me here.'

'What would come to find you, Molly?'

She shook her head, took another swig of her brandy and laughed. 'I'd thought the next time the reaper showed up it would be a personal call to collect yours truly,' she said. 'I never expected him to send an emissary with a gun.'

'Did he threaten you directly?' Alec asked cautiously, surprised at the sudden frankness and knowing that Molly could clam up without warning.

She swirled the remains of the brandy in the glass. 'A man with a gun is always a threat to those close to him,' she said obliquely. 'If you mean, did he point it at me, then yes, but only briefly. I think he wanted me to share the moment with him, to feel what he felt before he blew out his own brains and spared mine.'

Alec frowned. It was an odd thing to say even for Molly. 'What do you mean?' he asked, knowing even as the words fell out of his mouth that they were the wrong ones.

'Oh, for goodness' sake, man, I'm not speaking in Swahili. Or do you not comprehend plain English now?'

She got up and stuffed the brandy bottle back into the kitchen drawer. 'You ought to go,' she said. 'That wife of yours will be wondering where you've got to.'

'Naomi will be fine,' Alec said, but he knew he'd been dismissed and that he should obey. He'd overstepped some invisible line and Molly would say no more.

'Molly,' he asked as they reached the front door. 'Who's the officer in charge of the investigation?'

'Oh, someone called Barnes,' she said. 'Looked far too young to be an inspector. There was an even younger sergeant too, wanted me to call her Delia and kept asking me if I felt all right.' She inclined her cheek towards Alec and received his kiss.

'You've got my mobile number if you need me,' Alec confirmed.

'Of course I do.'

'And I'll call back and see you later in the week.'

'If you feel the need,' Molly said, but Alec knew she'd be glad to see him if he did. He also knew she'd be back in the kitchen and finishing his brandy before he'd left her drive.

Alec left, his head filled with misgivings. Something wasn't right here, something apart from the fact that a young man, as yet unidentified, had blown out his brains in such spectacular fashion. For the moment, Alec couldn't place what it was, but the sense of unease was stronger than that merely prompted by obvious circumstance.

Molly had almost told him something, Alec thought, but he'd made a wrong response and she had shut him out.

TWO

There were three teams of five. Each team had minimal contact with the others and also limited contact with the controller. In the event of anything going wrong each member had been issued with a passport, a legend and money in an offshore account. However it went down, immediately their part in the game was all over, they would disperse and, in all likelihood, that would be it. They would not see one another again and control would effectively erase their involvement from what few records had been kept. This was the way it had been organized for more years than Bud could guess at. He had been recalled twice, so far, so three very profitable jobs in total. He had no idea and didn't really care if this would be the last time or not. He'd be quite content to be forgotten after this.

Not that anything was ever truly forgotten, of course, Bud knew that. There were always those few record-keepers who had oversight of everything. The collators and gatekeepers whose sole purpose, the focus of whose existence was to keep the books on everything and everyone. *They* would not forget.

But this job was not going to go wrong. Months of planning, Bud had begun to suspect even years of pre-planning had gone into this and though he had never worked with any of his team of five before, they had gelled quickly. Even Ryan, with his sandy hair and freckles and ready grin, who looked like he should still be in school, operated with the same cool and efficiency as the rest of them.

Ryan was the only one of the team that he wondered about. He seemed too young to be this good at the game. But, then, Bud thought, you never knew about people, not really.

The road was narrow here, and midway between the two villages. Upper and Lower Stow were pretty but unremarkable locations, built in the local, Cotswold stone and Upper Stow still having a pub and a post office. Lower Stow was little more than a hamlet.

At this point between the villages the road narrowed and curved so any vehicle coming upon them would be unable to see the road works sign until they had turned the corner. Then they'd come up, suddenly, upon a young man with a stop-go sign and a reflective jacket and see the road half closed off with cones.

They'd been there about a half hour before the right car arrived. One of the local cars that had passed by had stopped and asked Ryan, the stop-go man, what they were going to dig up.

'Not digging up, mate, filling in. Council's sent us out to deal with some of the pot holes.'

'About time too.' The driver left with a cheerful wave at Ryan and Bud and the rest of them unloading the van. He was followed by a tractor and a blue hatchback.

Bud frowned at the little procession of vehicles as they passed him by. They were all on his mental list, all residents living within a few miles of the roadblock and just out on regular business, their activities having been checked and tagged over the preceding weeks, but he was still far from happy. They could do without additional traffic. He was relieved when the radio call came in a few minutes later, from a member of the second team telling them that their target was on its way and that there was nothing else on the road.

The unassuming black estate car came around the bend a few minutes later, right on schedule. It stopped obediently at the sign, the driver staring through the windscreen and down the road at the clearly empty lane ahead.

The boy with the sign grinned at him and then followed his gaze as though he too was checking to see the absence of traffic coming the other way.

Impatient, now, the driver lowered his window.

'Come on, man, let us through. There's nothing there.'

Ryan, still grinning, turned his sign around and the driver prepared to move away. The sight of Bud, pointing a gun at him through the side window changed his mind.

'Drive on, just drive on!' The rear seat passenger yelled at the driver and then shrank back into his seat as Bud glanced at him.

'If you'll be kind enough to get out, now.' Ryan was still smiling, but he had dropped his sign and he too held a gun.

The driver lifted his hands from the steering wheel and slowly eased himself out of the vehicle as Bud, helpfully, opened the door. The passenger needed a little more persuasion, but a few seconds later, he too had been herded into the rear of the van. The stop sign was thrown in after them. Bud closed the door and nodded to Ryan. A third member of the team now drove the car slowly forward, while the remaining two gathered the cones and stowed them in the boot. Bud hopped into the passenger seat of the van and belted up, glancing across as Ryan opened the valve that would bleed the gas into the sealed rear compartment.

It wouldn't kill anyone, but it would shut them up for a while.

Seconds later the van moved off, the car with the remaining three of the team following on behind.

A mile further on, at a T-junction, the car went left and the van right. Bud and Ryan passed through Upper Stow at two thirty in the afternoon and drove on, out into open country once again. Ryan fiddled with the radio, trying to find a classical station, crunching the gears as he changed down.

'Crap gearbox on this thing,' he complained cheerfully. 'Right, another few minutes and we say goodbye.'

Bud nodded. There was no sound from the back of the van. He assumed the two passengers were still alive, but wasn't that interested. He wasn't paid to speculate. He could feel Ryan looking at him, maybe indulging in a little bit of his own speculation, but the younger man said nothing and after a moment, returned his focus to the road ahead.

Bud slipped on a pair of thin, latex gloves and took a bottle of gel cleanser from his pocket. He poured a little into the palms of his gloved hands and rubbed it over everything he might have touched.

Ryan laughed. 'You know they're going to torch this thing, don'cha?'

'I know.'

'You always this cautious, man?'

'Twice your age and still around, Ryan boy. Work it out for yourself.'

Ryan laughed, but he glanced uneasily at the little bottle of gel. Pointedly, Bud placed it on the dashboard.

'It's there if you want it,' he said. Yes, he was always this cautious, he thought. In fact, he didn't think he was cautious enough. There would still be trace, still be something he'd not thought of.

They drove on in silence, Bud comfortable with that, but he could sense that Ryan, now the excitement was nearly over, wanted to talk. That was understandable. Ryan was young, like as not, this was his first big job, but talking, even with another member of the team, that was a bad thing. It could be a very bad thing.

'Mind if I offer you some advice?'

'You can offer.'

'Don't get drunk, don't pick up any girls and don't talk to strangers. Not tonight. Not for the next week or so. Get yourself on a train or a boat or a bus, buy yourself a ticket to somewhere you've never been and you're never likely to go again. Give yourself three or four clear days before you pick up any plans you might have had. Then whatever plans you might have had, even if you've mentioned them to no one, even if you've not even thought them through in your own head, change them. Do something else.'

Ryan laughed, a short, sharp uneasy sound. 'Man, but you're paranoid.'

Bud smiled. 'This is where we get off,' he said, indicating the sign for a lay-by up ahead. Two cars had been parked, the keys to both lay in Bud's pocket. He took them out, now, and offered them both to Ryan as the young man pulled the van in behind the parked cars. Ryan took a set without looking and Bud, getting out of the van, was satisfied to note that he had pulled on a pair of gloves and was cleaning down as Bud had done.

Bud paused before moving out from behind the van, wondering where the next team was located. They'd be close by, take the van as soon as Bud and Ryan moved away. He glanced at the key in his hand, matched it to the ageing Mondeo. Ryan was out of the van now, glancing back inside as though to check he'd not forgotten anything. His smile had faded, the first faint traces of anxiety showing in his eyes.

Bud nodded at him. 'Watch yourself,' he said and then strode off towards his designated car, checking the petrol gauge as he turned on the ignition. As expected, it was full. He still wore the rubber gloves he'd put on in the van and he left them on now. Flesh-coloured, no one would notice them at a casual glance. Not that his fingerprints were in the police system. They had been, once, a very long time ago, when he'd been Ryan's age or maybe a bit younger. He saw Ryan getting into his own car as he pulled away and turned back the way they'd come and, as he drove further down the road, saw, or thought he saw a figure slip into the van.

But he shrugged his shoulders and put the whole thing out of his mind. Ten miles on and he was drinking coffee and eating a burger and making use of the free WiFi to check his designated bank account. By the time he'd drained his coffee cup, the designated account had been emptied, the money shifting out into a dozen other accounts, each one a part of a shell company with more layers to their business than the average onion. One thing he'd learnt back when he was Ryan's age was to employ a good accountant.

Bud got up, tipped the remainder of his meal into the bin, his mind already elsewhere. Scotland was lovely at this time of the year, he thought, he could pick up his gear and lose himself up there for a few weeks. After that? Well after that would take care of itself.

THREE

It hadn't taken long for Alec to track down DI Barnes and the sergeant called Delia. He told the desk sergeant he was a relative of Molly Chambers – an almost truth – and that he was former DI Friedman, rather than just plain Mr – a definite truth, but not necessarily a helpful one. After a half-hour wait in reception, a young woman came through the glass doors and introduced herself as Sergeant Myers.

'You must be Delia?' Alec guessed.

She nodded, eyeing him thoughtfully as they shook hands. 'Mrs Chambers preferred to keep things formal,' she said.

'She would. I'm Alec Friedman. I was DI Friedman until about a month ago.'

She nodded again and Alec guessed that she'd already looked him up. She confirmed this by saying, 'You've had an interesting time this past year. I'm not surprised you went.'

Alec wasn't sure if that was sympathy or reprimand. This woman was an embryonic Molly, he thought. He followed her through to the back office and into a side room where a man with greying hair and dark brown eyes sat behind a desk. A kettle rattled as though it was about to boil. The man half rose and reached across the desk to shake Alec's hand. 'DI Barnes,' he said. 'Take a seat. So you're related to Mrs Chambers?'

'An honorary nephew,' Alec said. 'I think my mother is a second cousin once removed or some such. You know how it is with families?'

Barnes nodded, but Alec could feel that he still wasn't sure. 'So, what can I do for you?' he asked.

'Do you take sugar? We've got reasonable tea or bloody awful instant coffee,' Delia Myers asked.

Alec went for the tea. 'Any progress on identification?'

'No. Nothing. He appeared, shot himself. That's all we knew on the night it happened and apart from a few vital statistics that's all we have now.'

'Molly said he was a young man.'

'Best guess, from forensic analysis is older than twenty-five and less than forty. If asked to guess I'd say late twenties, but it was hard to tell. There was almost nothing left of the face. He was fit, looked like he worked out, had broken his collar bone at some point, probably as a child and his left arm in the past year or so. He'd had a tooth filled with an amalgam that's popular in Eastern Europe, but no longer in use here, other than that . . . well as I say, there wasn't a lot left that could be useful to us.'

'One small tattoo on his right arm.' Delia Myers sat down next to Alec.

'Oh?'

'Don't get excited. Just some sort of Celtic knotwork. It could mean anything and nothing. Oh and he had a scar on his right forearm, on the inside. Long and rather jagged, like it had needed stitching but hadn't been according to the doc.' She shrugged. 'That's about it.'

Alec sipped at his tea. He was a little surprised at the detail they had surrendered to him. Usually investigators were a little chary of talking so openly, even if the other party did happen to be an ex-policeman. The tone of the conversation chimed with the odd tone he had noted from Molly's earlier.

'So,' he said. 'What's really bothering you then? Apart from the obvious violent death.'

He saw the exchange of glances, but knew they'd made up their mind to tell him even before he'd entered the room.

'Did Mrs Chambers give any indication that she might have known the man?'

Alec looked from one to the other. 'What makes you think that? Did she say so?'

'Not exactly,' DI Barnes told him, 'but there is this.'

He reached for a digital recorder that Alec had noticed lying on the desk and pressed play. Alec listened to what he realized must have been Molly's call to the police. 'There's a man with a gun standing in my garden,' Molly said.

Alec listened as the call unfolded, the initial disbelief of the call controller and Molly's calm voice, edged with impatience that she wasn't being listened to. The controller calling her name as Molly must have lowered the receiver, a sound of something being said on Molly's end of the phone and then a bang, followed by silence.

The call seemed to end after that, with only the controller's voice on the line.

'She hung up?' Alec asked, puzzled.

'She says she dropped the phone, then kicked it under the bed as she panicked and ran down the stairs. The first officer attending found it broken on the floor,' DI Barnes told him.

'We've had the latter part of the call cleaned up,' Delia said. 'And Molly's voice isolated.'

Barnes pressed the play button again. At first all Alec could hear was the controller's voice trying to get her back on the line and then he heard Molly, not clearly but nevertheless unmistakably.

'Oh,' Molly said. 'It's you.'

'It's you,' Delia repeated, just in case Alec had missed the point. 'She recognizes him.'

Alec sat back and frowned at the little recording device. 'You've asked her what she meant?'

'And she told us she just thought she recognized him for a moment. That he looked like someone she had known when she was young and that she was shaken and scared and she got mixed up.'

'And that could be the case,' Alec said.

'Yes it could,' DI Barnes agreed. 'I can understand a moment of confusion when someone points a gun at you. But—' He shrugged.

Alec nodded. Molly had sounded so calm. Surprised, yes, but suddenly unafraid as though she'd been expecting something terrible to happen and was abruptly relieved. Molly had known the young man who had broken into her house and killed himself in such dramatic fashion. Alec was certain of that.

So why wouldn't she say who he was? Why the prevarication? Molly was direct to the point of bluntness; sometimes painfully honest. Why would she lie?

He was aware of the other two watching him carefully.

'She's withholding evidence,' DI Barnes said.

Alec was momentarily nonplussed. 'Maybe so, but this is a suicide. He killed himself, so—'

'So he killed himself. But it occurred to us that men with guns rarely just appear in someone's garden. They usually have history and so we looked for that history. The weapon had been used before. Twice – and those two incidents are definitely not suicides. There are two open murder enquiries, Alec, both linked to the same weapon so possibly to the same man. If he was the killer then we'd like to know; that way at least we know we can stop looking. If he's not, well.'

'And if your aunt is withholding evidence pertinent to two murder investigations, then that's a whole new ball game,' Delia said quietly. 'Alec, if you could get her to talk to you?'

'I don't know anyone that can get Molly to talk when she has decided not to,' Alec said. 'But I can try.' He thought for a moment. 'Look, I know I'm a civilian now, but if I could have access to the files, if I could know what I'm actually talking about, I might be able to put some pressure on.'

Again that exchange of glances, but again Alec knew that the decision had already been made. DI Barnes got up and indicated the now vacant chair. He produced a laptop computer from the desk drawer and set it on the desktop.

'Help yourself to tea or coffee,' he said. 'I'll have a sandwich sent in. Obviously, nothing can leave this office, but—'

Alec nodded his thanks and settled himself behind the desk. Oh, Molly, he thought, just what have you got yourself into?

FOUR

It was late afternoon when Alec returned to the hotel he and Naomi had been staying in, much later than he had expected to be and long enough after his expected return to make him feel guilty. As he had reminded Molly, Naomi was extremely independent and she and her big black guide dog well able to look after one another but still, he thought, she was in a strange place and didn't know anyone.

He and Naomi – and Napoleon, her big black guide dog – had been essentially nomadic for the past couple of months. Their house had attracted a few viewings and did have someone willing to make a cash offer – for somewhat less than they wanted. Alec was pretty sure they would agree to take it in the end; a house with the history theirs now had wasn't the easiest to sell at any time and the market wasn't exactly buoyant at the moment. They had stayed at a friend's place for a while and then decided to travel, without any clear aim in mind. The past six weeks had been a slow meander west, then south, then north again, visiting stately homes and antique shops – Naomi had a love of small silver, tactile pieces – and visiting friends and even acquaintances they'd not seen in years. House hunting too, in a random sort of way. If Alec spotted something interesting in an estate agent's window, they had gone to view it, but nothing had really felt right yet. The truth was, he thought, they didn't really know where they wanted to be. Apart from friends and family, they had nothing tying them to any specific place.

He parked his car in the awkward little space at the end of the hotel drive and made his way inside. They had chosen places to stay that were dog friendly, small enough for Naomi to find her way around very quickly, but large enough so that she didn't feel too exposed and could escape back to their room without anyone really taking notice. Their specific requirements had been the one thing that had directed their journeying. If they found an appropriate hotel, they went there, regardless of the location.

They would have to make some solid decisions soon, Alec supposed, but he wasn't sure when either of them would be ready to do that and he blessed the bequest of a beloved uncle that had left them with sufficient resources to ease any immediate pressure.

He ran up the short flight of steps outside the Edwardian hotel, once an impressive home for a mill owner called Fredericks they had been told, and was surprised to have Napoleon come to greet him in the hall.

'Hello, old man, where is she then?' He bent and stroked the dog's silky ears. The dog wasn't wearing his harness, which meant he was off duty; had it been otherwise he would not have left Naomi's side. Alec took this as a good sign. Naomi was obviously comfortable here.

'In here,' she called and he followed the big black dog back into the hotel bar. Naomi sat on a high stool, a cafetière and two cups on the bar top. A woman Alec didn't recognize sat on another bar stool and the hotel owner leaned against the rear wall, slowly polishing the already sparkling glasses. From the look of them, they'd all been there chatting for some time. Naomi was evidently relaxed and happy and so Alec relaxed too and shed the guilt that had been building as he drove back.

He took his wife's hand and kissed her. 'Sorry I was so long.'

'That's OK, I know what it's like when relatives get to reminiscing. This is Liz Trent, she's a local historian, writes books and also makes pots. We've had a lovely hour or two.'

Alec looked with interest at the other woman. She was tall, he guessed. She looked tall even sitting down. Her hair was defiantly white, as though it had skipped both the grey and silver stages. It was swept back into a silver clip at the nape of her neck. Her skin, pale and very English Rose, was still smooth, apart from the deep laughter lines around her grey green eyes. He guessed she must be in her mid-fifties and Alec found himself thinking that she must have been quite a beauty in her younger days. He extended a hand.

'Pleased to meet you. What sort of things do you write about?'

The woman called Liz smiled broadly. 'Whatever interests me,' she said. 'And when I can't think what to write I go and fire a few more pots. I like experimental glazes. The crystalline sort that have a massive failure rate and give me about one pot in four that actually does what I want it to.'

Alec laughed, a little bewildered. 'And how does that fit in with the history writing?'

She positively beamed at him now and Alec realized he had inadvertently hit on just the right question.

'Liz tries to recreate historically accurate glazes,' Naomi said. 'A great many recipes are completely lost, apparently.'

'You'd be amazed what went into them,' Liz said. 'But I think I've bored your wife long enough. Time to be off and I'll drop a copy of my book in. Alec can read it to you.' She laughed and hopped off the bar stool, then shook Alec's hand again.

He'd been right, she was tall, matching his own six feet two. She took Naomi's hand and patted it. 'Lovely to chat,' she said. 'I hope we'll meet again while you're still here.'

'And do we hope that too?' Alec asked quietly as Liz strode out of the door.

'Actually, I wouldn't mind. She's a bit intense, but she's really interesting. I've had a very funny afternoon.'

'Funny ha ha?'

'Funny ha ha, yes. And you?'

'More funny peculiar.' Alec sighed and took the seat Liz had vacated. 'Do you want a drink?'

'No, I'll wait until dinner. You sound as if you need one, though.'

'You could say that. When do you want to eat?'

'Soon, I'm starving. I bet you are too. Dealing with Molly always makes me hungry.'

'Not just Molly,' Alec said. He ordered a Scotch and sipped it before adding the ginger. He could see the moue of disapproval on Naomi's lips as she heard him pour it. She was of the opinion that if it was good enough to drink, then you took your whisky neat. If it wasn't good enough to drink in its pure form it was best left on the shelf.

Alec glanced at his watch. 'Want an early dinner?' he asked. 'I think I've earned it.'

Naomi reached for his hand and he clasped her fingers. 'You really should choose your pretend relatives with a bit more care,' she said.

'So how was she,' Naomi asked, feeling for her fork and turning her plate on Alec's instructions so that her vegetables were on the left and the chicken on the right.

'Oh, she's all right. No, that's not right. She's coping, but I think she was really frightened and I think that annoys her.'

Naomi laughed. 'It would,' she agreed. 'So, what *did* keep you? I can't see Molly wanting you there all afternoon.'

'No, I was dismissed when I made some faux pas I still can't identify. I went to see the investigating officers. They showed me the case files.'

'Oh?' An ex-serving officer herself, Naomi was immediately curious. Before she had been blinded, Naomi and Alec's career's had run roughly parallel. In his more analytical moments, Alec acknowledged that she'd actually been more ambitious than he had and would probably have ended up at a higher rank, had the accident not happened.

'They still don't know who he was,' Alec said. 'But they are pretty sure that Molly did, only she's decided not to tell.'

'Why on earth would she decide that?'

'Why indeed,' Alec said. Briefly, he filled her in on what DI Barnes and his sergeant had told him and what files they had permitted him to read. 'It's all a bit of a mess,' he said. 'Even for Molly this is odd. Whatever else she might be she's usually honest. If she's keeping something back she must feel she has a damned good reason.'

'And the two murders. You said two people had been shot with the same gun. What links them?'

'As yet, nothing. The first was eight weeks ago and the second ten days after that. Shooting number one was a man called . . .' he paused and felt in his pocket for his notebook, slid the elastic band aside and flicked through the pages. 'Ah, yes, Arthur Fields. He imported antiques, from the Far East, mostly. Specialized in Chinese porcelain and had a house out Stamford way He was in his late seventies and a member of the Rotary club. A school governor and a magistrate. He was shot once, in the head. The shot came through his kitchen window. They reckon whoever took the shot was bloody professional. It was dark outside, the shooter was looking into a lighted window, through old glass, you know, that mullioned stuff with the bullseye sections, so the parallax would have been a swine. But the shot was clean and from, they think, about a hundred and fifty feet away. They are assuming the sniper was up a tree at the end of the garden as that's about the only way he'd have got a clean shot.'

'And the second.'

'A younger business man. Name of Herbert Norris. Jamaican father, English mother, ran a little shop that sold vintage lighting in Newark, that's Nottinghamshire, apparently. Barnes tells me there are a lot of antique shops there . . .'

'And dog friendly hotels?' Naomi smiled at the evident bribe.

'I'm sure we can find something. Norris was thirty-seven. Again, no record. He'd been running the shop for eight years, unmarried, though it seems he had an on-off girlfriend for most of that time. She found his body.'

'Poor woman,' Naomi said. 'And no links to Arthur Fields.'

'Nothing yet. Herbert Norris was shot in his flat, above the shop. There were no signs of forced entry and the shot was at close range this time so the assumption has to be that he knew the killer or had some reason to let him in.'

'Or he answered the door to a man with a gun and didn't have much option about letting him in.'

'Or that,' Alec agreed.

For a minute or two they ate in silence, each running through the facts. At Naomi's feet, Napoleon snuffled contentedly.

Naomi eventually broke the silence. 'What if he'd come to kill Molly? What if he came, but something made him change his mind?'

'So, why didn't he just leave? If indecision is a reason to blow your brains out then we two are in serious trouble.'

Naomi laughed. 'Or he was afraid of whoever had sent him to do the job.'

'There is that, of course, but it still seems bloody dramatic. Most professionals have places they can go to ground if a job goes wrong. No, I don't really buy that one.'

'Most professionals don't suddenly change their minds. They take the money, do the job. If they have scruples about kids, dogs and old ladies, they state them up front, before anyone hires them.'

'And when did you become such an expert on professional assassins? No, but you are probably right. Molly said something weird.'

'Normal weird or weird for Molly?'

'Weird for Molly. She said he pointed the gun at her before turning it on himself and that it was almost as if he wanted her to share in the moment. To know what he was feeling.'

Naomi frowned. 'And why would she think that?'

'I don't know, but she'd obviously run it back and forth in her mind for quite a while and that was the conclusion she had come to. The way she talked about it, it was almost as though they'd shared something . . .' he paused, searching for the word.

'Intimate?' Naomi suggested.

Alec nodded. 'Yes, I think that's exactly right. I don't know, somehow that makes it even more disturbing. Would you like some more wine?'

He refilled their glasses, and took a sip. 'The gun was interesting.'

'Oh?'

'Yes, a real cold war relic, apparently.' He consulted his notebook again. 'Something called an MSP SP-3, 7.62mm, fired just the two shots, but the ammunition is internally suppressed. It's effectively silent.'

'Sounds rare,' Naomi said.

'Mostly KGB, apparently. It was used for close-range assassinations, the effective accurate range, I'm told, was no more than a hundred, a hundred and fifty feet. It's an unusual looking thing, not much bigger than a derringer, but looks a bit like a very short automatic.'

'Odd,' Naomi said. 'Why use something like that when you could have taken her down with a high-powered rifle? Not that I'm suggesting anyone should, of course.'

Alec shrugged. 'Beats me. It seems kind of personal, though, the same way stabbing someone is personal, you know what I mean?'

'I know what you mean,' Naomi confirmed. She frowned. 'So what do we do now? Stay here for a few more days and keep an eye on Molly? Or go chasing off to Newark to look for clues?'

Alec sipped more wine, considering. 'I think, if you don't mind, we'll stay around here for a while. I want to cultivate DI Barnes and see what more he has to say and I think Molly needs us.'

'She'd never admit it.'

'The day Molly admits she needs anyone will be the day they nail the coffin lid down.'

'She needed Edward,' Naomi objected.

'And the need was mutual. She and Edward made an excellent team. You know, if was one of those marriages where you never ever expected them to have children. They were kind of complete, all on their own.'

He paused and Naomi could feel him looking at her, wondering if he'd been crass. They had talked, last year, about starting a family. Alec had been very keen; Naomi not so sure. He'd pressured her for a while and then, quite abruptly, let the matter drop and she still wasn't certain what he really wanted. She had figured that he didn't either. Since then the subject of a possible family had been one he had taken pains to avoid. Naomi avoided it now.

'When do we go and see her?' she asked. She felt Alec relax.

'I don't know. Tomorrow, maybe? I want to talk to her again before Barnes decides to make it official.'

'You think he will?'

'I think he may have to. He's given me some leeway, says he wants me to see what I can get out of her first, but the phone call was pretty damning, no matter what she says about being confused.'

'Which could well be true, of course. Having a gun pointed at your head doesn't do a lot for logical thought.'

'True. But this is Molly we're talking about. She's spent most of her life in and out of war zones. I doubt, in fact I know for a fact, it's not the first time that's happened to her.'

'First time in her own bedroom, maybe.'

'Well, yes. Maybe that.'

'You think she's definitely lying to Barnes, don't you?'

'I think she recognized *something*. I think it's possible she did make a mistake and for a moment she thought this young man with the gun was someone else, but—' He paused and Naomi could almost hear the cogs turning. 'But I don't know what the but is,' he admitted finally.

'So, we go and ask her,' Naomi said. 'Molly prefers people to be direct. We'll be direct.'

'And get thrown out for our trouble.'

'Probably, but we've got to give it a shot.'

'If you'll pardon the pun.'

'Sorry, none intended. You want dessert?'

'I think I may. You?'

Naomi nodded. 'Alec, if Molly was a target—'

'Then someone may try and finish the job. Yes, I talked to Barnes about that. He tried to persuade her to go away for a few days but, well, you know Molly.'

'Police protection?'

'Out of what budget? She's a witness to a suicide. She's given the police no reason to think she may have been singled out by this man. There's no connection with the two dead men and, besides, she's told Barnes to take his offer of protection and, well, you know Molly.'

Naomi nodded. 'Whatever is going on,' she said, 'Molly will stand and face it.'

'She's too damned proud to ask for help,' Alec added miserably.

Naomi just laughed. 'Alec, if you think that then you've not understood the first thing about Molly Chambers.'

'What do you mean?'

'What I mean is, Molly won't ask for help because she views us all as incompetents that would only get in the way because we don't know what we're doing. The only way Molly would accept help from us is if we prove that we're not.'

*   *   *

Molly knelt beside the bed and pulled an old tin trunk out from beneath it. She really ought to burn this stuff, she thought. But she'd thought that so many times and never done anything about it. Inside the trunk were memories of her younger self, her travels, her marriage, her friends, photographed in so many places and at so many times. Invitations to parties. A pair of white silk gloves. Little notes from Edward and items of jewellery she no longer wore. She missed him terribly. The pain of missing him made her feel like she'd been sliced in two and all she'd wanted to do at his funeral was to climb into the casket beside him and face oblivion.

Downstairs there were photograph albums, many of them. But this old box housed the more personal reminders; those pictures and letters and little moments that were not for public consumption. The thought that, after her death, someone else might lay hands on these treasures, that her innermost feelings and loves and secrets might be laid bare for another's eyes, disturbed her deeply and she had always planned to dispose of the contents of this box before she went.

And this latest reminder of her own mortality had felt like a warning that it was time for the fire.

Oh, but it was so hard to think of letting go. Of the renewed pain that offering up such precious things to the flames would afford that Molly, tough as old boots Molly, could not bring herself to take that final step. It would be like another little death, another funeral.

Molly shuffled through the photographs, finally discovering the one she had been seeking. She had been so sure; so unequivocally certain when she had seen that young man's face, and yet, there was really no way it could be him. It was just some memory of a face superimposed upon that of another.

The photograph she sought had been taken in 1961 or maybe early '62. But no; they had left by then. She turned it over to check the date, scribed in pencil in Edward's hand. August '61, then. It was taken outside a hotel in Leopoldville as it had been back then. A group of young people, none of them more than mid-twenties, and all excited by the prospect of what might be achieved.

Edward was attached to the UN forces that had been sent to Leopoldville to try and keep the peace while this very new country found its feet. In all, there were around 12,000 troops there, drawn from across Africa, Europe and Asia; none from what could be construed as colonial powers. There were other armed men too, roaming the countryside. The 10,000 Belgian troops that had still not been withdrawn, even after independence, 2,000 of which were still posted in the secessionist state of Katanga. Ostensibly, they were there to protect what was left of the Belgian nationals, though the vast majority of these had left the year before, taking their possessions and their money.

Molly recalled reading somewhere that around $180 million had been withdrawn from the country in the two years before, as businesses had closed and left and individuals had packed their bags.

And then there were the mercenaries. The locals called them *afrits*, Molly recalled. The terrors, the frightful ones. She'd met a few and was very much inclined to agree, though on balance they were no better or worse than many special forces soldiers she had encountered across the world.

Molly sat back on her heels and sorted through the other pictures, smiling at the memories they evoked. One had been taken outside the UN headquarters on the Boulevard D'Albert, the main thoroughfare running the length of Leopoldville. Run down but beautiful Art Deco buildings lined the road. The UN headquarters was in the seven-storey hotel, Le Royal.

Molly laughed. 'Nothing very Royal about it, was there, Edward? The lifts didn't work, there was electricity for half the day if you were lucky and it was faster to run up and down the stairs than it was to try and get the phones to work.'

Edward had been in and out of the place several times a week, attending briefings and updating the various officials on the situation on the ground 'up country'. They had called the main briefing room 'the snake pit'. Edward always reckoned it was an apt description.

She peered more closely at the photograph, looking at the background of the picture. 'Oh, yes, of course. I'd almost forgotten. We ate there so many times. Dolmades and moussaka in the middle of the Congo. Utterly bizarre.' There'd been a Greek restaurant on the ground floor of Le Royal. It had seemed such an odd thing at the time, but they'd been grateful for the half-decent food in a city of shortages and high prices and where most of the UN forces and their tag-alongs – like Molly herself – lived most of the week on field rations.

'And I was too in love to care,' she said softly, touching her husband's face ever so gently. She had just married Edward and this had been their first posting together. Molly smiled remembering their little house with its long veranda and tin roof. They'd made a point of not staying in the colonial areas with the remaining Belgian and other European expats on the hill in Kalina. Edward believed he'd never gain any credibility with the local people if he separated himself from them. He'd be seen as just another white colonist. So he had moved his new wife into an enclave, mostly of local traders and merchants, on the edge of town. The smell from the dredging operations taking place on the river, attempts to improve its navigability, blew in on the wind. Much of the time, it stank, Molly remembered. It had been deafening when the rains came, too hot when the sun beat down. She had found a local man who had installed a false ceiling and a couple of fans and it had finally been bearable. It had been a tiny place, really, just a couple of rooms, one for living and one for sleeping and a primitive bathroom. The kitchen had been outside. A stove and a table beneath a thatched roof. It was all supposed to be temporary, but they'd lived in that little house for almost a year until the political situation worsened, and talks broke down and full civil war threatened to overtake them all. Molly and Edward had left, flitting in the middle of the night, only minutes ahead of the mob who had come to burn and steal and destroy.

She picked up the other photograph again. The group image she had looked for. Gently, she laid her index finger against each face in the photograph. Her younger self, all blonde curls and soppy smile. Edward, looking handsome and tall, his hair side parted and combed back from his face. That slightly crooked smile of his . . .

Molly felt her throat tighten and the pain in her chest like a lead weight.

Adam Carmodie, slightly out of focus as he always seemed to be, no matter how many photographs Molly had seen of him. He was never still, always off and doing. Piotre and Joseph and that girl who'd come over as a translator. . . . Genevieve, that was it. Molly had not known her so well, but Joseph had been smitten for a while. Then Paul and Adis, local liaison . . . she tried hard not to think of the night she had watched Adis die . . .

Gently, Molly laid the photograph back in the tin box. The face she thought she had seen, the one the young man had reminded her of, he looked back at her too. Eyes seemingly locked on hers, pale and blue, she remembered; they still looked pale and blue even in the black and white image. Drawing a deep and unsteady breath, Molly turned the picture face down and made to close the lid. Then she paused and, unwilling but knowing she must check, she dug down into the depths of the box and withdrew a faded green folder. Molly didn't trouble to open it; the weight and feel of it was so familiar she would have known if even a single page had been disturbed. Her fingers traced a single letter, stamped in red and enclosed in a circle. W, for Watch, for a file that should not have still existed, that should have been destroyed before they left back in 1961. She and Edward had carried this little scrap of forbidden information with them almost all of their married lives. Kept it, guarded it, worried about it and then, as years had passed, tucked it away with their memories and, even while they felt uncomfortable even acknowledging its existence, not quite felt right about its final destruction either.

Did it really matter now? Molly asked herself. She had thought not, but then the young man had come to her home and had died, right there in front of her and Molly could not shake the conviction that, even after all these years and all the changes, that those two things, the young man and this forbidden file were connected by a single, fragile, but unbroken thread.

FIVE

B ill was on his final patrol before going off shift at six a.m. He was ready for some breakfast and his bed and got the impression that Fred, the dog, felt pretty much the same way. Fred looked the part, but the truth was he was twelve years old and the night air didn't do a lot for his joints, and any way he was as soft as tripe. Bill sympathized with the joint problem, his own complained at the chill and damp, but he only had a year and a bit to go till he retired, so Bill figured he could mark time until then.

There'd been talk of retiring Fred, too and Bill was almost decided to offer the old boy a permanent home. Sheila wouldn't mind and it would be good to have something to walk of an evening, to help ease him into what Sheila kept referring to as normal hours.

They had just rounded the final turn of the perimeter fence when Bill became aware of a change in Fred's demeanour. The dog paused and pricked up his ears. Bill followed his gaze. Outside of the perimeter fence was a blue van, old and plain and badly painted and he was pretty sure it hadn't been there when he'd last made his rounds an hour before.

Man and dog drew level with the vehicle and Bill realized there were sounds coming from inside. His first thought was that it was a courting couple, thumping about. He smirked, knowingly, thinking that at least they had a bit more space than the back of a car and then thinking that it was a bit early in the morning or rather a bit too late in the night for anyone to be parking up to have that sort of fun. His next thought was that the sound was all wrong anyway and the thought that chased after that one was that whoever was inside was thumping on the back doors and shouting for help.

Fred growled, almost convincingly and Bill grasped the radio at his belt. 'Tony, something's up out here, I think we might need the cops.'

He frowned, he'd look a bit daft if it was only kids having a bit of fun at his expense, but . . .

Tony was asking what was wrong and Bill told him quickly.

'You sure?' Tony said.

'Just give them a call,' Bill said. 'I'll see if I can make them hear, them inside the van. If it's nothing, well, better safe than sorry, isn't it?'

He came closer to the fence. The exit gates were right round the other side of the factory and Bill didn't feel like making the trek if this really was nothing; he also had an odd feeling about this and it felt a bit better having the fence between him and the vehicle. He was aware that the dog wasn't happy either and Bill trusted the old boy.

'Hello in there,' he shouted at the rear doors of the van. 'Whatcha doing in there?'

The hammering increased in volume and the shouts for help were unmistakable now.

'Locked yourself in, have you?' Bill asked, though he couldn't for the life of him imagine how that could have happened. 'Don't you worry, police are on their way.'

The hammering became more frenetic and Bill wondered if whoever was inside could actually hear him. He raised his voice. 'I said don't worry, the police are on their way.' He eyed the closed padlock on the back doors. Something was really not right here, Bill thought anxiously They could hardly have done that from the inside, could they?

'Tony, you got an ETA on the police?'

'On their way, they said. What's going on out there? Want me to come out to you?'

Bill hesitated. There was supposed to be one of them in their little control room watching the cameras at all times. Not that anything ever happened. Or at least not that it ever had in the past. 'No, stay put, I'm going to head round to the gate, wait for the police there.'

It felt, maybe a bit cowardly, he thought, but he didn't want to be anywhere near that van. Something was just not kosher.

He gave the dog's lead a little tug and Fred followed him obediently away from the fence. Bill could hear the police car now, or at least he assumed it must be them. No sirens, but the sound of a vehicle travelling at speed through the industrial estate at that time of the morning wasn't likely to be anyone else. The sound of the engine was clear as it echoed off the warehouses and storage lots.

He reached the front gate just as they did and, glad that he recognized both officers, told them what was wrong.

'I figured some daft bugger locked themselves in,' he said. 'But there's a padlock on the back door; it's been fastened shut from the outside.'

'OK, we'll take a look. Want a lift round?'

'No, I'll follow on with the dog.' He paused, worried about being laughed at. 'It feels, I dunno, a bit odd,' he managed, noting the smirk on the face of the younger officer.

His older partner merely nodded. 'See you round there, then,' he said. The car pulled away and Bill and Fred followed, on the street side of the fence this time. As they turned the corner, Bill could see the police car pulled up beside the van and the older of the two officers – Bill struggled to recall his name; Prentiss, wasn't it? Tod or Tad or Tom or something – was banging on the back door, speaking loudly to those inside.

'We're going to need some bolt croppers,' he said as Bill arrived. He banged the flat of his hand on the van door. 'I've got to get bolt croppers,' he shouted. 'Get the lock off. Can you hear me in there?'

'They've gone quiet,' he said to Bill and it was clear to the security man that the police officer was now disturbed too.

The younger officer went to the front of the van and tugged on the driver's door. It opened suddenly, catching him off balance. He peered inside and then knocked on the rear bulkhead. 'Can you hear me?'

Tad Prentiss was speaking on his radio. 'You got anything in the boot you can lever that lock off with?' Bill asked, looking over the young officers shoulder. 'What's that there?' he added, pointing to something glimpsed between the seats.

The officer looked. 'Some kind of gas cylinder,' he said, 'and there's a valve and a pipe going—'

'Well you'd best switch it off then.' Bill was truly alarmed now.

The officer hesitated for a second, obviously worried about touching evidence. 'Christ's sake, man, they're dying in there.'

The policeman reached in to turn the valve. 'What the hell do you think it is? Think it'll explode?'

'I don't know,' Bill said, 'but we need something to lever those doors open.'

'Jack handle.' The younger officer ran to the back of his car and rummaged in the boot. He came back with what looked like a length of pipe, then wedged it against the van door, behind the hasp and staple through which the padlock was fixed. Bill watched as the man threw his weight against the lever. The silence from inside the van was now profound. Why had they stopped shouting? Bill gripped the length of pipe and added his weight to that of the police officer. Something gave with a sharp crack, launching Bill sideways. He scrambled back to his feet and examined the damage. Part of the hasp had pulled away from the body of the van.

'It's a start,' he said. 'Give it another go.'

Together they tried again, but the first attempt had partly bent the pipe. As a lever, it's effectiveness was all but lost. A second car pulled up alongside and Bill was profoundly relieved to see a young female officer pull a large pair of bolt croppers from the boot.

'Give these a go,' she said. 'What the hell's going on?'

No one replied; truth was, Bill figured, no one knew. But the lack of sound from those inside the van was now deeply troubling. What was going on in there?

Bolt croppers were applied and the lock gave way with a final reluctant snick. Handles were seized, doors pulled but refused to move. The now bent lever was pressed into service again, bolt croppers wedged in beside it and finally a small but definite opening was created between the doors.

'What the hell?' Bill had looked down to see if he could figure out what was holding the door closed. He touched the door sill. Tacky blue paint came away on his hand. 'It's been welded shut?'

'It's what?'

'Look at the bugger. Welded shut and painted over.'

All action momentarily stopped as officers and security man looked at one another. The female officer stepped away and Bill could hear her asking for an ETA on the ambulance and asking for additional support.

'Try again,' Prentiss said. 'Have we got anything else we can use as a lever?'

Bill rooted in the patrol car boot and came back with a nail bar, wrapped in a plastic evidence bag. Prentiss hesitated for a second and then took it from him. Together they launched themselves against the doors again.

The doors had bent, rather than opened and it was now possible to see inside. Two men lay slumped in the rear of the van.

'Can you hear me?' Bill shouted. 'The ambulance is on its way, we're going to get you out of there.' He glanced at Prentiss. 'What the hell is going on?' He stepped back from the vehicle and radioed his partner, fending off the anxious questions. 'Tony, do we still have that angle grinder? Right, I'm coming to get it, anything else you can find that might be useful for breaking into a van too, oh, and we'll need the genny.' He broke off. 'Be quicker if someone could drive me round,' he said. 'We've got a small generator; we got it when we had all those power cuts last winter.'

Prentiss's younger partner opened the car door and Bill slid into the passenger seat. 'Stay,' he told Fred. 'I'll be right back.'

'How long had the van been there?' the police officer asked.

'I'm certain it wasn't there last time I patrolled,' Bill told him. 'So it arrived in the hour between. There's a camera on that corner post, it should have caught something.'

They turned into the factory gate. Bill could see Tony coming down the front steps with the grinder in one hand and a portable power pack in the other. The generator stood at the top of the steps. Tony handed Bill the power pack. 'I've been keeping this in the car,' he said. 'My battery ain't so hot and I can't get another, not till next month. There might be enough juice in it for the angle grinder.'

Bill nodded and they loaded the equipment into the car. 'See if you can find when this van arrived,' Bill said. 'It weren't there the last time I went out.'

'Will do.' Tony disappeared inside. Bill could hear the ambulance, now, sirens on this time. It was almost light, the pale dawn reminding him that he ought to have been heading for home. He must call. Sheila would be worried if he came in late.

Back at the van he plugged the grinder into the power pack while the police officers hauled the generator out of the car and got it going. The draw would be too great, Bill thought, to keep the angle grinder going for long on the little inverter he was using. He started on the weld down on the bottom sill, going for the metal above and below, rather than cut through what looked like quite an efficient weld. The metal gave under the onslaught and Bill reached up to attack the weld at the top of the door. The power gave out as he'd almost finished, but the three of them hauling on the door broke what was left. They made way for the paramedics who clambered into the van through the one open door.

'Are they dead?' Bill wanted to know.

'No, but I think it was a close thing.' One of the paramedics crawled back out of the van and went to fetch a gurney. Bill peered into the space he had left. The man closest to him looked about mid-forties, Bill guessed. He was dressed in a suit and tie and polished shoes, like he'd been on the way to the office. His skin was ash grey and his lips blue. The paramedic fitted a mask over the man's face and Bill switched his attention to the rear of the van. It had been modified, he realized; a solid box created inside the body of the van. One small break in the blank interior attracted his attention. A valve of some sort. Metal flanges had been welded around the opening where the doors fitted so that when they were closed they fitted tightly against the frame. The external welding finished the job of holding them in place. The padlock, Bill realized, was really just for show. Just to slow down the rescue even more.

'They made it air tight,' he said.

'What?' PC Prentiss looked at what Bill was indicating.

'Poor buggers would have run out of air even if the gas hadn't got them first.'

Prentiss looked quizzically at him and then went round to the front of the van, opened the door. The two men peered inside.

'Look, that's where the valve goes through into the back,' Bill said, pointing. 'There's a pipe, leads somewhere to the front of the van, under the dash. We turned the valve off, but who knows how long it had been on for.'

'You're thinking carbon monoxide poisoning?'

Bill shook his head. 'No, their skin's the wrong colour.' He shrugged. 'Sheila, the wife, she's into all this crime drama stuff on the telly.'

Prentiss scooted back round to the rear. 'Best get them out fast,' he told the paramedic. 'I don't like the look of this.'

He got on to the radio and Bill got the impression he was trying to get the bomb squad called out. Bill moved back, away from the action. This was rum, very rum and Bill felt he was missing something. He radioed Tony back in the control room. No response.

'Fred,' he called to the dog, who got up reluctantly and nosed at his hand. 'Reckon you can give us another lift back round,' he asked, not really bothered which of the officers responded.

'Something up?' The young female officer looked up hopefully, like she'd welcome something to do.

'I can't raise my partner on the radio and . . . I don't know, I've just got a bad feeling.'

She shrugged, then led the way to the car. Another patrol had arrived, making her even more superfluous. She drove fast and Bill was grateful for that. He'd tried Tony again; still no response.

Man, woman and dog made their way into the building. 'What do you do here?' she asked.

'Not a lot. Most of it's been given over to storage. We sublet to one of those companies that charges people to keep their stuff here between house moves and what have you. Round the other side there's a couple of little industrial units. This was all one big engineering plant, back in the day, that folded and the owners subdivided. It's been up for sale this past year, but no one's even come to look.'

He led the way up the stairs to their little control room. 'We've got CCTV feeds from all over the industrial estate,' he said. 'Most people can't afford much in the way of security, we've got excess capacity now, so the owners repositioned and now rent out the other cameras. We watch it all from up—' He broke off, stopped dead at the door. Tony lay slumped half on and half off his chair, his head a mess of blood and bone.

SIX

September 24th

Slicing rain, the cold kind that felt like iced buckshot when it hit.

Adam thought, not for the first time, that he really ought to find somewhere warmer. Escape to the sun. Southern France,

Spain, maybe. Anywhere but endure months of the fickle-minded British weather. It was still only late September but the rain was wintry. Although, he argued, if he did leave, he would miss the hard, lustrous frosts and those precious mornings when he woke to find that snow had fallen and that the world was bright with it.

Adam quickened his pace, almost running along the narrow high street, pulling his coat collar high and wishing he remembered where he'd left his umbrella.

Traffic roared by, much too close for comfort, showering the filthy rain from the overloaded gutters over Adam's polished shoes and already too wet trousers.

He swore, irritably and miserably as the icy wetness soaked though his socks and into his shoes, then quickened his pace again.

Almost there now, a few more paces, then Adam Carmodie dived rapidly through a shop doorway and stood, slightly breathless, just inside the door.

'My God! Just look at you, you're soaked through. Get yourself into the back there before you catch your death and I'll make coffee.'

The woman bustled from behind the counter, all hands and good intentions, flicking his wet hair back from his broad forehead and fumbling with the large black buttons on his sodden overcoat.

Adam chuckled warmly and allowed himself to be relieved of his coat and ushered through to the back office. Billie had been with him for years and fussed over him like a mother with a rather wayward child, despite her being a good deal younger than himself.

'It's filthy weather,' he complained. 'I've only come from where I parked the car and look at me.'

Billie nodded sympathetically, and smiled a smile that framed her grey eyes in deep, upsweeping lines. She hung Adam's coat, lengthwise, over the backs of two swivel chairs placed close to the radiator and then turned to switch on the already filled kettle.

'You sit and get warm again,' she told him. 'I'll be back to make a coffee in a moment.'

Adam sat down and settled back with a deep sigh.

He was still at his happiest here. This tiny shop had been his first business and still, despite all of his success, the only part of Carmodie Electronics he felt to be truly his.

He glanced around him. Things hadn't changed much in all the years he'd owned the place. The little shop out front; the poky back room office and the storeroom beyond, filled with stock, mainly for the mail order side of the business.

Billie ran the place, really. Had been there long enough to view it as her own domain and, since last Christmas, had held a quarter share of the stock on her own behalf. A gift from Adam.

She knew the business back to front and inside out. Had a couple of part timers to help with the office work and packaging and Adam himself, though officially retired, came in on several days a week to keep his hand in.

He looked up as Billie bustled in to see to the kettle. Picking up, as she did so, the thread of a conversation with him she had been carrying on in her head since leaving the room.

'So the last ad in that new monthly, it's done us a power of good and there's been terrific interest in the catalogue.'

She filled the mugs and turned to him again. 'So you see, we were all telling you the truth, folk don't mind paying for a good-sized catalogue, especially if they get their cash back off the first order and even our Internet customers like something physical they can browse through.'

She paused and perched herself on the desk edge, handing him his coffee as she did so.

'There's a pile of new catalogue requests in the in tray. Do them, if you get around to it, will you. Judy phoned in sick this morning and I know I won't have time. And there are a few general enquiries, one about the range of those new transmitters. Oh, and there was this . . .'

She reached across to the other desk and picked up a plain, Manila envelope, handed it to Adam.

'I didn't open it,' she said. 'If you look at the address, it looks kind of personal.' She paused, as though about to say some more but then the doorbell rang and the shop door clanked noisily. Someone else in a hurry to escape the rain.

'Customers!' Billie announced with deep satisfaction, put her coffee down and left Adam to the mail.

Adam laughed softly to himself and drew the in tray close, preparing to work his way through the morning mail. Whoever it was who'd just come into the shop, they were likely to be there for quite some time. They might have come in only for a fuse, but they'd be sure to leave with a good deal more, even if it was only the memory of friendly conversation. Billie was just like that. It was as well, he reflected, for the sake of the business that mail orders didn't need any talking to.

He rifled quickly through the catalogue requests, separated out the more specific queries and then turned back to the Manila envelope Billie had handed to him.

The address was, to say the least, a little vague.

Adam Carmodie, Carmodie Electronics, Lentonstone. And that was all.

He slit it open and thoughtfully extracted the single sheet of headed notepaper inside.

A hospice? A request for charity, perhaps.

But no.

A letter that began, 'Dear Mr Carmodie, you don't know me, but I'm writing on behalf of . . .'

Curious now, Adam began to read, a small frown creasing between his eyes.

He read the letter twice and then, the frown deepened and he laid the page aside.

Joseph Bern. After all this time. Joseph Bern.

For several minutes, Adam stared blindly into space, his mind flooded with old memories.

It had been, what, ten years since they had last met. Their contact even before that had at best been inconsistent and erratic; sometimes, almost the closest of friends, then parting for months when some irritation had pushed them apart or Joseph had once more decided to travel.

And now this.

For moments more, Adam hesitated, his mind filled with the memories of their first meeting. The heat of the sun, the bright blue afternoon filled with green scents and the sounds of birds and buzzing insects. Joseph staggering on to the road and falling in front of Adam's car, blood oozing from a deep gash in his left cheek, his right arm cradled against his side and bloody footprints from bare feet, torn and abraded from long walking over hard terrain, marking the roadway.

Adam closed his eyes, all of those things as clear as morning, in his memory.

Then he reached out for the phone and dialled the number on the hospice letter head.

SEVEN

Bill sat in the front seat of the police car and watched the ambulance take Tony away. He was alive, they said, but no one was very hopeful. There were police everywhere and Bill felt like a spare part, watching them scurrying here and there, looking purposeful.

Fred snuffled sleepily in the rear seat and Bill wondered for a moment what would have happened if he'd been with Tony when his friend had been attacked. He had no doubt that Fred would have done his bit, but anyone capable of hitting someone as hard as they had obviously hit Tony, would probably have dealt with the dog just as harshly and efficiently. Bill could not help himself; he was glad that Fred hadn't been there and guilty because he felt like that.

He thought also about those two men in the van. Whoever they were, whoever had organized this, those men had been considered expendable too. Someone had sealed them into that van, known that when they woke up from whatever gas had been pumped into the space through that little valve in the bulkhead, they'd be sure to make a racket, sure to try and get out. They'd counted on someone hearing the noise and on someone going to help. They'd counted, specifically, on Bill hearing them and calling for help. On Bill and probably Tony as well, leaving the building so that whoever it was would have had access. If Tony had been with Bill and Fred and the police officers on the outside of the fence, he wouldn't have been hurt. Whoever it was would have gone in, got what they wanted and that would have been that.

And even while he wrestled with that conclusion, he couldn't help but wonder at how elaborate this ruse had been. It went, in his mind, from making little sense, to making none.

Prentiss came out and opened the car door, and crouched down beside the passenger seat. 'We're going to need you to come back in and take a gander at the system,' he said. 'It looks like someone wiped all the CCTV records for the past week, maybe longer. Do you have back ups?'

Bill shook his head. 'The recording is on a loop,' he said. 'The past ten days will be kept, the first of the ten drops off as a new day is recorded over the top. It's a digital system,' he said more hopefully. 'I hear they can recover digital records even though they've been wiped or overwritten.'

Prentiss shrugged. 'Let's hope so,' he said. 'Apart from that I need you to come and look inside at the storage units, see if you can see what they might have got into. It all looks locked up tight.'

Bill nodded and got out of the car. 'Why'd they have to hit him so hard? Tony wasn't a big lad, he'd have given them no bother.'

Prentiss gestured that he didn't know.

'He should have been with me,' Bill said. 'He offered to come out and I said to him, no, rules are one of us stays in the viewing room. One inside at all times, that's the rules.'

'The rules your boss laid down?'

'Company rules,' Bill said. 'The day shift is the same. One person in the control room, one to go and patrol. We switch round every two or three patrols. Tony liked to watch the telly, so I generally did the two last walks. We never had trouble here. Worst we got were drunk teenagers and a couple of graffiti artists. And they got scared off when Fred barked at them.'

'I don't know, Bill, I really don't. But the thing that strikes me is how bloody elaborate it was. Those two in the van . . . no one would go to that much trouble just so they'd be a diversion. It's like they already had them available, in the van, so someone thought they may as well put them to another use.'

Bill looked sideways at Prentiss. 'I thought the same thing,' he said. 'It seems like too much trouble to go to, just to get us out of the building.' He laughed harshly. 'Didn't even work for that, did it?'

'Not your fault, Bill. You mustn't even start to think that.'

'Hard not to.'

Prentiss led the way to the back of the building and the storage units that had been in Bill's care. 'There's no sign of forced entry anywhere, Bill. Anything you see that's different, that's unusual? CSI would like to know where's best to make a start as there's a hell of a lot to go through.'

Bill stood back and looked at the row of storage lockers. This had been one big room; the owners had sectioned it off with stud walling and put cage doors on the front, secured with padlocks, all of which appeared to be in place. There were a row of lock-ups along each wall and a double row down the middle of the big space.

On the face of it, the lockers seemed solid and secure, but Bill knew the stud wall between was cardboard thin. A good punch and you could put your fist through it.

He began to walk down the row, patrolling now as he did every night; not that he'd ever expected to find anything wrong but just because that was what the job description said he had to do. Normally, he'd have tugged on each of the padlocks. He told Prentiss so and the officer handed him a pair of gloves.

'Do what you usually do,' he said.

'What if they've left prints?'

'They won't have left prints,' Prentiss asserted.

Bill absorbed that. Slowly, he walked down the rows, glancing at the numbers on the front of each cage and that linked, somehow, to the computer records. He looked through the little window in the cage door, trying to remember how the stacks of boxes and shelves had looked earlier that day. He tugged at each of the locks, checking as he always did. Prentiss paced slowly behind.

The first row and there was nothing. The second row, again, all seemed to be as he expected. Bill turned back down the row of central cages and pulled the padlock on the first enclosure. He paused. Looked inside again. Had something been moved?

Not certain, he moved along the row, but something nagged at him that he couldn't quite place and once he'd finished checking that block, he headed back and looked again.

'I'm not sure what it is,' he said. 'But I'm sure something's been shifted about in there.'

'OK.' Prentiss beckoned to the waiting CSI. 'It's as good a place to start as any.'

Bill nodded and slowly checked the final block of cages, but the more he thought about it, the more he was certain only that particular one had been disturbed. He came back round to where the two CSI had now cut the lock and opened the door.

'It belongs to an old woman,' he said. 'I remember her. She came in about a year, eighteen months ago, picked up an old chair and then came back maybe six months ago and fetched a box. Just an old tin thing. I remember her because she got a taxi all the way from town and had it wait for her while she came in. It was before the day shift came on, that was what struck me, both times. She came early. I remember the fight she had with the driver of the black cab because she wanted to take the chair back in the cab and he said he didn't carry furniture.' Bill laughed. 'She won that one. I got the impression she won most of her arguments, come to think of it.'

Prentiss nodded. 'Can you find her address?'

'I can't, it'll be on the computer at head office. The people who use these lockers, they have a key and a pass card. I scan the card and it comes up with their number, then I show them where the locker is. Actually, it's not usually me. Usually the day shift. Most people don't arrive in the middle of the night. The customer then lets themselves into the cage and they're responsible for locking up after themselves.

'And what sort of people use the storage facility?' Prentiss asked.

'Oh, all sorts. Mostly they leave stuff here for a month or so. The company lets them out in a three-month block, but usually it's, like, people who are moving house and there's a gap of some sort between the moves. The lock ups are quite small, so if you've got to store your furniture, it can mean hiring two or three of them, and for a three-month block even if you don't need it. It's not the cheapest around, but a lot of people like the fact there's always security around and that if they need to they can come any time. We get a lot of early starts on moving days, vans turning up here just before I go off shift and that, not so many at three in the morning.'

'And that's when the old lady arrived?'

Bill nodded. 'You remember that sort of thing. Not that I'd have forgotten her anyway. She was a right . . . character.'

They stood and watched as the CSI moved carefully inside. Everyone seemed a bit jumpy, Bill thought, but then, in their place and after what he'd seen in that van, he'd have been a bit jumpy. Thoughts of bombs and booby traps jostled in his head and he took an involuntary step or two back, then told himself not to be a daft sod. If something blew in here, he'd need to be a lot further away than he could reasonably get. The desire to leave was suddenly overwhelming. Bill took a deep breath.

'You said you wanted me to look at the control room?'

Prentiss nodded. 'See anything?' he asked the two CSI.

'Looks like a box might have been moved. The dust's been disturbed back here.'

Prentiss nodded. 'We'll leave you to it, then,' he said and, much to Bill's relief, led the way back upstairs.

EIGHT

Alec and Naomi had gone out house hunting. Truthfully, neither of them really wanted to settle in this current location in the Northamptonshire countryside, beautiful though it was. It was just that bit too far from the sea for Alec's liking. They examined what Alec told her was a very nice looking bungalow in a quarter acre garden and while Naomi agreed that there seemed to be lots of space in the big rooms and the roses in the garden were lovely, the kitchen and one of the bedrooms smelt of cats and she wasn't convinced that even stripping out the carpets and scrubbing the boards would get rid of that particular stink. Napoleon forgot himself for a moment and hoovered eagerly at the new scents, then remembered he was supposed to be working and pressed himself close to Naomi's leg.

'Who lived here?' she asked.

'An elderly lady,' the estate agent told her.

And her cats, Naomi added silently.

'And, yes, it does need work. We said that in our details.'

'New kitchen and bathroom for a start,' Alec said.

'Well, yes, but once it's done . . . she was a very elderly lady. Had to go into a home and then she died.'

So, what happened to the cats, Naomi thought.

'And now the family want a quick sale, so hence the good price.'

'Not so good once you take account of all the work that would have to be done,' Alec objected. 'New kitchen, new bathroom and we'd have to install an en suite and the windows look like they haven't been painted in decades . . .'

'I'm sure they would be open to offers,' the estate agent said firmly. 'It's still a very good buy . . .'

Naomi tuned them out and listened to the sad little house. She could hear how large the rooms were and almost catch the sounds of the ghosts that had once loved this place. It could be lovely, she thought, but it was not for them. She wondered what was.

They returned to their car and, without bothering to ask her, Alec phoned and cancelled their next booked viewing.

'It's not working, is it?' he said.

'Not really. No. Maybe we should just go back home? Try and make it ours again.'

'Do you think we could?'

She hesitated and then shook her head. 'No. You know what's strange, Alec?'

'What?'

'The one place I keep thinking about, thinking maybe I could settle there was that little cottage down in Somerset.'

She could feel Alec's disbelieving stare. 'I'd have thought that was one place you'd never want to go back to. Naomi, I nearly lost you there. I couldn't . . .'

'Alec.' She laid a hand on his arm, stroking the smooth fabric of his shirt. 'I know it isn't logical, but you know, I won that one. I scored a victory. It turned out all right. Since then, not much has. You know?'

She could almost hear the wheels turning as he processed that and tried to work it out. Alec started the car, signalled and pulled slowly away.

'That last place stank of cats,' she said.

'Yes, I noticed. The bowls and litter tray were still in the kitchen, four bowls so presumably four cats. And there was a book on the living room chair. It had been left open and there was a pair of glasses next to it and a cup on the table and hair brushes on the dressing table. It was as if she'd just walked out.'

'I think she died there,' Naomi confirmed. 'Despite what the agent said. People don't like to think about that, do they? Even though it's inevitable if a house has any age to it.' And if the death had been a violent one . . .

'Alec, accept that cash offer for the house. I don't think we'll better it, not even if we wait.'

'You could be right,' he said. 'OK, love, I'll give them a call tonight. Want to do the Molly thing, now?'

'We may as well,' she agreed. 'Then let's do something fun. Go and see a film, find a park and feed the ducks. Anything really.'

He reached out, briefly, and clasped her hand. These sudden depressive moods had hit her recently and he could understand why. He felt the same. It was as though nothing would ever feel settled or safe ever again.

Molly opened the door to them and for a moment Alec thought she wasn't going to let them in.

'Back so soon?' she said. 'Two visits inside a week. Be careful, Alec, I might get used to it.'

She bent, then, to greet Napoleon. 'Hello, dog. You are a fine fellow, aren't you? Never had a dog since I was a girl. We did far too much travelling about, but there was this old brown mutt I had as a child, followed me everywhere.'

'Can we come in, Aunt Molly?'

'Well, I suppose you can, yes. Kitchen all right for you, is it? Or are we going to get all fancy-pantsy and go into the drawing room?'

'Just as you like, Molly,' Alec said. He gripped Naomi's hand, wishing he'd taken her back to the hotel. They followed Molly into the kitchen and sat down at the table while Molly first fussed with the kettle and then opened the kitchen drawer and set the glasses and bottle on the kitchen table. 'I'll get another glass,' she said. 'And I expect the dog will want some water.'

Naomi thanked her and Molly hmmd rather than harrumphed, which, Alec thought, was a good sign, of sorts.

'Sorry,' Alec apologized softly as Molly went through to the other room to fetch a suitable glass.

'What for? I know what she's like. I'm not exactly unprepared.'

Molly returned and set the glass down, poured three large measures and pushed Naomi's glass towards her. 'It's by your right hand,' she said 'You like brandy.'

It wasn't really a question.

Naomi raised her glass, Molly seemed to be hesitating about something. Naomi knew all about her usual toast but guessed it was something Molly would be unsure about sharing with a relative stranger. She chose words that were close enough in meaning to Molly's little ritual. 'To absent friends,' she said. She sensed Molly relax, just a little.

'Absent friends,' Molly agreed 'The whole damned lot of them.'

Naomi sipped her drink. It was very fine brandy. It deserved far better than exile in a kitchen drawer. She was about to ask what it was when Molly interrupted with, 'So, to what do I owe the pleasure this time?'

Alec drew a deep breath. 'I went to see the investigating officers.'

'Detective Barnes and "call me Delia".' Molly laughed. 'You said you might. What of it?'

'What of it? Well, for a start, they think you've been lying to them, Molly.'

'I don't lie,' she said flatly.

'I don't believe you.'

The silence that followed Alec's statement was leaden. Naomi heard the kettle boil and then click to off, but Molly made no move to deal with it. Instead, she heard the older woman refill her own glass and then top up Naomi's, even though it had barely been touched. Naomi lifted her glass and cradled it in her hands, out of Molly's reach. She sipped again, feeling the warmth of the spirit spread through her body, relaxing her to the bones.

'I don't tell lies,' Molly repeated. 'I said something foolish. People do. And do it more the older they get, I suppose.'

'You recognized him.'

'A momentary aberration. He reminded me of someone I knew a long time ago. The mind plays tricks, Alec, sometimes very painful ones.'

'He's killed before,' Naomi said. She took another sip of the spirit. 'Twice, at least.'

'No, my dear. The gun he carried was used to kill at least twice before. That does not necessarily mean that the young man who chose to end his life on my landing, took the shot. I'm told you can rent a weapon and five rounds by the week if you know who to ask.'

'Five rounds?'

'Well, I agree it's excessive. If you can't get the job done in one, you should probably find another, more suitable occupation. But five rounds is standard, I believe. I always wondered if you got a refund for any unused.'

'Molly!' It wasn't like Alec to be sharp, at least not outside of the interview room. Naomi was startled; Molly just chuckled delightedly.

'Oh, are we playing good cop, bad cop? Really, Alec, isn't that a little bit of a cliché?'

Naomi could feel his frustration. She wondered what was really going on here and it occurred to her that Molly, like so many before that Naomi had encountered in a professional capacity, really *did* want to tell. That whatever it was she was hiding was weighing heavily, but that the thought of just coming out with it was . . . well was impossible. She needed that permission, that coercion, so that admission would not be her responsibility.

But she didn't think that Molly would be quick to give in. She tried a different tack. 'What makes you think the dead man hadn't killed the other two?' she asked.

'I didn't say that was what I thought.'

'No,' Naomi agreed. 'I just got the impression you'd thought that.'
There was another silence while Molly considered this, but it
was not so leaden this time. She heard the bottle raised and poured
again, and moved her own glass well away.

'He stood in my garden,' Molly said. 'Just stood there, like some
little kid who'd been sent to stand outside when the party was going
on inside. He looked . . .' She seemed to scrabble around for the
right word. 'Lost,' she said. 'No, just puzzled. It was as if . . .' She
shook herself and the moment seemed to pass. 'I'm an old woman,'
she said. 'What could I possibly know about such things?'

'Molly, please,' Alec said. 'This is important. Other people could
be at risk. You could be at risk.'

'By your own logic, that's not likely,' she said. 'Alec, if he'd
been sent to kill me then he failed. Dramatically. If you are right
and he killed those other people, then he is no longer a risk to
others, is he? If it was someone else, then nothing I can tell you
will help, will it?'

'And what if he was sent for you? If someone else comes?'

'Then I'll be dead and you'll have your answer, won't you? Alec,
I told that policeman and I told that Delia woman, I won't be frightened out of my home and I've lived far too long to be intimidated
by what *might* be. None of us know how long we have. Sometimes
we cheat death when others beside us don't. Sometimes death decides
it really is time to turn our card and comes to find us, no matter how
we try to stack the deck. One thing I've learnt, Alec, is that death
is everywhere. I've spent my life with him breathing on my back;
sometimes you just have to turn around and face the inevitable.'

Naomi frowned. Then, on impulse, she held out her glass in
Molly's direction. Molly laughed harshly and filled both their glasses.

'Are you at least going to pretend to sample yours, Alec? A toast
isn't a toast unless the spirit touches the lips.'

Reluctantly, Alec raised his glass.

'To the lost ones,' Molly said.

'Are they finding their way home, Molly?' Alec asked.

'Maybe they are,' she said. 'And if that's the case there is nothing
to be done.'

They left half an hour later. Half an hour during which Molly had
turned the tables and interrogated them on their future plans and

where they planned to settle down. She made it plain that all other conversation was closed, and every time Naomi or Alec attempted to steer it back, she eluded them. Eventually, even Alec's patience thinned and Naomi took his hand and told him it was time to go.

Molly watched through the window as they drove away down the cul-de-sac. As Alec's car turned on to the main road, Molly slumped down on to the old armchair set beside the window. It had been Edward's favourite seat, bought in a second-hand store in Brighton only a few years into their marriage; it had been in and out of storage all their married lives, and finally come home properly when they had. One of the few, tangible constants in a life that had been full of intangibles; negotiations, cautious friendships and uneasy domiciles.

Oh, but she would not have missed any of it. Not for worlds of security.

But she missed the man she had shared it all with. Missed him even more acutely every single day.

'Oh, Edward,' Molly breathed. 'I need your wisdom, now. This is all beyond me.'

The phone conversation had been brief and disappointing. Nothing in the locker answered the description.

'One box with documents in, and a couple of photo albums, but nothing like you said there'd be.'

There was a silence from the other end of the conversation that spoke volumes about dissatisfaction and a degree of scepticism.

'There wasn't much in the locker. Some bits of furniture, a few old books and . . .'

'Books? You went through them all?'

'Well . . .'

'But you brought the papers with you, I hope.'

It was not a question.

'Yes, I've got them in the car.'

'Then I'll send someone out to collect. But I'm disappointed, Colin, I truly am. I hope you realize that.'

The conversation ended and Colin let out a deep breath and then looked across at the passenger seat. His companion shook his head. 'Not a good man to cross,' he said. 'So what now?'

'We deliver the box and get ourselves lost for a while,' Colin

said heavily. 'And we hope that security bloke lives. Did you have
to hit him that hard?'

'Why do you care? Shouldn't have been there, should he.'

'Start to finish it was just stupid,' Colin said angrily.

'Going to tell *him* that, are you?'

Colin said nothing. He just started the car and pulled out from
the side road where they'd been parked up and back into the traffic.

NINE

June 1961.

'What the hell!'
Adam jerked the steering wheel around, his body
swerving, reflexively, even before the car slewed across
the road.

Had he missed the man? Not by more than inches if he had.

Adam was leaping from the driving seat even as his hand reached
to cut the engine.

My God, I've hit him!

The man had fallen. Front wheels of the car poised over his left
hand as though he'd reached out to stop it and been pushed aside.

I've hit him . . .

Where the hell was he bleeding from? Did he hit his head on the
road when he fell?

'Are you all right! No, no, don't try to move. You can hear me,
can't you? Are you all right?'

The man on the ground turned his head slowly and managed a
lip cracked half smile.

'Not dead yet, am I?'

'What? Oh, I see.' Adam laughed breathily. 'Yes, I mean no. No,
you're certainly not dead.'

For a moment the man closed his eyes, seemed to grow limp and
passive. Then he moved his head slightly and stared at Adam.

'Where?' he managed. 'Tell me where I am.'

Adam stared at him, taken aback by the unexpected question.

'Er, Leopoldville,' he managed. 'Well, near as damn it. It's about five miles that way.' He gestured loosely up the way he had been headed. Then, 'My God! What happened to you? I thought I'd hit you when you went down like that.'

Again, the man smiled, faintly, his lips cracking and bleeding with even such slight effort.

'Argument . . .' he whispered. 'Argument . . . with a friend . . .'

'Some friend!'

Adam frowned. It was clear he wouldn't get his answers now, and the main thing was to get this man some help.

'If I help you, can you stand?' he asked.

'Got this far, didn't I.'

'This far? Where . . .? No, never mind, let's just get you into the car.'

Kneeling close beside the stranger, Adam slid an arm beneath his shoulders, apologizing rapidly and nervously as the man winced.

'It's all right,' the man said. He leaned heavily against Adam, catching him a little off balance and causing him to stagger as, together, they pushed to their feet. The man groaned sharply at the sudden pressure on his right side. He clung convulsively to Adam's arm, waiting for the worst of the pain to pass away.

'I'll be all right now.' It was more of a gasp than separate words.

Bloodstained spittle clung to the stranger's mouth. Adam eased him gently towards the car and hoped, fervently, that it came only from his cut and bleeding lips.

He pulled the passenger door, sharply, and lowered the man gently into the seat. It wasn't easy, posting him in sideways, then swinging him around to get his legs inside.

He slammed the door, ran around to the driver's side and slipped into the seat.

'Just do me a favour, huh?'

The man turned his head, questioning.

'Don't die on me on the way.'

Joseph Bern smiled and whispered softly. 'I'll try hard to cause you no more . . . inconvenience,' he said. Then closed his eyes and seemed to sleep.

September 24th, Present Day

Evening. Only just past five and yet as dark as midnight. Thick cloud, most of it still raining, Adam drove as quickly and as safely as he could, but the journey had been a slow one.

Worcester an hour ago, gone to bed early and strangely empty, the foul weather having driven all but the most determined back inside. The last fraction of the journey was the most tiresome. The network of side roads confusing both him and the satnav. Twice he took the wrong turn. Twice had to backtrack and by the time he turned the car into the broad, overgrown driveway of the converted house, he was both very tired and very irritable.

He brought the car to a halt and stared up at the old house, it's lighted windows, mostly semi-screened by heavy curtains or by broad, vertical blinds.

The hospice doors stood atop of five stone steps. A ramp had been added at the left-hand side. In the half-light that fell upon it from the windows, it seemed to have a temporary aspect, somehow unfinished. The original, heavy wooden door stood open. An inner glass door partitioned the hallway. Adam could glimpse movement, figures passing across the broad hallway and the hard edge of what must be the reception desk off to one side.

Adam sighed deeply and unfastened his seat belt and killed the engine.

Now he was here, he felt a strange uncertainty, born, he thought, of the long journey and the driving rain and the tiredness that came with it.

What did Joseph want with him after all this time?

He thought of that first day, the journey back to Leopoldville, Joseph slumped in the car beside him, opening his eyes just as they entered the first sprawling outskirts of the city.

'What's your name?' Adam had asked him. 'I thought I'd run you down and I don't even know what to call you.'

The man had turned his head and smiled that pained slow smile again. His face, half in shadow, turned to Adam, the other half, oddly white in the harsh sun. Slowly, he'd extended his left hand across his body, reaching towards Adam as though he might shake his hand.

'Joseph Bern,' he had said. 'They call me Joseph Bern.'

They call me Joseph Bern . . .

Slowly, reluctantly and yet, with the kind of nervous, excited apprehension Joseph had always managed to inspire in him, Adam got out of the car, crossed the brief expanse of sodden gravel drive and made his way up the steps and into the hospice reception.

TEN

Naomi and Alec had eaten early and then retired to the bar and sat in a quiet corner enjoying a drink. The hotel was in a residential area that lacked a pub of its own and they had discovered that quite a few locals used it casually in the evening, coming for a meal or just a pint. Naomi listened abstractedly to the buzz of chat and clink of glasses. It was a friendly sound, normal and familiar.

'I'm hungry,' she said.

'You just had dinner.'

'I know, not that kind of hungry, more the going to see if there's any cake left, kind of hungry. You know, like at home, when we drifted into the kitchen and had a late supper, just because we wanted to.'

Alec laughed. 'You have to have your own kitchen if you want to do that,' he said. 'The chef seems the friendly type, but I'm not sure he'd let you raid his fridge. But I'm sure we can get dessert if you want some.'

She thought about it and shook her head. 'I think it's more wanting the whole kitchen thing than the whole cake thing, if you know what I mean.'

'I know what you mean,' he agreed. 'Which brings us back to what next?'

It was the first time she'd said anything like this and Alec took it as a sea change in the way Naomi was feeling. 'I think it's a kind of homesickness,' he said.

She nodded. 'That's exactly it. Alec, I think I want to go home.'

'You want me to phone the buyer, tell them it's not going to happen?'

She shook her head. 'No, it's a bit late for that. I think what I mean is we need to just decide on a place to be, buy somewhere that will do for now, that can be home while we figure out what we actually want. I mean, we're in a very lucky position, we've got money to do a cash sale, how many people can say that? We can find somewhere that will be OK for now and then sort it out later, can't we?'

Alec nodded. 'Sounds like a plan,' he said.

'But we've got to sort out this Molly thing first,' Naomi said flatly.

'We don't have to. We can just walk away and let the police deal with it.' He laughed. 'See what I did then, I talked about the police like it's them and us. I'm getting better at it.'

'Hmm, a little. We can't walk away, Alec, you know that, but what I want to do is put a time limit on things. If Molly won't help herself well there's not a lot anyone can do. We stay another week and then we move on. We do all we can to help out in that week, but after that, she sorts it out herself or she gives in and lets DI Barnes and his people help her. Agreed?'

'I'll drink to that,' Alec said. 'So, where do we go looking for the "it'll do" home?'

She smiled. 'We could try sticking a pin in the map,' she said.

Alec harrumphed, then realized he sounded like Molly. 'I seem to remember we did that before,' he said. 'It didn't work out so well that time.'

Molly sat alone with her own thoughts. The radio was on and a classical concert played softly, but she wasn't really listening. She was remembering the concerts she'd attended with Edward and the music they had danced to. Edward always loved to dance, even as they grew older and the idea of dancing all night was just a fond memory, he had still been a fine mover. Elegant and upright. But that was just Edward, wasn't it, a man so upright and so convinced he knew what was right and what was wrong and Molly had believed whatever Edward said . . . even when she didn't.

She closed her eyes and recalled that young man coming up the stairs, gun in hand, pausing on her landing. It was his breathing that had warned her, told her he was unprepared for this. She could hear the tension in his chest as he drew the air into his lungs. It was that which had told her and she'd felt so insulted that they'd sent a mere beginner, an *amateur*, after *her*. Just because I'm old, Molly had thought, doesn't mean I'm bloody helpless.

She remembered how she'd squared her shoulders and cast aside the now useless phone. Dimly, she could hear the woman calling her name, but Molly had tuned her out, knowing she'd only have seconds to act and that she had to get it right, sirens from the approaching cars cutting through the night, approaching far too fast, now. The help she had summoned arriving both too early and too late.

Molly opened her eyes and stretched, unwilling, for the moment, to think about what had come next, not because it bothered her but because she had to keep her story straight.

'You think only about your legend,' Edward had told her. 'Replay your legend until it becomes the truth. Nothing else, no other thought, no uncertainty. Make *your* truth *the* truth. There can be nothing else.'

'Nothing else,' Molly said softly. 'I never lie.'

ELEVEN

The television report was vague, Bill thought, but then the whole event had been a bit vague. He'd finally got home for lunch, leaving the police still there, attended now by his colleagues on the day shift.

News from the hospital had not been good. Tony was in intensive care, his wife had called Sheila twice, but there was nothing new to tell. He'd come through an operation and they were worried about pressure on the brain, that was all she could say.

'She doesn't blame you,' Sheila had told Bill. 'There's nothing you could have done. Bill, it could just as easily have been you.'

They'd watched the television news obsessively all day, wondering if reporters would come knocking at their door and hoping not. There were reporters at the warehouse and at the hospital, but the police liaison officer they'd spoken to seemed to think the fuss would die down soon enough.

'So far as the media know, a security man was attacked during a robbery,' she'd told them. 'Bill, I know that's not the whole truth, but the investigation won't be helped by a lot of speculation. You understand that? We don't want whoever did this to know exactly what we know. We want to keep them off balance, so we're only releasing certain facts.'

He'd nodded, not sure he agreed, but well, what could he do. He'd had to tell Sheila, though, about the men in the van and his efforts to get them out and the police arriving and then that awful moment of realization, that all this was just a decoy, some elaborate plot to get the warehouse clear for some strange kind of robbery.

'It's not right,' Sheila said, echoing Bill's thoughts. 'They've not said anything about those poor men in the van. I mean, they could be dead and we wouldn't know. What about their families? It's getting like a police state, them telling us what we can't say.'

'It's not like that, Sheila, love. They just want to be able to investigate without falling over reporters, I suppose. Like the police-woman said, they want to keep the criminals in the dark too.'

Sheila was obviously not convinced and to be truthful, neither was Bill. He'd seen that van, seen how elaborate and strange the events had been and he knew, he just felt it in his water, that this was much bigger than they could guess and likely bigger than the police could guess either.

Several hundred miles away, Bud was channel surfing. There was a nag at the back of his brain that wasn't usually there once he'd finished a job. Something about this one refused to let go. Bud wasn't in the business of having a conscience about his actions, so he knew that the nag had nothing to do with that. It was more, he recognized, that the whole project felt unfinished; unresolved, which seeing as he wasn't usually in the business of bothering about what happened after he'd been paid, was an equally strange sensation for him to be indulging in.

He'd caught something on one of the rolling news channels earlier and that had got him thinking too. It was only a vague hint of a report, not repeated in the next bulletin, but there'd be an item about a warehouse being broken into and a security guard badly injured, and then that small scrap of information; that an ambulance had been called out to the scene a half-hour earlier in response to some incident with a van. The report implied that this had, maybe, been a simple RTA, and the reporter had clearly not been told if the two incidents were related. The van had been missing from the next bulletin, had scant mention in the third, but Bud had been watching closely by then, looking behind the cordon as the reporter spoke to camera, and he had caught just a glimpse of the van and it had confirmed his suspicion. It was the van he had briefly driven in with Ryan the afternoon before.

The niggle left the back of his brain and came and perched on his shoulder. So, what's this really all about, the niggle said.

'It's about none of my business,' Bud told it, but a few minutes later he was down in reception, checking out and telling the curious receptionist that he'd had a call from his wife and needed to head for home.

Since leaving Ryan, Bud had changed cars twice, an hour later and he'd changed his ride yet again, and was heading further north and east, and the niggle had now grown into a fully fledged nag, that

sat beside him in the passenger seat and told him to keep driving and
not to stop.

TWELVE

Anywhere but the Congo in 1961 and the meeting Adam had
just left would most likely have been impossible. Adis
Ngouba, French schooled but British trained, aide to the
embryonic Ministry of Trade. Duane Emerson, an American techni-
cian, doing his best to put his government's case. Piotre Vasse, a
Ukrainian engineer, who spoke English as if it were a language
worth strangling. Edward Chambers, some kind of attaché with the
British mission, who had flown in three days before, with his young
bride, Molly, in tow. And Adam himself, another Brit, his specialty
communications and electronics.

The four men had met a dozen times in the past three weeks, then
Edward joining the conversation late, but coming quickly up to speed.
Twelve meetings, suffused with a heady mix of political manoeuvring
and technical discussion. And an awareness that the country stood
on the brink of civil war and that all the talk and planning could
well come to nothing.

Today Adam was glad to get free of the meeting. The conference
room of the Leopold Hotel, the only neutral ground all five men
and their backers could agree upon was stiflingly hot. Ceiling fans
did their best to revive the stale air and all the windows had been
thrown open, doing little to alleviate the heat, just letting in the
noise and dust of the street below.

Adam forced himself to remember how important these meetings
were. The future of the entire country was being decided by men
like him in rooms like this. Mostly the excitement of being in on
the ground floor was enough to keep him going, but today, it wasn't
working for him.

He was hot and tired and sick of cloudless skies.

Out in the street, traders were shutting up shop and clearing their
goods off the streets.

There will be rain, they told him. Get inside.

Looking up at the polished blue of the sky, Adam found it hard to believe them but his body, aching with the heat and clammy in his sweat-soaked shirt, wished they could be right.

It was only a short distance from the hotel to the single-storey, wooden building that passed for a clinic here on the outskirts of Leopoldville, but Adam decided that he had no energy to walk. Besides, if the locals were right and the rain was coming, he'd be glad of the transport. So he drove, keeping his speed down on the narrow streets blocked by wandering people and stray dogs. Streets so dry that however slow his pace he raised a dust storm around the jeep that choked his lungs and filled his eyes with dirt.

Christ! But he wished the rain would come.

Adam got his wish just as he reached the hospital and cut the engine. In those brief moments the sky had lost its brilliant blue. Clouds, thick and black with rain, boiled and surged like some cauldron in a skyward hell. As Adam sprang from the jeep, the first rain began to fall, heavy and torpid and dropping with such force upon the dusty ground that the dirt exploded, fizzing into the air.

Adam ran across the open area and thundered in hard boots on to the veranda. Then he paused to look back as the few leaden drops of rain became a solid curtain hiding the world from view and the sooty clouds created night at mid-afternoon.

'I've come to see Joseph Bern,' Adam told the woman at the desk.

She smiled. 'If I could just have your name, sir,' she said to him, 'and you'll need to sign the book.'

Silently, Adam did as he was asked and waited for her to tell him where to go.

This wasn't Africa, he reminded himself, and this wasn't then. Not that hot afternoon that turned to vicious rain. Back in a time that seemed another life ago. Neither was it Venezuela or Cuba or Bosnia or any of the theatres in which he and Joseph had played their part.

He followed the directions he had been given, down the corridor and into a small room towards the back of the converted house. The room was quiet and cool, a ceiling fan turned slowly, lazily, as though it tried hard not to break the peace. Joseph lay in a too neat bed, arms resting on the outside of the blue coverlet as though he had been carefully arranged and now lacked the strength to move.

Adam was shocked. So shrunken. Joseph was younger than him by a good five years, but his face was so drawn and dry he appeared almost mummified.

As Adam stood uncertainly just inside the door, the head on the pillow moved and the eyes opened. Still that piercing blue. Joseph stared at Adam and the lips moved. 'Where?' he managed. 'Tell me where I am.'

Adam stared at him, taken aback by the unexpected question, but then remembered that day, back when Joseph had first tumbled into his life, lurching out of the trees, bleeding from a wound to his head. Barefoot, his feet leaving reddened tracks in the dust. 'Tell me,' Joseph had asked him. 'Tell me where I am.'

'This isn't the Congo my friend. This is England.'

Joseph smiled. 'You can tell them apart?'

'Just about. The rain is colder here. What happened to you?'

Joseph tried to laugh. 'Always to the point,' he commented. 'Cancer. I have maybe a few days or maybe only a few hours. Not long.'

'I'm sorry. I truly am.' Adam crossed the room and pulled up a chair, angled so that Joseph could see him easily.

'Come to my funeral?' Joseph asked.

'Of course.'

'You must be sick of funerals. Mine will be the fourth, I think. This year, I mean. There have been too many to count before that.'

'How did you know that? About the four this year?'

'Oh, I read the obituary columns and there are mutual friends who keep me well informed. I was too ill to make it to any of them, I'm sad to say, but I remember Duane and Piotre. Adis died long ago, of course. You were there, I recall.'

Adam looked away, shaking the memory before it took hold. 'I was there,' he confirmed. 'We're all getting older, Joseph. Death is bound to be a frequent visitor.'

Joseph laughed again. 'Death was always a frequent visitor, Adam, wherever we were he was certain to be invited. But this has nothing to do with old age. I have proof of that.'

'Proof? Of what?'

Joseph closed his eyes, his strength seeming to ebb. He coughed, then gasped for breath, the effort shaking his fragile body. Adam wondered if he should call for the nurse.

'The drawer,' Joseph managed finally, between painful gasps. 'Red folder, in the drawer.'

Puzzled, Adam reached into the bedside drawer and withdrew a fat, red file wrapped about with a half dozen elastic bands.

'Take it and go,' Joseph told him. 'I don't have the strength to talk any more, but I'm glad you came.'

'What is this?' Adam demanded. As always in his dealings with Joseph he had the feeling he was being set up for something; he suffered from the annoyance that he came back for more every bloody time.

Joseph Bern smiled, it lit his face and danced in his eyes and, in that moment, Adam remembered just why he kept coming back.

'Bosnia,' Joseph managed. 'Other things too, but mostly Bosnia and Congo. Read it, I prepared it for you. You could say that it is my legacy.'

He closed his eyes then and Adam watched as his old friend and sometimes enemy fall into sleep. He wondered if he'd wake again.

He paused at the desk to speak to the nurse, telling her that Joseph seemed to be having trouble breathing and to make sure the hospice had his contact details for when the inevitable happened.

'He's had very few visitors,' she said. 'He has no family?'

'No. There's no one left now. You'll let me know if any arrangements have to be made.'

She smiled. 'It's all been taken care of,' the nurse told him. Joe has organized it all. 'Some people feel the need, you know. It makes them feel happier if they've put everything in order.'

Adam nodded, thinking wryly that logistics had always been Joseph's forte. Then thinking it odd that the young woman should refer to him as Joe. No one, in Adam's experience, ever had.

He drove home, the red folder lying on the passenger seat. Adam eyed it suspiciously from time to time, wondering what it contained, wondering if he'd be better off not knowing. If he should just keep it until the funeral and then bury it, unopened, with the man who had compiled it. He no longer wanted any part in such matters as their mutual past had brought.

Joseph stirred, the pain in his lungs interrupting his desire for sleep. He too remembered that first day, but his thoughts strayed to the hours before he had met Adam Carmodie that first time.

He recalled the grit beneath his nails. The ground hard under his back and pinprick rough against the line of bare skin where his shirt had been pulled free.

Insistent voices, too far off to make out the words or even the language. Like voices off stage. Out of the action.

And then, there were hands. Hands pulling him upright. Steadying him when he thought he was about to fall. Arms, thrust beneath his own, keeping him on his feet.

Joseph could not move. Joseph was certain that he could not move, but they dragged him forward.

His head dropped towards his chest and the sun-baked ground scraped against his feet as they manhandled him, pulling him towards the half open tent flap.

They must have taken his boots.

Grit beneath his nails. Sandy, fragmented earth rasping against his skin.

He tried to move his feet, place them flat on the ground but Joseph found that he couldn't quite remember how.

His legs buckled but they dragged him on. Pain in his right side as one of his captors pushed close, recalling the sharp memory of someone kicking him there. Throwing him to the floor, kicking at his side with hard-toed boots.

The pain grew worse as they forced him to bend beneath the tent flap. Then the brightness as they turned his face towards the sun.

Joseph could feel his skin begin to tighten under the sudden heat and he could smell the sweat on his own body, pungent and musky, mixed with the scent of sun-dried earth and summer dust. The smell of sunlight, hot and harsh, breathed into pain-scorched lungs.

He could smell them too. The one's that held him. Sweat long dried on unwashed bodies. A smell that matched his own, strong and sour, and filled with too much heat.

Joseph felt what little strength was left in his legs diminish. Pouring out through his feet and into the dust. And then the other one was there.

Joseph fought hard to put a name to the scent. Put a face to the man who came now, to stand, almost companionably at Joseph Bern's left shoulder; to speak so softly in his ear. This one's scent, clean and newly washed, redolent with soap and fresh drawn water, laced with just the merest tang of woodsmoke.

'I'm letting you live, Joseph. Letting you go. We will agree to differ on this matter and you will agree to leave.'

Joseph could see the other's face, now, in his mind's eye, as clearly as if he stood before him, blocking out the blinding brilliance of the sun. The sweet half smile, the pale blue eyes, soft with regret as though he had no wish for any of this unpleasantness.

And that was all.

They dragged him forward once again, feet scraping the ground as they moved him far too fast for his feet to gain a purchase.

Then lifted by the arms, thrown face down on to the wooden flat of an open truck.

Pain cut into him, lancing into his belly and drilling into the ribs on his right side. Vibrations of pain as the truck engine started.

Rattling and shaking through his frame, a network of pain, resonating with an almost musical cruelty orchestrated by the engine noise, the shifting gears, the bumps and ruts of the mean excuse for a track that they were travelling along.

Joseph moaned, tried to shift his weight a little to ease the pain on his right side.

Joseph could feel the wood, rough and splintered, beneath his outstretched hand and beneath his cheek. Sun-warmed. Trapped heat. Trapped scents of wood and oil and dirt.

He tasted blood in his mouth.

And there was grit beneath his fingernails . . .

'Mr Bern.' A soft hand touched his face and then came to rest, gently, on his shoulder.

Joseph opened his eyes.

For a moment, he was back in Africa, back in that filthy flatbed truck with the pain vibrating though his body, lancing, knife-like, as he woke and moved.

But it was a woman's face he saw when he opened his eyes, and a woman's voice he heard and the pain was now, not the pain of more than fifty years ago.

And there was no sun, here. Only a patch of grey cloud, seen dimly through a blinded window and the lash of late September rain against the glass.

And the ironic thing, Joseph thought, was that back then he had not been the one to have taken the moral high ground. That time, it had been Clay.

'Do you want some water?'

'I'd rather have a whisky.'

She smiled. 'In a little while, Joe. I'll bring it before I go off duty. You've already had too much today.'

'Won't kill me,' he said and laughed harshly.

She lifted him and put the glass to his lips. It was getting harder to swallow. They'd offered him more pain relief. A morphine pump that he could control himself, but he'd resisted, knowing that really would signal the end and he wasn't quite ready yet.

She laid him down and Joseph turned his face towards the window, so he could watch the rain.

He'd arrived in the Congo before the rest of them, getting there just before the elections in May of 1960, paid by one of the big mining corporations to look at the logistics involved in shipping out the copper they planned to mine. The infrastructure wasn't as badly neglected as some places Joseph had known. Katanga, the state that produced almost two thirds of the Congo's mineral exports, had been shipping copper for fifty years. So, there were roads. More or less.

Joseph had surveyed for the company by day and watched as the political situation unfolded, going into Elizabethville most nights. There'd been something like eighty different political parties, Joseph remembered. But only two men stood out from the herd; Patrice Lumumba and Joseph Kasavubu.

Joseph heard the nurse coming back into his room.

'I thought you were going back to sleep,' she said.

'Too much on my mind.'

'You want to tell me? I like your stories.'

Stories, Joseph thought. That's all they were to her, this young woman, probably not even into her thirties.

Probably no older than he'd been back then.

'Sit, then,' he said. 'I'll talk for a little bit.'

He waited until she sat next to him, leaning her arms on the bed and putting her head close, so he didn't have to raise his voice.

'The Americans were scared,' he said. 'Lumumba had the backing of the Belgian Communists and the AAR and he'd persuaded some of the Belgian businesses to stay.' Joseph managed a harsh laugh. 'Not that he wanted them. Wanted the white colonists out, just like that Nkrumah, in Ghana. Said they should drive all the white colonists out of Africa.' He smiled. 'You know how many attempts there were to kill him? Man was like Castro, seemed to have a charmed life. CIA even sent him poisoned toothpaste.'

'I heard they sent Castro an exploding cigar.'

Joseph choked out a laugh, but his eyes were closing. He felt her move, then tuck his hand beneath the sheet before leaving softly.

He recalled how he had continued with his survey and he and that geologist . . . Joseph could not recall the man's name. They had discovered what looked like new reserves. The only fly in the ointment was that they were on *Baluba* land. Not, Joseph thought, that anyone actually cared what the *Baluba* thought. A favourite sport of the mercenaries that Joseph remembered from Elizabethville, was to go out hunting the *Baluba*.

The *Baluba* didn't seem to have any part in this new and promised world of independence and profitability.

Joseph shifted awkwardly on to his side. It was all in the file he had given Adam, all of Joseph's guilt, all of his mistakes. But more important than that, there was Clay, running through every page; guilt, written in blood. Joseph knew, had he been less of a moral coward, he might have revealed all this years before. But he was implicated; as guilty, as bloody as any other, and to betray Clay would have been to betray himself.

The pain had receded just a little and finally allowing his eyes to close, he drifted into sleep.

THIRTEEN

If asked for a description, the one thing people always said about Clay was how pale his eyes were. There had always been light, but looking in the mirror – which he bothered to do only when shaving – he had to admit that the passing years had leached even more of the colour from them.

The second thing people said was that his eyes changed with his mood. That often that strange shift from blue to almost steely grey was the only clue to what he really thought about anything. The only clue they had that life was about to get that much harder. At rest, when he felt happy, when he woke from sleep the pale blue was almost the colour of washed-out forget-me-nots and, since retirement, or what passed for it in his world, the man had actually been happy more of the time than he'd been enraged or frustrated or simply irritated, which was good news for those who happened to cross his path.

Right at this present moment, though, he was anything but and the young man with him was both conscious of the potential threat and, oddly, amused by it.

'Secrets,' Nathan said.

'Not the ones we are looking for.'

'Were they ever?' Nathan allowed himself a smile. Clay did not intimidate him; he'd known the man too long, grown up in his shadow. Seen the moods and tides too often to be afraid. Besides, Nathan wasn't sure he knew how to be afraid.

'Maybe Annie was right,' he said. 'Maybe there is nothing left for anyone to know. Maybe no one ever knew as much as you thought they did.'

One of Clay's dogs wandered over to where he sat and lay a muzzle on the arm of his chair. Nathan stoked it absently. Clay had two of these great big hounds, Hugin and Munin he called them. Thought and Memory, like Odin's ravens. Nathan liked them both; big and impressive looking, but gentle as lambs, they seemed at odds with everything else Clay embraced.

Clay frowned; that in itself was a rare expression of emotion and Nathan logged it thoughtfully. In his opinion and in Annie's, Clay was obsessed about something that no longer concerned anyone. The fears and anxieties of his youth had come back to haunt him and neither Annie nor Nathan could quite put their finger on why. Had something actually happened that had raised Clay's concerns? Or was it, as Annie had suggested in a seemingly outrageous moment, the onset of senility?

Nathan had known she had a point, but they'd both just looked at one another for a moment and then Nathan had shaken his head. 'No, not Clay.' And Annie had pretended to agree. Neither of them had mentioned it again until the day that Clay had finally consented to see the doctor and the doctor had referred him for a brain scan and the results of that had been . . . .

'You should have sent someone to just talk to Molly Chambers,' Nathan said.

He'd said it before, Clay had disagreed then and he did now.

'Molly wouldn't talk, not to anyone. Any more than Edward would, we none of us *talked*.'

Nathan shrugged. True, he thought. The old guard and their code of silence. Or was it just the old guard? Annie was probably the only one alive who knew Nathan's secrets and, for that matter, Nathan was probably the only one who knew hers. As far as Clay was concerned, that would mean that they'd both confided in one person too many.

Clay assumed he knew everything, Nathan supposed. It was what Clay did; it was unlikely he would have even conceived of a situation in which secrets could be kept from him. That, in Nathan's view, was perhaps his one weakness.

'Sometimes you could just ask, you know. Once people are dead, they're a little on the silent side. Shooting them before they can tell is not always the best option.'

Clay looked at Nathan with those cold grey eyes of his and said nothing. Most people would have been intimidated by that and, for a brief moment, Nathan considered it. He discarded the idea immediately. 'Clay, why now?' He voiced the question he and Annie had mulled over. 'What happened to make all of this stuff break surface again? It's ancient history.'

Clay shook his head and Nathan watched as he seemed to wrestle with that concept. 'Not to me, it isn't,' he said finally. 'It's as clear as yesterday and just as important. Lives depend on us, you should know that more than anyone. Identities, Molly knows too many of them. We have to protect our own, Nathan.'

The younger man nodded solemnly. He didn't think it was the right moment to remind Clay that most of those they counted 'their own' were dead anyway and the rest were either so well hidden even they couldn't remember who they'd once been. Or they were like himself and Annie. Outside of it all, except when they chose to become involved, bound only by habit and what, he supposed, they still owed to the likes of Edward and Molly and Clay.

He glanced over at the older man. The old man, Nathan corrected himself. He wasn't sure how old Clay actually was; Annie doubted even Clay knew how old he actually was, but older than the likes of Molly and Edward Chambers, that was for sure. And a man who'd given his entire life to the job he'd done. He knew nothing else.

Nathan knew that Annie felt sorry for their one time mentor and Nathan had asked her once if she actually liked Clay or if she knew anyone that did. She had thought for a moment and then shaken her head. 'Nothing to like,' she said. 'Respect, yes, feel grateful, yes, but like? No, I don't think so. It's a bit like you can admire, respect, even see the beauty in something like a great white shark, but would you really bring it home to meet your parents . . . always supposing you had parents for it to meet.'

'Always supposing another great white hadn't got to them first,' Nathan had joked, knowing he was the only one she'd ever accept such humour from.

'Supposing that,' Annie had agreed.

Nathan studied the man with pale eyes. They were closed now as if he'd fallen asleep. Nathan always found it wisest to assume that he had not. In repose, the lines on the tanned face were pale, a whole network of them spidering out from mouth and eyes and down on to the jaw.

And Nathan wondered if Annie was right about something else. It there'd come a moment when it was down to them, to Annie and Nathan to put an end to all this. To either finish what Clay had started . . . or to finish Clay.

FOURTEEN

DI Barnes took both Naomi and Alec by surprise and turned up at their hotel just after breakfast. They found a corner of the bar, not open at this time of the morning and drank tea by the big bay window.

'So?' Alec prompted when the small talk had run dry.

'So, have you spoken to your aunt?'

'Spoken to and been told what to do with our advice and that she knows nothing more.'

'And do you think she's telling the truth?'

Naomi laughed. 'Molly always tells the truth,' she said.

'What Naomi means,' Alec interpreted, 'is that Molly's sins are always one of omission rather than commission. She only tells anyone what she thinks they need to know or would want to hear. The rest, as they say, is silence.'

DI Barnes sighed. 'And your feelings are?'

'That she didn't necessarily recognize *him*. The man who shot himself may not have been known to her per se, but she knew what he was; recognized the type, maybe something about him that she had seen or known about before. Molly's been around the block a few times.'

'I'm not sure I completely understand. Recognized what? That he was a killer? I think the gun might have been a giveaway there.'

'Ah, but he didn't, did he? Kill her, I mean,' Naomi pointed out. 'And maybe that's the most interesting question. Why didn't he?'

'I have two murder enquiries,' DI Barnes said, 'The SIO of each one is waiting to see if I can provide information that might break the case. They, in turn are being pressured to now close what seem to have been solved cases, in the who did it category at least, even if we're no further on as to motive. Having a name, would be an advantage. The media like names and our bosses like to satisfy the media.'

'I mean, she recognized him as a professional,' Alec said. 'Bill, this wasn't some random stranger wandering into another random stranger's house and blowing their own brains out. Naomi's right. We've talked about this and we've no doubt that your other victims were killed either by the same man or the same organization and there must be a link. Why—'

'Organization?'

Alec ignored the interruption.

'So, Naomi is right. The interesting question is, why the hitter didn't make this hit.'

Barnes was silent for a moment, considering, then he said. 'Neither of you seem terribly surprised that someone would want Molly Chambers dead,' he said. 'You'll excuse me if I find that a little peculiar.'

Naomi laughed again. 'You've just not spent enough time with her yet.'

'That aside,' Alec said. 'Molly and her husband, Edward, spent almost their entire married life attached to some embassy or other, Edward and I suspect, Molly, though she's never told me directly, were involved in negotiating truces with Afghan Warlords, Beirutie kidnappers and Venezuelan opposition parties, and that's just the little bits I know. They made powerful friends and even more powerful enemies. I know Edward retired almost ten years ago, but I also know that retirement didn't mean pottering in his garden. He acted as consultant to a number of government agencies and some very big corporations. I don't think his security clearance was ever revoked. Get a map of the world and stick a pin in it and I'd bet you a damn good dinner Molly would have been there or know someone that had. It was what they did. What, I think, she'd always done. Get her to show you her official photo albums, Bill, they're a who's who of every damned world leader, of whatever political persuasion from here to . . . Zanzibar. Edward lived for this stuff and Molly . . . Molly lived for Edward.'

'And you think this shooting, this suicide, was something to do with her diplomatic past? I don't see how that links to our other victims. Or even if it does.'

'Oh, there'll be a link, and it's one that whoever authorized this wants to be identified,' Naomi said. 'Think about it. What assassin

uses the same, unusual weapon, three times over? It would flag up
in a half dozen different searches. Someone is sending a message;
you just need to figure out what it is and who it's for.'

'Couldn't they just send a bloody postcard?' Barnes grumbled.
He paused thoughtfully. 'Look, I'm not sure you are right about
any of this, in fact I hope you're not, quite frankly. I prefer my
murders to be straightforward, not all cloak and dagger. Look, Alec,
I'm meeting a colleague of mine later today, at the flat of the second
victim, Herbert Norris. I've got permission for you to tag along if
you'd be interested.'

There was a long pause. Naomi voiced what they were thinking.
'And how many arms did you have to twist?' she asked.

'Ah, well, that's the thing,' Barnes said uncomfortably. 'It wasn't
actually my idea at all. It was, shall we say, suggested that I invite
you to consult.'

'Who by?'

Barnes shrugged. 'Directly, by my DCI, indirectly. . . . Alec, no
offence, I'd welcome a new pair of eyes on this of course, but don't
expect me to be comfortable with being told what to do and who
to do it with, and especially don't expect me to be comfortable with
the conclusion that someone well above my pay grade is thinking
along the same lines as you are. Given all that . . .'

Alec hesitated and Naomi could feel the thoughts and memories
writhing in his brain as acutely as if they'd crawled across her skin.

She knew he would say yes, he couldn't not. Curiosity and concern
for Molly would conspire to draw him in, but it still disturbed her.
This felt too much like the events they had both been through so
recently. Events that had led them to the indigent lifestyle they now
followed. She knew what kind of life Molly had led, Alec had told
her some of it and Alec's father filled in some other details. She
admired Molly, rather than liked her. The older woman had a spirit
and energy that Naomi hoped she might possess when she was
Molly's age, but she also sensed – no it was more than that; had
grown *sensitive* to the undercurrents, dangerous and deep, that she
and Alec had fallen into earlier that year.

The experience then had been painful and stressful and she had
no wish to repeat it now.

'Alec?'

'I'm not sure I want to go with you,' Alec said.

'Any particular reason?'

'Same reasons I had for leaving the job. I don't want to be dragged back in again.'

'A quick look round a flat, that's all it will be, a few thoughts on some notes I've had sent over. Alec, I don't think I like this any more than you do—'

'Oh, believe me, I don't think you have a clue how I feel about it.'

'Ook-aay,' DI Barnes breathed. 'Look, no one can force you, but I know you care about Molly and I also know, because I've done some digging about, that you're a first class investigator. I could use your eyes on this, Alec.' He paused. 'I suspect, so could Molly.'

'That sounds awfully close to blackmail,' Naomi commented.

'It probably is,' Bill Barnes agreed. 'I don't want the hassle of facing my boss and telling him that former DI Friedman told him to stick the idea.'

'Oh, poor you.' Naomi was caught between amusement and downright annoyance. but she knew which way this discussion would go. She was right. She heard her husband set his cup down and ease himself into his seat. He clasped her hand, silently asking for her approval and, reluctantly, she nodded.

'Give me five minutes,' Alec said, 'and I'll be ready to go.'

FIFTEEN

It had been close on eight months since Bob Taylor had seen his wife and the first he knew of her return was the smell of toast and bacon that reached him as he came through the side gate and crossed the garden. The dogs knew what it meant too; their owner never cooked breakfast, making do with a pot of strong tea and whatever he thought to pick up from the fruit bowl on the kitchen table, before disappearing into his studio.

Bob paused, standing beneath the apple trees and wondering for a moment how he felt about her being there. Fly, the youngest of the two dogs had no such reservations, yipping excitedly, his short body whipping side to side in a frenzy of tail wagging. Rabbie, older and more sensitive to his master's thoughts, looked up expectantly as though waiting to be told that he could celebrate. Bob fondled the old dog's silky ears. 'OK, so she's home,' he said, knowing that if he had a tail to wag he'd be doing so as well.

Annie was by the range, turning bacon in the pan and dancing to music on the radio. She turned, smiling at them. 'Hey. Thought you'd be along any time now. I borrowed your robe, couldn't find mine and I've put my stuff in the spare room, hope that's all right.'

She flipped the last piece of bacon and set the tongs down on the star-shaped brass trivet at the side of the stove. Bob folded his arms around her, inhaling her scent. She'd used his shampoo; he always put her things away when she left. It was easier not to have her stuff around during her long absences and, besides, he was never absolutely certain that she *would* come back. Not really. He could never really be sure of anything where Annie was concerned.

'Oh, but that feels good,' she said, hugging him tightly and then lifting her face for his kiss before pulling away.

'Eggs,' she said. 'You do have eggs?'

He pointed to a blue, covered bowl on the dresser.

'Oh, that's new. Very pretty.'

'I saw it in the antique market last month. I loved the colour.' He took a deep breath and asked the most important question. 'How long are you home for?'

Annie grinned at him. 'A couple of weeks, if that's OK, then I'll be off for about ten days, but then, if it's OK with you, can I stay until Christmas, maybe a bit longer.'

Christmas. That was months. Even in the early days of their marriage when Annie had tried so very hard to settle down, to be the wife she knew he wanted, she'd never been around for that long at any one time.

Friends and family told him he was crazy to put up with her. Bob didn't need telling, but he knew he'd be even crazier if he stopped.

'Why?' he asked. 'I mean, yes, of course it's fine. It's wonderful, but . . .'

'I've got a teaching job,' she said.

'A *teaching* job?'

She giggled. 'There's no need to sound so shocked. I'm fully qualified, you know and someone made me an offer I just couldn't refuse. It's only a few hours a week, and it's a temporary contract, but Bonnie told me about a friend of his over at the Arts Centre at Benton Place. You know they've just got a whole load of new funding? Well, they need tutors. And I applied and I start in October. If it goes well there'll be classes next spring too.'

She finished with the eggs and dished bacon and toast on to warm plates. Slid the eggs on top. 'Sit. I've already made tea.'

'But . . . teaching who?' He sat down and checked the strength of the tea in the bright red pot.

'Whoever turns up. It's mostly going to be adult returners, but Dan, that's the college director, he reckons that I've got a strong enough reputation in the business that we should attract a good calibre of student.' She laughed at his incredulity. 'I earned my living that way before, you know.'

Yes, and you hated it, Bob thought, but he said nothing. She was back, and not just for a few weeks this time. He knew she'd go again. Annie just could not settle, not even with the man she loved and Bob knew she loved him. He also knew that she couldn't change, not ever, not really.

'You really should remember to lock your doors,' she said as she attacked her breakfast. 'Anyone could just walk in.'

'No one locks their doors round here,' Bob reminded her. He paused, just looking at her. The thick, wavy black hair was still damp from the shower and her skin was tanned from whatever part of the world her latest adventures had taken her to. A small scar on the back of her hand was new. It stood out, still pink, against the brown skin. Green-grey eyes laughed at him. She had the most perfect, oval face. He'd sketched her so many times over the years but never quite managed to capture her in oils. To freeze Annie in the moment was an impossibility and eventually he had given up on trying. His wild girl, as he thought of her in secret moments. She had come hurtling into his life ten years ago and he, thirty years her senior and a confirmed bachelor – so confirmed that even close friends had assumed he must be gay – had fallen utterly and completely in love.

'I saw the posters for the new exhibition in the hall,' she said. 'They look wonderful. You've got to show me the new work after breakfast.'

'I'm pleased with it,' he admitted. 'And you'll be here for it.' He smiled.

'Yep, sure will. Not that I've missed one yet, you know.'

That was true. Sometimes it had been a close run thing, but she'd always returned for the important things in his life. Opening nights, birthdays, anniversaries. 'You were away a long time,' he said quietly. 'The longest time yet. I'd begun to think—'

She reached out across the table. 'I know,' she said. 'I'm sorry, my love. I stayed away for far too long. It won't happen again.'

'I didn't mean—'

'I know. But *I* did. I missed you. Bob, I may never stop being a nomad, but maybe it's time, you know, to try and be a bit less of one.'

He wanted to believe her and he knew she meant it, as far as Annie could ever mean anything like that. He clasped her hand. 'Good to have you home,' he said. 'Very, very good.'

SIXTEEN

The drive to Newark took a little over an hour. Dual carriageways gave way to a good, but narrow A road which swung off to bypass the town as Barnes and Alec continued on. The land was flat, here, not quite fenland but smoothing out as if in preparation. In the distance Alec glimpsed the chimneys of the sugar beet processor; they had crossed a river some minutes before with a small marina packed with boats. Off to the left he glimpsed the newer road rising and guessed the river too headed off in that direction.

'Newark on Trent,' he read on one of the painted signs. 'Of course, this is Nottinghamshire.'

'Just,' Barnes confirmed. They were in town now, passing the curtain-walled ruins of a castle which jogged some memory in Alec's brain that a civil war battle had been fought close by.

They turned left and Alec glimpsed the wide space of the market square. A little further on and Barnes pulled in outside a shuttered shop.

'He lived above the shop,' Barnes said. He nodded a welcome to a woman getting out of a car across the road. 'Alec, this is DS Tupper. Stevie, this is Alec, I told you about him?'

Stevie Tupper was in her thirties, Alec guessed, noting with interest that her short brown hair had been cut very precisely and she wore a bright red lipstick. Her handshake was firm, but she looked puzzled, even faintly disapproving. Alec felt like apologizing for being there but decided against. It wasn't his fault.

'We'd better go up,' she said. 'But I don't know what you expect to find that we haven't seen already. The boss says you can bring him back to look over the notes,' she said to Barnes and Alec figured that the handshake had been the full extent of her acceptance. She probably figured she'd done her duty towards him now. Barnes, obviously recognizing this too, shrugged apologetically.

This was going to be fun, Alec thought, already regretting his decision to come. He followed the officers up the stairs and into the flat above the shop. A door opened from the narrow lobby and he guessed that must be the private entrance into the shop. He decided he'd like to take a look before they left, thinking that the objects Herbert Norris chose to stock in his little shop might shed more light on the man himself. DI Barnes held the door open for him, Alec went inside.

'There's no lock on this door,' he said. 'Only a bolt.'

'Which has been painted over so many times it doesn't work,' Stevie Tupper said. 'You need a key to undo the downstairs door and there's a dead lock and two bolts. Same as on the shop door. I suppose he felt safe once those were fastened.'

'So. Whoever shot him, must have, what, rung the bell on the street door, Norris must have come down and let him in, then brought him back up here. Or been forced to bring him back up here. Any CCTV?' he asked hopefully.

Stevie laughed. 'Two cameras in the shop itself. Nothing inside and nothing in the street. This is not a high crime area.'

'And the footage from the shop over the past few days?'

She sighed. 'If you want to waste time looking it over, be my guest. We've had officers on it. Nothing of interest that *we* can see.'

Alec ignored her tone. Slowly, he walked the scene. It had been cleared for entry now, the CSI had collected every scrap of possible evidence and there was no defined path to follow, but Alec walked the perimeter anyway. Hands thrust in his pocket, as they always were when he was deep in thought. A fine dusting of fingerprint powder covered the shelves and coffee table and in the second room, the dining table had been given the same treatment. Kitchen counters, two cups on the draining board . . . in the bedroom the headboard shimmered with a faint veil of silver grey.

But there were no fingerprints. Only the evidence of the CSI's increasingly frustrated search.

'The place has been cleaned,' he said. 'Not just wiped down. Deep cleaned.'

Stevie said nothing; she just glanced non-committally at DI Barnes. 'What about the shop?' Alec asked.

'Untouched, so far as we can tell. I mean, there are fingerprints everywhere from customers handling stuff and so on.'

'So you've dismissed the CCTV.' Alec didn't mean it to sound so judgemental, but that was the way it came out. 'Because you think the killer would have cleaned up after himself if he'd ever been there as well.'

'We're assuming nothing,' Stevie Tupper said coldly.

Alec shrugged. He was discovering that there was something liberating about being an essential outsider.

He wandered back into the first room, noting the markers on the floor that defined where the body had lain. 'One shot,' he confirmed. 'Can I see the pictures?'

'Back at the station,' she said.

Alec grimaced. 'I always like to look at them on scene as well,' he said. 'It helps get things clear.'

'Well, I'm very sorry for the inconvenience—' Stevie began.

'Please,' Barnes interrupted. 'We're all on the same side. Alec doesn't want to be here any more than you want him, but if there's anything *useful* to come out of this, then I want to hear.'

Alec wondered if he should apologize; decided he didn't want to. Stevie Tupper turned her back on them both and went to stare out of the window.

A long, art deco sideboard took up most of the space along one wall. On it stood a lamp in the shape of a rather extravagantly elongated, deco nude, a few rather pleasing silver boxes and a couple of photo frames lying face down, their backs removed. Alec had noticed them on his first circuit of the room. 'The CSI did this?' he asked.

'No,' Stevie said without turning from the window. 'The photo frames were empty when we first got here. The girlfriend says they were family photos.'

'Did she say who of?'

'I don't think she knew. Some aunt or something, I think. And yes, we found that strange too, not just that someone would go to the trouble of removing family photos, but that a long term girlfriend would seem so vague.'

'Long term.'

'A year or two, closer to two since they met. She had a key, but didn't live with him. Said they both still needed their space.'

Alec nodded. 'Any more photographs?' he asked.

She pointed to the sideboard. 'Some albums in there, we took them. You can look later, but it seemed like the usual stuff to me.'

'No photographs on show of Norris and the girlfriend out on display? Can I speak to her, do you think?'

For a moment she looked like she'd be saying no, then she shrugged. 'I've been told to let you do pretty much what you want,' she said. The idea obviously really pissed her off. 'And no, no pictures on show except the two that are now missing.'

'Has the girlfriend been offered protection?' Alec asked.

'What for?' Stevie asked frostily. 'She's at her mother's, in Grantham. They've got someone checking in with them.'

Grantham, Alec thought. That was Lincolnshire, wasn't it? So a different force, different jurisdiction. Had they been told to cooperate with him too? He wondered who was pulling strings here, then wondered if he really wanted to know.

'You think the girlfriend might need protection?' Barnes asked.

'I think this is complicated,' Alec said. 'OK if we take a look at the shop, now?'

Stevie Tupper sighed and led them back down the stairs.

SEVENTEEN

Annie stretched out on the bed, listening to her husband singing in the shower. Welcome home sex was always good, she thought, it left her feeling content and sleepy and reminded her of just how much she was missing when she left him behind.

Bob Taylor was a good man. A loving, funny, talented man and Annie was always troubled by the thought that he deserved more. The truth was, she was more than a little afraid of remaining with anyone. It had taken encouragement on the part of her oldest friends to accept Bob's proposal of marriage because she was afraid.

'You love him,' Nathan had said. 'He loves you. What is there to think about?'

'Because I might lose him. He might . . .'

'We all die, Annie. Fact of life.'

She closed her eyes and snuggled back beneath the smooth sheets and warm blankets. Bob didn't like duvets. She knew exactly where the fear sprang from and knew that Nathan was right and as she inhaled Bob's scent on his pillow, knew that she really did want to stay, this time. If she could. That she was ready to try. The memory of the first time she had met Nathan Crow swam into her head and she let it. Time was, she'd have tried hard to push it away, but over the years she'd learnt that Edward – God rest him – and Nathan had been right. Memories are what make you who you are and if you don't acknowledge them they'll rise up and bite you on the bum, just when you least need it and lately, she'd learnt to let the memory come. To acknowledge and even enjoy it, seeing it as the start point, the birth really of the Annie she'd become.

She closed her eyes, remembering. The scene so vivid, even after all these years.

A man in a shabby uniform stood just inside the door, watching her with detached interest. He cradled a gun in his arms. She couldn't tell what it was, only that it was some kind of semi-automatic – she recognized that much from one that had been in her father's collection.

She supposed the man by the doorway must be some kind of soldier, but the word didn't quite fit; she was at a loss to find another.

'You must be Annie.' It was the man behind the desk that had spoken not the armed man by the door. She swivelled round to look at him. He came around the desk, his hand extended ready to shake hers. It was the first time an adult had ever offered to shake her hand.

'I'm Edward,' he said. 'Your father and I were friends, a very long time ago.'

'Why have you brought me here?' She shook his hand automatically. It seemed impolite not to and her parents had raised her to have good manners.

'I promised him that I would look after you if ever the need arose. And so I have.'

'And my mother?'

'I'm sorry,' Edward glanced at the man beside the door. 'We didn't get to her in time.'

'So, they're both dead,' Annie said. She was startled at how flat her own voice sounded. Shouldn't she cry or something? Looking at Edward's face she could see that he thought so. Somehow, she felt too numb to cry. Yet.

Annie took a deep breath and, feeling that something more was required of her she said, 'Thank you for trying, anyway.'

Edward nodded as if satisfied and returned to his desk. Annie knew that she had been dealt with; this Edward, whoever he was, had done his duty.

'Annie,' the man beside the door gestured to her to follow and she turned obediently. Why couldn't she cry?

She followed him down a corridor, trying to figure out what kind of building this was. It was underground, that much she'd figured out and they'd arrived in the dark, the sound of gunfire echoing through the city behind them as they drove in. Down here, everything was almost uncannily quiet in contrast, just the vague hum of something electrical in the background and the occasional sound of footsteps.

'Are we staying here?' Annie wanted to know.

'For tonight, and tomorrow day. Then I expect we'll be moving on.'

'On? On to where?'

'To another safe place. Don't worry, Annie.'

'I'm not worrying. I just want to know.'

The man opened a door and gestured Annie inside. Two field cots had been made up and placed by opposite walls. Through another door she spied a toilet and washbowl. Clean clothes had been spread out on one of the cots, jeans, T-shirt, what looked like a warm sweatshirt. It suddenly occurred to Annie that she was cold.

On the other cot sat a boy of about her own age. He sat cross-legged, playing some kind of hand-held computer game and barely glanced up as she came into the room. His hair was as dark as her own and needed cutting, sticking out at odd angles from behind his ears. He frowned at the screen he was holding, and his thumbs moved rapidly on the controls.

'This is Nathan,' the man said. 'Get yourself cleaned up and changed and I'll have some food sent in for the pair of you.'

He closed the door then and Annie was left alone with the boy and the beeps of the electronic game and, at last, the sudden, overwhelming desire to cry.

EIGHTEEN

The phone rang at two and Molly didn't reach it in time. It rang again a half hour later, just as she was passing through the hall. She grabbed the receiver and rattled off her number as she always did. Silence on the other end of the line.

'Bloody auto-diallers,' Molly muttered to herself. Then more loudly, 'Look, if I wanted double glazing or insurance I'd find someone else to buy it from. It sure as hell wouldn't be anyone like you, shower.'

She paused and listened, thinking vaguely that this didn't sound like an auto-dialler. There was emptiness on the other end of the line. 'Who is this?' Molly demanded. 'Get off my phone.'

Impatiently, she slammed the receiver down and headed for the kitchen, only to have it ring again just as she reached the door.

'I'll disconnect the bloody thing. See if I don't.' She turned and lifted the receiver again, listened once more to the silence. 'Oh bugger off, whoever you are,' she told them and reached out to unplug the phone from the wall.

'That's not very polite, Molly. I thought you had better manners than that?'

Molly felt her chest tighten and for a moment she couldn't breathe enough air even to frame her reply. 'Well,' she said, 'If I'd known it was you, I'd have cursed with a bit more imagination.'

The man laughed. Molly knew that laugh so damned well. Soft and mellow and utterly, utterly humourless. 'Your boy came to my house,' she said. 'But I seem to still be in the land of the living.'

'For now.'

'He killed himself,' she told him. 'Is that standard operational procedure, now? If so, I can only say it's bloody wasteful.'

Silence met the comment and now Molly's irritation grew beyond her fear. 'Look,' she said. 'I'm old, not stupid. If you want me dead, then I suppose I'd better start on the funeral arrangements, but I'm damned if I'm going to play your games. Like I said before, you can bugger off. I just don't want to know.'

Before she could lose her nerve and wait for a response, Molly slammed the receiver down again and then unplugged the line. She stood in the hall, breathing heavily and staring at the phone.

So, Molly thought, it really wasn't over yet. Even when she'd seen the tattoo, even when the man had died on her landing, she'd still kept that tiny scrap of belief that this was something else; that this was nothing to do with *him*. That the whole thing was some insane coincidence.

'Right,' Molly said and squared her shoulders. 'So that's the way it is.' Well she would die as she had always lived and not let the fear get the better of her. Whatever else happened, Molly would go down fighting.

On the outskirts of Grantham was a modern estate, approached via a roundabout and a left turn at the Muddle Go Nowhere pub. Typically, Alec and DI Barnes missed the turn and sailed on down a long, curving hill with no easy place to spin around. Alec glanced at the Victorian and Edwardian houses set on either side of the road. They looked prosperous and comfortable, nicely settled into their gardens and set back from the road. He caught himself looking out for the 'For Sale' signs.

At the bottom of the hill the traffic bottle-necked at a mini roundabout, the main road swinging off to the left and on into the market town, the right heading off the roundabout and into a supermarket car park. Barnes took the supermarket option and they turned around and headed back up the long sweep of the hill.

'Isaac Newton,' Bill Barnes said.

'What?'

'He was born here. It's a pretty little town once you manage to get into it. Might be worth a look while you and Naomi are still wandering.'

Alec added it to his list. They'd talked of very little of any consequence on the way here and Alec sensed that not only was Barnes a little embarrassed by Stevie's attitude, but was also still not entirely comfortable with Alec's exact role in the investigation. Alec, in his shoes, would have felt exactly the same. Perhaps in response to this, they had talked of random things in the hour and a bit journey from Newark to Grantham. Hour and a half if you included their last little detour.

The housing estate at the top of the hill was modern and ubiquitous, contrasting with the more historical town below. It was OK, Alec thought, but definitely not the kind of thing he and Naomi were looking for. He chided himself again for slipping back into house hunting mode when he should have been focusing on a murder investigation, then changed approbation to vague congratulation; it just went to prove that he'd made the right decision. Alec the serving officer was slowly but surely sliding into a box marked 'old Alec' and although he wasn't yet sure how to define 'new Alec' he did feel that he was making progress.

Barnes pulled up outside a brick semi with shallow bay windows and a neat scrap of lawned garden. 'This must be it,' he said.

They were a little later than they'd estimated in their phone call and the front door opened as they walked up the truncated path between the lawn and the off-road parking space in front of the white garage door. The front door was white too, Alec noted. That UPVC stuff he could see the point of but didn't really like. Barnes was apologizing for their lateness to a woman with pale hair and an even paler complexion. She looked like an older version of Tricia, Herbert Norris's girlfriend, whose photographs Alec had seen in his flat. The mother, Alec supposed.

'It's OK,' she told Barnes. 'She's in the living room. Go through and I'll make some tea or something.'

She had, Alec thought, the look of a woman worn out by someone else's grief. Tired, and then guilty about being tired and then even more guilty about being tired *of* . . . Alec smiled at her. 'Tea would be great,' he said. She nodded briefly and fled down the hall, and closed the kitchen door.

Tricia Needham sat close to the window, curled up in a red armchair and with an old-fashioned patchwork quilt spread out across her legs. She was even paler than her mother; hair, skin, even eyes a washed-out blue. She had been crying, her eyes reddened and the pallor blotched with red so vivid they looked like incipient bruises.

Bill Barnes introduced them both and asked if they could sit down. She nodded and pointed to a chair opposite. Barnes seated himself there and left Alec to choose between the sofa some feet away from the girl they had come to see or the odd looking, large, upholstered stool set right in the bay window. He decided on the sofa. He was planning on leaving most of the talking to Bill anyway.

The room was long and quite narrow, a flat screen television occupying the far corner and a mock Adam fireplace not quite managing to be the focal point of the room, halfway along the wall. Family photos crowded the mantelpiece and Alec noticed one of Herbert

Norris and Tricia. They seemed to be at the seaside, leaning against a railing on the promenade. He noted that all of the family photos were mounted up in very similar wooden frames whereas this one was in a much more elaborate curling metal. Had she brought this with her? Alec wondered. It didn't look as though it really belonged.

'I've read your statements,' Bill said quietly. 'We wondered, was there anything you'd like to add? Anything more you can think of?'

She shook her head. No.

'Herbert's behaviour in the week or two before he was killed. Did he seem any different? Worried about anything? Had he had any unusual phone calls or visitors?'

Again the vehement shake of the head.

'When did you last see him?'

'That's what's so bad,' Tricia said and Alec could see the tears had threatened again. 'I'd not seen him for a couple of weeks. He said he'd got to go away on a buying trip, but he never went. The neighbour said they saw him and Syd who runs the shop when he's not there. She said he came back two or three times when he'd told me he'd be away for the whole time. That's why I'd gone to the flat. He was supposed to be coming back and I went to cook him a meal. Surprise him, like, and I found him, just lying there.'

The tears began in earnest just as her mother returned with a tray of mugs and a teapot. Alec caught her expression as she set the tray down, the look of resignation and also irritation, soon concealed and no doubt stimulating yet another layer of guilt to grow.

'Tricia?' Alec asked. 'There were two photographs missing. The frames had been left but the pictures were gone. Can you remember what they were pictures of?'

She stared at him for a moment, a look of surprise on her face as though he'd shocked her by asking the wrong question. She sniffed loudly and her mother handed her a box of tissues. Alec couldn't help but wonder how many she'd got through.

'He said they were family,' she said. 'There was an old woman and a little girl, in one. A black woman and a white kid with red hair. She looked about five or six, I suppose. He didn't talk about them much. He said they'd died.'

'And the other picture?'

She shrugged. 'Two men. I don't know. He said one was his brother, but the guy was Asian. When I asked him about it he said something about brothers not always being blood. He was funny

like that, always talking about family but not real family like aunts
and uncles and so on. I think he was an orphan.'

'You think?'

That shrug again. 'He never talked about it. He didn't like to talk
about himself or his family. He said we should live in the present
and not in the past.'

'You said two men?'

'The other was older.'

'Asian as well?'

'No, a white guy. He was a bit fuzzy, like he'd been looking at
something and moved his head. Older, though.'

'Did he ever tell you their names?'

'I . . . maybe . . . I don't remember.'

'Herbert could be a little odd about some things,' Tricia's mother
said. 'He was a nice enough young man, but he was . . . private,
I suppose. Very generous, though, very nice . . .' she trailed off
as though trying to think of something more useful to say and
failing.

'Did you often let yourself into the flat? You didn't live with
Herbert, did you.'

A look of embarrassment passed between mother and daughter.

'He didn't know Tricia had the key,' her mother said. 'She
borrowed his keys and had it cut one day. I think she just wanted
to surprise him, like she said.'

'He was shutting me out,' Tricia blurted. Pain and anger now
winning out over the grief. 'I mean he didn't even have our picture
up in the flat, not even after he promised me he would. I'd been
going out with him two years or more and he . . . he . . . then I go
there and I find him dead on the floor.'

She gave in to the tears again and her mother sighed, then crossed
to her, perched on the arm of the chair and hugged her tight, a
resigned expression in her eyes.

'I think you'd better go now,' Tricia's mother said. 'She's told
you all she knows.'

That was probably very true, Alec thought as they took their leave.
He'd be willing to bet that Tricia hadn't known Herbert at all, not really.

'You think he was trying to keep her out of the way,' Bill suggested
as they got back into the car. 'Lying to her about going away for
that two weeks?'

'Either that or they'd broken up and she'd not noticed,' Alec agreed.

'Have you looked through the photo albums? Anything else that sounds like the woman and child or the two men in the missing pictures?'

'Not that I remember. It was mostly pictures of the happy couple, with and without accompanying friends. I get the feeling Tricia made up the albums. She was certainly in most of the pictures.'

Alec nodded thoughtfully.

'Look,' Bill Barnes said. 'If you think it would be OK with your wife, Stamford is only forty minutes from here, down the A1. Fancy a trip?'

'I'll let her know,' Alec said. 'I don't think she'll mind. She's made friends with a local historian and I think they plan a trip to the local cemetery or something.'

Barnes laughed. 'Some people really know how to enjoy themselves,' he said.

Naomi was, in fact, enjoying herself very much. Liz was good company and the fact that from time to time she seemed to forget altogether that Naomi couldn't see actually scored points in Naomi's opinion. She could cope with occasional neglect far more easily than with overweening attention.

'This is an ancestor of mine,' Liz was telling her. 'He was an industrialist, a mill owner. Apparently he made broadcloth, heavy stuff used by sailmakers and theatrical painters?'

'Why would they need it?' Naomi asked.

'Backdrops. They painted scenes on it. I suppose that makes sense really. You wouldn't want to be running into seams all over the place. Well that's what I've been told anyway. Someone else told me that sailcloth is a particular weave and maybe wouldn't have been so good for painting on so it's on the list for winter research.'

Naomi laughed. 'Is winter your research time, then?'

'Oh yes. October through to March you'll find me tucked up warm with my books and my computer or else ensconced in some corner of a library. I do my best writing in winter.'

'I miss libraries,' Naomi said. 'I miss books, actually. Alec is great and so are our friends and audio books are a godsend, but I do miss being able to browse the shelves and that moment when you find an author you've never heard of, but is right up your street, you know. And I miss the book shop experience, I used to love second-hand book shops. You know there's nothing quite like the smell of old books.'

'Apparently they're fermenting,' Liz said. 'It's some kind of fermentation process, breaking down the pages. That's what the lovely smell is.' She laughed. 'I like to think it's possible to get just slightly drunk inhaling the scent of old books.'

'It sounds like the perfect drug,' Naomi agreed. 'You were telling me about your ancestor?'

'Oh, yes. Well his name was William Haversham – like the mad woman in *Great Expectations*. His wife was Betsy and she's down as relict of the same. I'm not sure I'd like to be anyone's relict. It sounds like some kind of leftovers.'

'Maybe you could fry it up with bubble and squeak.'

'Well, quite. Relict and chips with mushy peas. Anyway, their grave is pretty standard. It's a bit of a monstrosity, actually, topped off with the most miserable angel you ever did see. The poor thing looks bored to death, but what really makes me interested is the tombstone next to it. It's just a tall flat slab with a central panel, but the interesting thing is, it's to his manservant. His valet, or gentleman's gentleman or whatever. His name was Eric Doyle and it says he: "*Entered the service of Mr Haversham in the year of Our Lord, 1752, aged twelve years. Remained, in the service of our family for the next forty seven, finally succumbing to a sickness of the lungs and having, in that time, risen to become the personal servant of Mr William Haversham. He left, at his death, the sum of two thousand pounds, with instruction this be used for relief of the deserving poor. May God rest his soul.*"'

'That's a lot of money for back then,' Naomi said.

'It is, isn't it? He must have just saved everything, from the year dot, don't you think? Sad, though, he never had a life outside of the Haversham household.'

They walked slowly back to where Liz had left her car.

'Naomi, do you know anyone round here?'

'No. Why?'

'Because there's been a man watching us ever since we arrived. I wasn't sure at first. I thought I was just being over-imaginative, but he got here when we did and I've spotted him several times since.'

'A fellow historian,' Naomi suggested.

'Well, I would think that, except that he's now leaning against my car.'

'Oh.' Naomi felt her heart sink. Of course, it could be nothing, someone waiting for them so he could make a perfectly innocent enquiry, but somehow she didn't think so.

'What does he look like?'

Liz had halted, obviously not at all certain what she should do. Beside her, Napoleon, who'd been plodding ahead of her in duty mode, and, Naomi suspected, slightly bored, was now unmistakably wagging his tail. You recognize him, don't you, Poly, Naomi thought.

'Not young,' Liz said 'Tall, greying hair. Kind of rugged-looking.'

Naomi frowned. Liz's description could fit a great many people. She moved Napoleon forward. 'We'll never find out standing here,' she said.

Liz took her arm and Naomi wasn't sure if the gesture was protective, wary or both. Together they approached the car and she heard a sound as though the man had moved towards them. The description might have been vague, but the voice was instantly recognizable, even though she'd only heard it briefly before.

'Hello, Naomi,' he said.

'Gregory?' Naomi could not keep the shock from her voice. 'What in heaven's name are you doing here?'

Arthur Fields, late importer of exotic porcelain, must have led a very pleasant life, Alec thought as he looked around the cottage in Stamford that had been his home.

The mellow stone glowed in the late afternoon sun and the walled garden at the back of the house seemed to have sucked in a whole day's worth of heat. Peaches had been trained against the far wall and apricots closer to the house. Herbs overflowed from raised beds and the scent of roses permeated the still air. It was a beautiful spot. Though the garden was a little small, he supposed. He'd want a little more land.

He immediately chided himself for slipping into house hunting mode and wondered at his willingness to consider this house as a possible home, even though there'd been a violent death here, when similar circumstances made theirs suddenly impossible to live in.

DI Barnes led him through a small door at the end of the walled plot and out into a broader sweep of lawn and flower beds beyond. Mature trees lent shade and somewhere Alec could hear the sound of running water. Naomi and Napoleon would love this, he thought. So much space. You could shut the world out at the front door and still not feel confined.

'The CSI reckoned the killer climbed that tree,' Barnes told him. 'He'd get a clear view over the wall and through the kitchen window. It wouldn't have been an easy shot, but that would be the best vantage point and it lines up with the trajectory. There were scuff marks on the bark up there.' He pointed to a sturdy-looking branch that pointed back in the direction of the house. 'Escape route is easy; there's a low fence down there where the garden backs on to farmland.'

Alec nodded. 'So, what's the link between Fields and Norris? And what, if anything, links them to Molly? There was nothing taken from here?'

'No. The wife was at home and they had friends round for dinner. Arthur Fields had gone through to the kitchen to fetch another bottle of wine, the guests heard the sound of breaking glass and thought he might have dropped something. His wife went through to the kitchen and found him dead.'

'How long before officers were on scene?'

'Paramedics got here in twelve minutes, the first police officer arrived when they did. But before that, one of the Field's guests had gone out with a torch. He saw nothing.'

'That was a little foolish.'

'That was a retired colonel. A man called Finch, old friend of the Fields family apparently.'

'And Arthur Fields, was he ex-army too?'

Barnes shook his head. 'He was a civil servant of some kind,' he said. 'You can read the files; I'm having everything faxed over for you.'

'Why?' Alec asked.

'Why what?'

'Why do you want me involved?'

Barnes looked away for a moment, then said slowly, 'Because I'm curious.'

'About?'

'About why the bosses of my bosses are so keen to have you involved. It makes so little sense I'm now intrigued.'

So am I, Alec thought. And if I've got any sense I'll walk away now, before any of us find out.

Liz knew a local pub that, she assured Gregory, sold a good range of decent beers. She gave him directions and then set off in the lead.

'So, who is he then?' she demanded almost before Naomi had her seat belt fastened.

'He's—' What was he exactly? 'He's someone we met during an investigation,' she said.

'When you were still on the force?'

'Well, no. It was earlier this year. Liz, it was a bit complicated. He's not someone I know particularly well.'

'Oh, intriguing,' Liz said. 'So, a good idea to take him to a neutral place, then. The pub, I mean.'

'Yes, I suppose it is,' Naomi said. She was aware of Liz, waiting expectantly for more information, and knew she wouldn't give up easily.

'Gregory and I, we had a mutual friend. A journalist, I'd known for years. She'd moved to London, found work there . . . Anyway, she died and Gregory wanted to find out what had happened. That led him to us and the rest, as they say, is history.'[1]

'Died?'

Naomi sighed. 'She was murdered,' Naomi admitted. 'It was horrible. Liz, if you don't mind, I really don't like to talk about it.' She could feel Liz's gaze still fixed on her and ignored it, resolutely. She really wasn't ready to talk about this, about the death of her friend.

'So, you *really* don't know him that well?'

'No.' Naomi could feel the unspoken questions, the lack of logic Liz would have identified. If they didn't know him well, Liz was thinking, then why had Gregory gone to the trouble of finding Naomi, of turning up so unexpectedly? It was something Naomi was wondering too. She'd asked how he knew where they'd be and he'd said he'd asked at the hotel. Liz had seemed to accept that, but it raised more questions in Naomi's mind. One being how had Gregory known where they were staying? Only a couple of their friends were party to that right now. The second was that she was pretty sure she'd mentioned their plans to no one at the hotel and even if they had, it seemed like an odd thing for the hotel to impart to a complete stranger.

'This is the place,' Liz said and Naomi felt her pull off the road and on to gravel. 'Hang on till I come round and help you out. The ground's a bit rough. He's . . . um he's quite a good-looking man, isn't he? This Gregory.'

'I wouldn't know,' Naomi told her.

---

[1] *See Night Vision*

'Oh, no . . . of course not. I'm so sorry.'

Naomi laughed. 'I'm told he's kind of rugged.'

'Oh, I go for rugged,' Liz said. 'I'm not so into smooth.' She giggled like a teenager and Naomi wondered what Gregory was going to make of the obvious interest her new friend was exhibiting. She wondered if she should warn Liz that he was not the kind of man she should be getting involved with, then figured that would lead to even more questions and she didn't really think it would put Liz off anyway. Probably the opposite.

Liz helped her from the car and handed her Napoleon's harness. 'Hello again,' she said, presumably to Gregory. 'There's a nice quiet bit at the back, if we go through that door there. I don't know about anyone else, but I'm hungry and they do decent food.'

'I could eat,' Gregory agreed.

He had an interesting voice, Naomi thought. She'd not really had much time to listen to him before; their last encounter had been a somewhat rushed affair, but now she listened, she couldn't quite place the accent. There was something of a West Country burr to it, perhaps.

'How have you been?' he asked as they crunched across the gravel.

'We've been all right,' Naomi said cautiously. 'You?'

'Oh, I've been fine. I've taken a bit of a holiday. First one for a long time. I think it's been a good thing.'

'And now?'

'And now there are just a few things I need to attend to before I leave again. I liked the holiday. Think I might make it a permanent thing.'

'Sounds like the best idea,' Naomi agreed. She could feel Liz straining to listen, her curiosity palpable.

'You're planning on early retirement, then,' Liz asked brightly.

'I hope not,' Gregory said. 'I'd like to have time to enjoy life first.'

'Oh.' Liz sounded puzzled and Naomi hid a smile. Retirement had a somewhat different meaning in Gregory's business, she thought. She heard the sound of a door being opened and felt solid concrete and then wood beneath her feet. She allowed herself to be steered into a seat and settled Napoleon on the floor beneath the table. Naomi's mind buzzed with possibilities and at the heart of all that buzzing Molly sat like a queen bee.

'OK, so what are you doing here?' Naomi asked, taking advantage of the few minutes while Liz left them to find the ladies.

'Sorry to just turn up like this.'

'Which is another question. How *did* you find us? The hotel would never have told you, even if you really went there.'

She could almost feel Gregory smile. When he spoke, he sounded amused. 'Your young friend, Patrick, said you were travelling. I called in a few favours. You've got GPS on your mobile, that makes it easy, if you know how.'

'You spoke to Patrick?'

'Off to college soon. I hear. He'll do well. I like his work.'

'You've seen his work? Gregory, I don't understand. Why keep tabs on us?'

He shrugged. She heard the creak of the chair as he moved. 'General interest,' he said. 'Anyway, as to why, particularly, an old acquaintance of mine was shot a few weeks ago. I was curious as to what was going on, then the same gun turns up—'

'Molly Chambers,' Naomi said. 'I just bloody knew it.'

'She's quite a character,' Gregory agreed.

'You know her too?'

'Only by reputation. It's a small world, Naomi, especially in my line of work. You get to know, or to know about, everyone of any importance in the end. So I wondered if I could take you and Alec out to dinner, maybe, so we could talk about old Molly.'

Old Molly, Naomi thought. He'd never get away with calling her that to her face. She was about to tell him so when Gregory said, 'So how's the house hunting then?' and she guessed Liz must be heading back.

'Oh, you know. Not going very far,' she said.

'What's not going very far?' Liz asked as she sat down. 'Ah, looks like food's arriving. I'm starved.'

'Always ready for a good feed,' Gregory agreed. 'Naomi was just telling me about their house hunting.'

'Oooh.' Liz's voice was knowing. 'Not much luck so far. Mind you, this is a pricey area, for what you get, I mean. Lovely villages, but then the price is loaded to reflect that and if you're in one of the catchment areas for some of the best schools that can load the price, again, by ten grand.'

'Really?' Gregory asked. 'So where would you start looking, then?'

This is like a bad joke, Naomi thought. I'm sitting in a pub, having lunch with a potter and an assassin for hire, chatting about the state of the property market.

At her feet, Napoleon, smelling the arrival of lunch, snuffled approvingly.

Oh, what the hell, Naomi thought and settled back to enjoy her meal and regale them, as she knew was expected to, with tales of elderly ladies and cats and bungalows with rotting floors.

'So where would you like to live?' Gregory asked at last. 'What part of the country, I mean?'

Naomi found her thoughts drifting back to the little cottage in Somerset. The last place anyone with any sense would want, thinking about the memories it held for them, but . . .

'I think maybe the West Country,' she said. 'We spent a holiday down on the Somerset Levels and it was so peaceful and so quiet. It was like time had just walked out on it, if you see what I mean.'

'Sounds like a good place,' Gregory agreed.

'There was this little house, right in the middle of nowhere. Not very big, but with a great garden and you could smell the sea. I don't know, maybe somewhere like that.'

'A friend of mine died recently,' Gregory said. 'He had a lovely home out at Stamford, just outside of town. It had this beautiful little walled garden and then you went out through a door into the orchard. Beyond that it was all fields and a little stream. Very rural, very lovely.'

'Very pricey,' Liz said wistfully. 'I'd love a bigger place, but it isn't going to happen. Still, mustn't grumble. It's a fine little house and I've no mortgage to speak of. When my parents died, I sold their place and put all the money into getting somewhere of my own, so I've been very lucky really. And there's room for my kiln in one of the out buildings and I've got a little studio.'

'Really? Gregory said. 'What do you do?'

Naomi smiled and listened as the two of them flirted over glazing formulas and wondered what Liz would think if she knew what Gregory really was. She had a sneaking suspicion Liz would find it exciting.

The dead friend, Naomi thought. Was that the friend who'd been killed? The first of the murders Alec had been drawn into, that was in Stamford, so obviously, it must be . . . what was the man called . . . Arthur, that was it, Arthur Fields a man who imported fine china from somewhere or other, or was it Chinese porcelain he bought? She really ought to have paid more attention. Maybe she was, finally, shaking off her police persona. She wondered where Alec and DI

Barnes had got to and how they were getting on and felt an odd moment of resentment at Alec being called away and a less odd moment of resentment against Molly Chambers.

She's an old woman in trouble, Naomi reminded herself and then began to wonder exactly how old Molly was. Alec would have told her at some point, but somehow, things Molly, beyond the fact that Naomi found her deeply irritating, had never really sunk in.

Belatedly, she realized that Liz was asking her something. Pudding? Right, get back with the programme Naomi, she chided herself. 'Oh, yes, that would be nice. What do they have?'

Having selected brownies and ice cream, and being unable to attract the attention of any passing waiting staff, Liz took herself off to the bar to order dessert and coffee.

'Penny for them,' Gregory said. 'You were a long way from here.'

'Sorry, I suppose I was. I suppose I wanted to be.' That sounded rude, she thought, but somehow knew Gregory understood. 'Is anything ever over?'

'No, I don't think it is. Some things just get put on hold for a while. Sometimes a long while, but they always come round again. You know that bit in the Bible that talks about the sins of the fathers being visited on future generations?'

She nodded.

'Well I never figured that as being an instruction, you know, more like a statement of fact. What we do, well it can echo down the years until we've almost forgotten what the sound of it was in the first place, but echoes always bounce back at us.'

'And this has to do with Molly?'

'Molly Chambers and others.'

Liz returned, with news of dessert and a waitress followed with a tray of coffee.

Echoes, Naomi thought. So often they were amplified by time, not diminished. She didn't want any of this any more. She wanted peace and quite and a place to settle, and no more problems. No more threats.

Liz was chatting again and Naomi knew she ought to join in, but a great weight seemed to have descended upon her and sapped what energy she had left. Beside her, Napoleon sat up and laid his head against her knee, sensing her mood. Absently, she stroked the silky black ears and pushed dessert she no longer wanted around her plate.

'I'd best be going,' Gregory said at last.

'Oh, must you? We must do this again. I mean—'

'It's been nice,' Gregory said. 'Naomi, I'll give you a call, later.'

'OK,' she nodded. 'I'd best be getting back to the hotel, if that's OK, see if Alec's back.'

'Oh, of course,' Liz said, though she sounded slightly puzzled and a little disappointed at being abandoned.

'He's nice,' Liz said as they drove back. 'Is he single?'

Naomi laughed. 'I don't think he's had much time for romance,' she said. 'Gregory travelled a lot with his job. Some government contract, I think. He doesn't talk about it a lot.'

'Oh, man of mystery,' Liz said. She sounded pleased about that. 'It would be nice to, you know, maybe meet up for a drink or something.'

'I'll let him know you asked,' Naomi promised.

Clay had called twice on her mobile, but she'd ignored him; now, with Bob busy in the studio, she knew she couldn't ignore the third call.

'I'm assuming you've been playing the good wife,' Clay said.

'I'm not *playing* at anything. What can I do for you?'

'The documents we needed, they weren't in the car or the storage locker.'

'Did you really expect them to be? It was always a long shot. I saw on the news about the men in the van. Why did the security guard have to be hurt, Clay? He didn't do anything.'

'He shouldn't have been there,' Clay said petulantly. 'It was a waste of time anyway. There was nothing in the storage locker.'

'So, maybe there's just nothing to find, have you considered that?'

'Considered it and found it flawed. Molly must still have it. Molly or Adam.'

Annie sighed. So he was after Adam now, was he? 'So go and talk to him. Let me go and talk to him.'

'I don't talk to traitors, Annie.'

Oh, for fuck's sake, she thought. 'Time was you were all on the same side.'

'Things change. Sides change. For some people, morality becomes blurred.'

'But not for you, I suppose. What does Nathan say?'

She knew it was the wrong question as soon as she asked it. Clay did not respond. 'Look,' she said, 'it's maybe just time to let things go. Past is past, Clay. Sometimes you just have to let it go.'

Silence built on the other end of the conversation.

'Your husband, what do you think he would say if he knew about the real you, Annie?'

'Blackmail, is it, Clay? Look. Bob knows all about me. He knows everything he needs to know. You leave him out of this.'

'I hope I can, Annie, I really do, but events may well overtake all of us. Sometimes nothing can be done about it.'

He hung up on her and left her cursing softly. 'So help me, Clay, I'll bloody kill you one of these days,' Annie promised the now silent phone and realized with slight shock that she meant it.

Alec returned to the hotel just after five, kissed Naomi in a rather distracted manner and dumped a folder down on the bed. She could hear from the sound it made that he was not a happy man.

'What's that?'

'Case-notes.'

'You're retired or resigned or whatever it was you did. Remember?'

'I remember doing it. Doesn't look as though anyone took any notice.'

'We could just sneak away tonight,' she suggested. 'Let them all get on with it.'

'We could,' he agreed. 'But you could just bet they'd come and fetch us back.'

'We could go abroad.'

Alec laughed. 'Don't tempt me.' He flopped down on the edge of the bed. 'How was your day?'

'Oh, interesting and not just because of Liz's dead ancestors. Guess who turned up at the cemetery?'

'Don't want to guess. I'm not sure I want to know.'

'Gregory,' she told him. 'We all had lunch together.'

There was a moment of silence as Alec absorbed that. 'Right,' he said finally. 'Where abroad? I quite fancy Mongolia. I hear property is cheap there or we could buy a yurt, join the nomads.' He groaned and lay back. 'Don't tell me, he's a friend of Molly's.'

'No, apparently he just knows her by reputation, but he was a friend of the man killed in Stamford. Arthur Fields. And he wants to meet up and talk.'

Alec groaned. 'Just what I need,' he said. 'I don't suppose he knows who did it?'

Naomi found herself laughing. 'I don't think so,' she said. 'I got the feeling he'd like to know, though.'

Alec groaned. 'That's all we need,' he said. 'A hired killer on the case as well.'

'I don't think he's been hired this time,' Naomi reminded him. 'This time, it seems like it's personal. Alec, maybe we should just stand back, out of the way and let him get on with it.'

'Seriously?' She felt his weight shift as he turned to look at her. 'You know I can't do that, even if I wanted to.'

'Actually, you can and I think you do want to. If it wasn't for Molly . . .'

'If it wasn't for Molly,' Alec agreed. 'But it is for Molly, isn't it? I can't just—'

'Walk away? No, I know that. Tempting though, isn't it?'

Alec sighed and sat up. 'You can't imagine how tempting,' he said. 'No, love, I don't think even you can.'

Nathan called her late in the early evening. Bob was out walking the dogs again while she cooked; creature of habit that Bob was, Nathan would have guessed it was a good time to call.

'Can you talk?' he asked.

'Yes. Clay called earlier. What is it with that blasted man? Nathan, I swear—'

'I know,' Nathan soothed.

'No, you don't. He threatened Bob. I'm not having that, Nathan. No one threatens my husband and gets away with it.'

There was a beat of silence as Nathan absorbed that; she could almost hear the shift in his thinking as he measured this new position. 'No,' he said finally. 'No one should be able to do that.'

'So, what do we do now?'

'You've seen the news?'

'The robbery at the storage warehouse, yes. Any news on the security guy?'

'Nothing good. Hopefully he'll make it, but . . . you know who the two in the van were?'

'No, there've been no names released, so far as I know.'

'Gilligan and Hayes,' Nathan told her and Annie laughed, unable to help herself. 'Well, Clay still has a sense of style; you've got to give him that. What's he trying to do, start a war?'

'Wouldn't be the first time. No, I think it was just personal revenge this time. He was happy to make use of them when he was on the winning side, but with all the post colonial complaints coming into the courts now, I think he felt they knew too much about Clay and what he might have been up to. He's not said much. I'm guessing.

'I get the feeling the police weren't supposed to get the van doors open. Clay wanted them to wake up long enough to make noise, but not long enough for anyone to let them out.'

'What did he use?'

'Xenon to knock them out, apparently. Simple CO2 to finish them off, on a very slow seep. Too slow as it turned out.'

'Will they make it?' Annie asked, curious rather than concerned. Neither Gilligan or Hayes registered very high on her scale of 'people to be worried about'.

'Don't know,' Nathan told her. 'Annie, any chance you could take Bob away for a bit? Have a holiday somewhere?'

'Can't be done,' she said. 'He's got a new exhibition coming up, I've got a new job to start. Whatever has to be done will have to just work around that. I can't just try and drag him away.'

'No, that's fine,' Nathan said and she could hear the cogs turning. 'OK, well, just watch your back, I'll keep in touch.'

Annie put down the phone and turned back to the range. Nathan was worried, she thought, she could hear it in his voice, even though she knew no one else would have noticed. Closer than brother and sister, they had grown up together since Annie had been thirteen, and Nathan however old he had been back then. Annie sighed and wondered if anything ever truly came to a proper end.

NINETEEN

Naomi hadn't really expected to hear from Gregory so soon, so was surprised by the phone call half an hour or so after Alec's return. He asked if they could meet him later, in the hotel bar.

'Dinner is still on,' he said. 'But I think Alec may be too tired to want that tonight. I thought a drink might be better.'

Naomi did not respond immediately; she took in the inference that Gregory knew about Alec's day and then agreed to meet up with him around nine.

'*Do* you think he's working for someone?' she asked Alec.

'Could be I suppose. From what little I found out about him, his old associates are mostly retired or dead. It could be he's freelancing or it could be just as he told you, he's curious about the death of an old friend. I don't imagine you acquire a great many friends in Gregory's line of work. I suppose you come to value those you do hold onto.'

'I suppose.'

'He's right about Arthur Fields' house, though. The one out at Stamford. Lovely place, not too big but the garden is just gorgeous and it's made of that golden limestone that looks like it should be sandstone, if you know what I mean. The sun was on it and the whole house positively glowed.'

'Think they'll put it on the market?' she asked.

'I wouldn't know. But you know a man was killed there, don't you? How does it make it different from our place?'

'Because. . . . it would have happened before we lived there, if we bought it, I mean. And because it wasn't someone out to get to us.'

'There's no logic to that.'

'Did I say there was?'

'No, you didn't say there was.' He flopped back on the bed. 'I met the girlfriend today, Herbert Norris's. You know, when I went to his flat, it struck me. No pictures out on show of the two of them together. Not a one. There were plenty in an album that she'd put together, but it was as if, at some point, she'd become his girlfriend and he hadn't noticed.'

'You want to talk about it, or eat, or both?'

Alec shook his head. 'No, I think I want to eat now and prepare for whatever Gregory has to say. You do realize we've agreed to have drinks with a wanted criminal?'

'Wanted for what?'

'Oh, I'm sure there's a list a mile long.'

'Yeah,' Naomi agreed. 'But it's not likely to have his actual name on it, is it?'

Alec chuckled. 'No, I don't suppose it will. OK, I'll walk the dog. Then we go down and eat and then we see what our man of mystery has to say. And I suppose I should check in with Molly.'

'Shall I do that, while you're out with Napoleon? She can be rude to me just as easily as she can be rude to you.'

'Do you mind?' He was already off the bed and fumbling for his shoes.

You agreed to that a bit quick, Naomi thought as, reluctantly, she reached for her phone.

TWENTY

N aomi had the feeling that something was really worrying Molly and that it was something new; not directly about the young man that had died in her house.

'I'm just making sure you're all right,' Naomi had said.

'And you could do what about it if I wasn't?'

'Probably not a lot,' was Naomi rejoinder. 'But if there's anything we *can* do—'

'Then I would be the one calling you.'

Naomi paused. This was rude, even by Molly standards. It was clear the older woman must have thought so too because she said, 'I'm sorry, Naomi. I know you mean well. I expect I'm just tired.'

'Just tired. Molly—'

'I'm fine, my dear. Some days I just feel my age. I resent that, I suppose. Ageing is such an unjust process.'

The call had ended shortly after, but Naomi was left with a sense of words that had been absent from it. As though Molly had been on the verge of admitting to something and then resisted that urge. It was nothing she could put her finger on . . . or could she? Yes, she decided, there's been something slightly anxious about the way Molly had answered the phone. A sense that she had been relieved to hear Naomi's voice, not because it was Naomi but because it was not someone else.

For a moment, Naomi thought about calling back and asking Molly directly, but she knew she wouldn't get a straight answer; there'd be more evasion, maybe even more outright deception and she really wasn't in the mood for that right now.

The urge to run away and forget about it all was almost over-whelming and Naomi had the sudden thought that if she had still been sighted then Alec would come back to the hotel to find their bags packed, the bill settled and Naomi waiting for him in the lobby, car keys in hand.

It was a stupid, random thought that stopped her; the notion that she wouldn't know for sure if she'd managed to pack everything and that Alec would only have to come up to their room to check. A random and such a slight excuse, Naomi told herself, but it was enough to stop the idea dead in its tracks. If you were going to run away, then you didn't do it without your shoes – metaphorically speaking. You did it spontaneously and you didn't go back to check the bathroom or the bottom of the wardrobe. You just went.

Alec returned a few minutes later, Napoleon lay his head in her lap and beat his tail rhythmically against the side of the bed. She stroked the silky ears, enjoying the familiar feel of the dog's bulk pressed against her side.

'You know that ultimatum. That week I gave us,' Naomi said.

'Yes. You revising it, are you?'

'I'd like to, yes, but I will give this a week to go wherever it goes and then we walk away. We can't spend *our* lives living other people's for them.'

'OK,' Alec said slowly. 'So what did Molly say to you?'

'No, it wasn't Molly. Or at least, not just Molly. Alec, all our lives we've done what other people needed. Or we've responded to other people's demands. Our working lives were spent sorting out the muddles the rest of the world threw our way and . . . and I want us to sort our own out now. I think, what I'm saying is—' But she couldn't finish. Naomi rarely cried; generally she didn't see the point and even when she felt the urge she tried to restrain it. But she cried now, wept bitterly and loudly for all the lost people and broken lives that had littered their past and that, she was afraid, might still be there, walking the road ahead.

Molly had just been relieved that it wasn't Clay. There'd been a time when she'd faced him down, told him what he could do with his demands.

'He who must be obeyed,' she had called him, joking with Edward and skitting on Rider Haggard. Edward had never liked that, he'd always been a little overawed by Clay. It had never caused rows between them because Molly hated anything that caused conflict between herself and Edward. She'd made a point of not rising to the bait when Clay, aware of their difference of opinion, tried to drive the wedge. Her marriage, her love, was far too precious to allow anyone and especially '*that man*' to widen even the smallest chink in their collective armour.

She had made some allowance for Clay, knowing that sometimes they needed his help and expertise and his resources, always far greater than their own.

'Some good did come out of it,' she told herself. 'Some good out of all that evil.' Hadn't it?

She thought of the children, now grown and prospering, like Nathan and Annie and young Adis – though he'd changed his name and Molly no longer knew where he was. He still contrived to send her a birthday card, but there was never any hint of a return address. For a moment her heart seemed full; a warmth and relief growing there.

There'd been others too . . . others they had helped.

And then she thought again of Nathan and of Annie and the rest and how they still seemed in thrall to Clay and her heart emptied. Had they really made life better?

Molly went and sat down again in Edward's chair. She fancied she could still catch the faint essence of cigar smoke and the even fainter hint of the lemon trees that had once grown in their garden, or of the spice market, a few streets away, when they had been stationed in . . . oh where was that?

She closed her eyes, trying to fix that one place among so many places, the smell of spice and citrus and incense. But the scent that filled her nostrils, came unbidden, choking and hated, was the smell of fire and dust and blood and war.

'Edward, Edward, why did you have to leave me alone? I can't bear it without you. I'm not strong enough without you.'

Tears pricked, but she blinked them away and wiped her eyes on the cuff of her blouse.

'No, you're right,' she said to the shades of her lost love and all the rest that crowded around her, filling the little room and pressing close to Edward's chair. 'This is war. My last war. And I'll not lose without a fight. I promise you all that.'

TWENTY-ONE

Annie and Bob stood in his studio, talking about his latest work. These canvases were larger than usual and there were also several boards, large and traditionally gessoed with chalk and rabbit skin glue, painted in a mix of his usual oils but with the addition of egg tempera.

'It's a technique that goes back to the fifteenth century,' he said. 'I saw a couple of examples in an exhibition and thought it looked interesting. You get this real luminosity, such a play of light.'

Annie stepped back, the better to take in the picture. It depicted a wood; she recognized it as the stand of birches and oaks not far from the house. Bob regularly walked the dogs there. It was autumn and golden leaves floated down and settled heavily on the forest floor. The light was strange, as it was in a great many of Bob's pictures. Not quite day and a bright crescent of moon hung in a vibrant blue sky. The shadows seems to be cast by two sources of light, sometimes separately and sometimes overlapping and it was only when you looked and then went on looking that you realized there was a setting sun, half hidden by trees and then this almost too bright sliver of moon, Annie thought. It worked, but she wasn't sure why and it was also oddly unsettling, as though the day had been unwilling to relinquish control and the night not quite strong enough to snatch it away.

It was liminal. Ghostly.

Between the trees ran figures, some in such deep shadow she couldn't quite make them out, but they reminded her of wolves and men and men-shaped wolves; wolf-shaped men. The figures in the middle ground were clear and sharp. Men and women, hinds and stags, running through the forest. Reaching out for one another but not quite touching. Some smiling out at the viewer, others with their faces deliberately turned away. They were dressed in costume that was at once medieval and modern as though, Annie thought, they had been permitted to raid some elaborate and costly dressing up box.

'It's beautiful,' she said. And meant it. 'You stole my dream?'

Bob laughed. 'I didn't think you'd mind. I don't know, it kind of helped me forget you were so far away. I started it the day after you left.'

She took his hand. He'd depicted her dream so eloquently, she knew that she would never again be able to recapture the original look and feel of it. The memory would be subsumed by this picture; by his vision of it. It was a dream she'd been having most of her life. Since her parents died and Clay and Edward had . . .

'Do you ever wonder about me?'

'Often.'

'No, I mean—'

'Annie, I know you have a past, we all do and I think there are probably things in your past that are . . . out of my range of experience.'

'I mean,' he laughed, 'look at your friends.'

He paused. 'Your family,' he corrected himself. An ex-mercenary and a . . . well, I'm not sure I have the vocabulary for what Nathan is.'

Bob smiled. 'Annie, I know I probably don't know all there is to know and I really don't care about that. If there's something you want to tell me . . .'

She could almost see him holding his breath, anticipating some revelation he wouldn't know how to handle. Annie kissed him, silently cursing Clay and all the secrets and the lies. She kissed him more hungrily, leaning into her husband's body, pressing close, wanting to be even closer.

'You've captured my dream,' she said. 'Pinned it to the canvas.' And she didn't know if she felt elated or bereaved by that.

TWENTY-TWO

'He's here,' Alec told Naomi. She'd already figured that out from the slow beat of Napoleon's tail against her leg. Dog liked Gregory, for some reason and, against all reason or logic, Naomi was inclined to agree with him. At least, she thought, you sort of knew what you were getting with Gregory.

They paused while Alec ordered drinks at the bar plus another of whatever Gregory was drinking.

'I'll bring them over to you,' the barman said.

Alec led her over to their favourite corner table and she heard the scrape of chair legs on wood as Gregory stood up to greet them. He shook hands with Alec and then took Naomi's. 'Sorry for being so dramatic, today,' he said.

'Are you?'

'Well, maybe not.'

They sat down and Naomi asked, 'How did you find me today?'

Gregory laughed, softly. 'No great mystery,' he said. 'I called Patrick and asked him where you were staying. I'm surprised he didn't warn you?'

'Patrick probably didn't think it was a bad thing,' Alec said wryly. 'I suspect that to Patrick it would just be like an old friend wanting to get in touch.' He didn't sound as though he agreed.

'So, I arrived this morning, just in time to see you and Liz drive away.'

'So you followed.'

'So I followed. Had you not been here, I'd have found somewhere quiet to sit and wait or left a message at reception.'

'Just like that? Like a regular thing.' Alec sounded both amused and irritated.

'Sure, why not? I can be that regular guy just as much as you can.'

'So, not at all really,' Naomi said.

There was a beat of silence while the waiter brought their drinks over from the bar. Naomi raised her glass. 'Do you toast the lost ones too?' she asked.

'No,' Gregory told her. 'Seeing as I'm probably responsible for their being lost, I think that might be a little crass, don't you? Good health and long life.'

They echoed his wish and then Naomi set her glass down. 'So,' she said. 'What do you want, Gregory?'

'I'd like to know why Arthur died,' he said. 'He lived a long life, a dangerous life, perhaps, but I think he assumed he'd be safe enough, retired and living in a place like Stamford. I think he believed that all those who might still bear a grudge were either dead already, or too old to care any more or at the very least retired. It seems he was wrong.'

'It seems he was not an importer of Chinese porcelain, then?' Alec observed wryly.

'Oh, he was that too. He specialized in Oriental materials, but he was also something of an authority on early Islamic. He had some truly lovely pieces in his private collection.'

'And what else was he? Some kind of spy?'

There was a smile in Gregory's voice as he said, 'Something like that. He gathered intelligence, he made friends in high places, he told those who needed to know where the right kind of pressure could be applied. Unlike me, he was strictly white collar, I suppose.'

'And he knew Molly?' Naomi guessed.

'Molly, Edward, Clay . . . others too. They all moved in the same circles. Sometimes worked for the same employer. All had fingers in the same pie and all had the same sidelines, I think.'

'Sidelines?'

Gregory was silent for a moment, then he asked. 'Do you know what an economic hit man is?'

'Can't say I do, no,' Alec said.

'Well, in essence, he is someone a government, or a big corporation will send in to another government or corporation to coerce them into accepting loans, favour or some other inducement.'

'Sorry, don't get it,' Alec said.

'OK, well, if you have, say, a newly independent state, one which is rich in natural resources, but a bit lacking in infrastructure, or skills or reliable government or cash flow. Say, for instance, that you are a more developed state or big corporation and you look at this new country and you think, yes, I'd like a slice of that pie. Well, you might just send a representative over, authorized to offer some very nice little package of loans and expertise, of private security, perhaps, just to ensure that the people most sympathetic to you might be the ones with enough clout to get the best positions in the new government. In return, of course, you might ask for oil or mineral concessions and offer to build the roads and airports or ports that you need to get those minerals out – all to help this new, emergent state and its fledgling government, of course.

'Nine times out of ten, your offers will be accepted and a few years down the line, the government of the country you now all but own will realize that these loans are accruing frightening levels of interest and the only people really profiting from the new infrastructure and investment in mining or drilling or whatever it might be are living it up half way round the world. Meantime, you can't afford food or education or homes for even a fraction of your

population, because all the money you might have had from your
mineral reserves or your coffee production or your oil is going to
pay back loans and interest on loans for something that was meant
to benefit everyone.'

'That sounds very simplistic,' Naomi commented.

'Oh and it is. And I'm missing out the fact that those in power
are also the ones benefiting from the money paid by these foreign
powers and they probably don't now give a damn about anyone
else. And that most of the time, as I said, these offers get accepted
with little or no argument. And not always because of corrupt
governments, sometimes just out of pragmatic, political and
economic need.

'Sometimes, quite often in fact, there is more than one foreign
power trying to curry favour. You get a bidding war. You get factions
wanting to take up one offer or the other. You get conflict.

'Or, sometimes, just sometimes, you might get a government or
a president or a dictator that tells the foreign power to go to hell,
they're going to do things their own way and foreign investments
will not be welcome.'

'And your economic hit man?'

'Is sent in with a bigger, better deal. Is sent in to find the cracks,
the leverage points, the people who can be coerced, blackmailed or
simply paid off. Sometimes it gets a little more dramatic than that
and the odd individual in a key position might need to be eliminated.
Taken right out the picture. Sometimes, it means triggering an actual
conflict. Sometimes even a major war.'

'Seriously?' Alec laughed. 'Sorry, Gregory, but it sounds all a
bit conspiracy theory.'

'Maybe it does. But it happens and has happened, for centuries
in one form or another.'

'And your friend? Is that what he did?'

'In part. He had a talent for gossip, for finding the scandals, the
tiny chinks in the armour. The less than honourable deeds of otherwise honourable men.'

'So he made enemies,' Alec said. 'So the pool of those who might
want him dead is pretty big.'

'Large and deep and wide,' Gregory agreed. 'Though, mostly
well in the past. As I said, most of his one-time enemies are dead
or old or retired. But evidently someone out there thought they had
unfinished business.'

'And what does this have to do with Molly and Edward and, you mentioned another name, Clay, wasn't it?'

'Clay. Yes. I think I need another drink. What would you like?'

'I take it you aren't driving tonight,' Naomi said.

Gregory laughed. 'Still the police officer,' he said. 'No. I have a friend collecting me later.'

He gathered their glasses and went to the bar. The noise in the lounge had increased now as the evening drinkers arrived and settled. Naomi recognized a few of the voices and assumed these must be regulars.

'You think he's telling the truth?'

'Why not?' Alec said. He sounded tired and deflated.

'He hasn't mentioned Herbert Norris. Do you think he's part of all this?'

'Why don't we ask?' Alec sighed. 'You know that week you gave me? Do you feel like downgrading the offer?'

Gregory returned and set down the tray. Naomi heard the rattle of ice in glasses. He set one down close to her hand. She could feel the chill of it.

'And what part did Molly play in all of this?' she asked.

'Where to begin?' Gregory said, but she had the feeling he had already worked it out and was just looking for the right words.

'She met Edward in Kenya,' Alec said. 'In Mombasa, I think. She said she was just strolling along the beach one day and there was this man, just standing by the water and they got into conversation. They were married three or four months later and stayed together until Edward died.'

'Nice story,' Gregory said.

'You don't believe it?' Naomi asked.

'More that I don't really care, I suppose. Who do you think actually runs the world?'

Naomi laughed. 'Oh, God, we're back to the conspiracy theories again, are we?'

'No, we're back to a very simple question.'

'Bankers,' Alec said. 'People with money.'

'Clay used to call them the three B's. Bankers, Big Business and Bureaucrats.'

'Clay. You keep mentioning him. So what's the connection to Molly?'

Again the pause as Gregory took stock. He seemed to find the

start point of his story and he began. 'In 1961, Edward was
dispatched to Leopoldville as part of the British trade mission to
what had been the Belgian Congo. For about a century the kings
of Belgium and later the Belgian government had treated the country
as their personal piggy bank. When the country finally got independence in 1960 and elected their own president, big business and big
governments were lining up, ready to negotiate their own deals; get
their own piece of the pie.'

'Dag Hammarskjöld,' Alec said abruptly. 'The UN guy that was
killed. Plane crash, wasn't it?'

'It was,' Gregory agreed, 'and by the time Edward and the others
arrived, trouble had already begun. One of the richest states, Katanga,
wanted to secede from Congo. It wouldn't have worked in practice.
They were rich enough in mineral resources and the like, but didn't
have enough agricultural land to feed themselves. Anyway, their bid
for freedom was backed by some very big corporations, bankrolled
by those who hoped to take control if the secession succeeded. The
country as a whole had got its independence in June 1960 and
Patrice Lumumba had been elected president in May of that year.
Many considered him to be too impetuous to be a good politician,
but he'd been elected as part of a democratic process, so—'

'And Molly and Edward were mixed up in this? I still don't see—'

'Let me get to it. Clay had been sent in ahead. His job was to
take advantage of whatever situation seemed to be emerging. To
make whatever promises he needed to make to secure economic
and political footholds in what was then an emergent and potentially
very rich country. He wasn't the only one, of course. You've got to
remember, this was the middle of the cold war and the Russians
and the US had sent their own big hitters into play.'

'And Edward?'

'Was a lot further down the food chain. Edward loved Africa. He
never settled as easily anywhere else. And he wanted things to work
out well for the Congo. He'd been sent because not only did he have
close friends in the newly elected government, but he also knew some
of the big players. You've got to understand, usually we apply the word
mercenary to the foot soldiers who are called upon to do the actual
fighting, and, believe me, there were plenty of those in the Congo back
then. But there are what I'd call executive level mercenaries. The top
level economic hit men I was telling you about.'

'Like your friend, Arthur?'

'Like him, yes. As it happens, Arthur wasn't there at the time. His role had already been taken by Gustav Clay and, back in 1961, Clay's opposite number, who happened to be working for the USSR at that point in time, was a man called Joseph Bern.

'I can't be sure that Edward and Bern knew one another before this time, but they certainly got to know one another back in Leopoldville and they continued to work together for years. For that matter, so did Clay, though for the purposes of our Congo story, Clay and Bern were technically on opposite sides. Clay even tried to scare Bern off by beating him senseless and keeping him prisoner in some little Bakuba village for several days. You've got to understand, I'm piecing all of this together second-hand. I don't know all the fine detail.'

'Why not just kill him?'

'Because that's not how the game was being played. Had Clay killed Joseph, then the Russians would have sent someone to deal with Clay. The whole operation, on both sides, would have been forced into a state of flux and no one would have been able to operate effectively. The odd beating was seen as an occupational hazard.'

'So, where do Edward and Molly fit into this and, forgive me, Gregory, this is all very interesting but what does it have to do with the current murders?'

'You asked me for a start to the story,' Gregory said. 'This is the closest to a beginning I can think of.'

Naomi sipped her drink. The ice was melting rapidly. She allowed a small piece to sit on her tongue before biting into it. 'Did you know the other dead man?' she asked. 'This Herbert Norris?'

'I know what he was, I think I can guess how he fits into our story, but personally, no, I didn't know him, though I suspect Arthur may have done.'

'So . . .'

'If you don't mind, I need to fill in some of the background, first. Every act has a history and I think you need some grasp of the history.'

'OK,' Naomi said. 'So . . .'

'To cut things short, things went very wrong very quickly. The country stood on the brink of civil war. The UN had moved in and brought troops with them, Hammarskjöld had insisted that no troops should come from any country that may have an interest in the outcome. This was the biggest test, so far, of a very young United

Nations. Their first real test as peacekeepers and it all fell apart around them.'

'They fled in the middle of the night,' Alec said. 'In the back of a flatbed truck. Molly said that as they drove up into the hills, they could see their home burning behind them.'

'And that was the start of things,' Gregory said. 'I hesitate to use the word friendship, but associations were formed back then that caused other things to happen. Decisions to be made that, I believe, are finally catching up with all of them.'

'What decisions?' Naomi asked.

Gregory paused for so long that she began to think there would be no answer. That he would finish his drink and walk away and they would never know.

'A child,' Gregory said at last. 'It was the decision to save a child.'

TWENTY-THREE

B ud watched the morning news with more than usual interest. He'd found a little boarding house in the Highlands and from there moved into a holiday cottage he'd discovered in a small valley. It was empty and deserted, the season already coming to an end. A query at the local post office and a phone call later and Bud had rented the place for a week. Mr Briars, as he'd become for the purpose, left his rental in cash with the postmistress.

He was still not being careful enough, Bud thought, but a feeling of resignation seemed to have settled upon him. The feeling in the pit of his belly told him that this was not going to come out well and equally that there was not a thing he could do about it. He'd either survive this last job and go on to enjoy the money it had made for him or he would not. Nothing he could do now would make an ounce of difference. He could feel it.

So he watched the news now and noted with interest rather than anxiety that the reports of two men found in a van close to where a warehouse robbery had taken place, was now on every channel.

'Police were called by a security man at the warehouse. He'd been alerted by someone hammering on the van doors from the inside, but by the time the emergency services had arrived, the sounds had apparently stopped. Police broke into the van to find the two men inside, already unconscious. It's understood that one man never regained consciousness, while the other managed to speak briefly to a police officer. He too is believed to have died during the night.

'Police will be releasing a statement later today. It is not yet known if the families of the two men have been informed of their deaths or even if the authorities are sure of their identities.

'The security officer injured in the raid on the warehouse is still in a critical condition in hospital. He has not yet regained consciousness. It's understood that the warehouse, a former car plant, is now used as a self-storage facility. It is not known if any of the lockers were broken into or what, if anything, was taken. Customers are asked to call this number, which will appear on your screens in just a moment, if they have immediate concerns. The number will also be available on our website.'

'So,' Bud mused, 'what was it someone wanted from the lockers?' He jotted the number down and stared at it as though it might enlighten him. He thought about the other members of his team and wondered if they too were wondering about the circumstances; the organization, the complexity of it all. Usually, once a job was over, Bud just walked away; as far away as he could get. Put the whole thing out of his mind. So what was so different about this time? What was it that wouldn't let him loose this time?

Bud's phone chirped softly. He picked it up and stared at the screen. Hardly anyone had his number. He opened up the message and looked hard at the few words there. The weight in the pit of his stomach grew heavier.

'We need to talk,' the message said. There was no name, but then, Bud thought, there didn't have to be.

'Where and when?' he texted back and then repacked the few possessions he had with him. Within an hour he was headed south again.

DI Barnes arrived at the hotel in time for breakfast. He had a selection of morning papers with him, which he dropped on the table beside Alec's plate.

'Developments,' he said. 'And yes, I will have some breakfast today, I think I'm going to need it, and then I want you to come with me to see Molly Chambers.'

Alec groaned. 'Oh, God, what now?'

'Have you seen the news today? Take a look. Front page of these two and page three inside. No, not that page three.'

'Thanks for that,' Alec said.

Naomi heard the sound of paper rustling and pages being turned. 'What's it about?' she asked. 'Alec, where's my knife gone? And can someone pass me the butter, please.'

'That warehouse robbery,' Alec said. 'All that stuff about the van. We heard it on the news this morning. What's it got to do with Molly?'

'Butter's there,' DI Barnes placed it beside Naomi's hand, reminding her of Gregory the night before and how carefully he had set her glass down. 'I don't see a knife.'

Alec passed it to her. 'Molly?' he said.

'Ah, well it's this. One locker seems to have been broken into and the rental is in the name of—'

'Molly Chambers,' Alec guessed.

'Well, strictly speaking, Molly and Edward Chambers. But yes. I've been asked to talk to her on behalf of the investigating team, but no doubt they'll be wanting a word later.'

'No doubt,' Naomi said dryly. 'Do we know what was taken?'

'Not sure. The security guard thinks it's a box missing. The lockers are really just glorified cages, with a bit of thin wall in between. It's a cheap and rather tacky set-up, done to maximize the number of lockers they can fit into the space and put together as cheaply as they could get away with. That's about all I know as yet. They want me to take Molly over there to examine the contents, tell us what's gone, so I'd like you to come along.'

'You afraid of one defenceless old lady?' Naomi asked.

'Defenceless old ladies don't bother me, no. Molly Chambers is something else.'

Naomi laughed. 'True. What about the two men in the van, do we know who they are?'

'Well, yes and no. We know who they are supposed to be, but there are complications, it seems. Identification on the victims suggests that they are Gilligan and Hayes, from a firm of financial consultants of the same name. There was apparently a Bern, but he seems to have retired and the name had been dropped.'

'Joseph Bern?' Alec said.

Instinctively, Naomi wished he hadn't.

'Yes. Why? Do you know him?'

'I've heard the name.' Alec said. She could hear that he regretted it too. He tried to backtrack. 'It's an unusual name. It stuck in my head.'

Barnes waited for Alec to elaborate and when he did not he said, 'So we collect Molly Chambers, take her out to the warehouse and find out what she had stored there. See what it was that almost cost a man his life. The security guard is still in a very bad way.'

Guiltily, Naomi realized she had forgotten about the man who'd been injured in the raid. 'Will he be OK, do they think?'

'Too soon to tell. Tell me, where did you hear of Joseph Bern?'

'Molly might have mentioned the name,' Alec said. 'I don't remember.'

Naomi could feel Barnes staring at her husband. Alec was such an appallingly bad liar. 'And why do you think Gilligan and Hayes might not be, if you see what I mean?'

Reluctantly, Barnes allowed himself to be diverted. 'Because we found a number of other identities in their safe,' he said. 'Passports, bank cards, driving licences.'

'Theirs. Or were they dealing?' Alec asked.

'I've not been told. The search is still ongoing. I've a feeling it might be a long day, Alec.'

'I've not agreed to go with you yet.'

Barnes seemed nonplussed by that. 'No,' he agreed. 'I'm presuming. Sorry. But I'd be grateful if you would. I don't think Mrs Chambers is going to cooperate just because I want her to.'

'Or because I do,' Alec added. 'But I'll come and talk to her. And if she agrees then I'll come with you to the warehouse, but I'm not going to commit further than that. I left the job, remember. I didn't resign just so I could be the unpaid help.'

Naomi raised an eyebrow. It was unusual for Alec to be so acerbic. It was a sign of the strain he was under. She knew he hadn't slept well the night before. The conversation with Gregory had disturbed him, even though Naomi could not think of anything specific that had been said to be so upsetting. He had left them soon after telling them a little about the child but Naomi was still hazy about the details. Apparently a translator Edward had worked with had been murdered and Edward had assumed responsibility for the man's son.

Then Gregory had left and they had learnt no more.

'His name was Adis,' Gregory had told them. 'He was named

after his father. I know very little about him apart from the fact that Clay must have facilitated the process, helped get him false papers, that sort of thing.'

'Why would he do that?'

Gregory shrugged. 'It's always useful to have leverage,' he said, 'even over those on the same side as you are. But I know that Adis was not the last child Edward and Molly rescued, or the only secrets they kept.'

Annie had left Bob in the studio and walked down to the village shop, taking the dogs with her. She was unsurprised to see Nathan walking up the lane towards her.

'I called you at home,' he said. 'Bob told me where to find you.'

'You called the landline?'

'I brought you this.' He held out a new mobile phone. Annie took it.

'Trouble?'

'I don't think Clay has been able to access your home phone. I think the security on that is still good, but I don't want him logging our calls. If you need me urgently, text the number in that phone. It isn't registered and I've changed the sim card anyway.'

He fell into step beside her. 'How's Bob?'

'Well, excited about the exhibition. But I'm worried, Nathan. Clay is—'

'I won't let anything happen to Bob, I promise you. I've called in some reinforcements, nothing Bob will be aware of, but—'

'How bad is this getting?'

Nathan shrugged. 'I'm not sure. You heard about Hayes and Gilligan. That they died?'

'On the news. Yes.'

'But you won't have heard about Joseph.'

'Joseph? He's gone then?'

'Early hours of the morning. Inevitable.'

'I'm sorry. Sort of. I liked Joseph Bern. Will you go to the funeral?'

'I don't think so. Clay wants me to check on the house.'

'And will you?'

Nathan shrugged. 'I'll go. Frankly, I don't think Clay knows what he wants to find anyway.'

'He's losing it,' Annie said.

Nathan shook his head. The dark curls bounced against his forehead. 'He's gone beyond that,' he said.

TWENTY-FOUR

Molly welcomed them with her usual asperity and very reluctantly agreed to go with them to the warehouse. 'I'll go,' she said, 'but I need a favour in return.'

'You aren't doing us a favour, Molly. This is part of a murder investigation.'

Molly continued as though he hadn't spoken. 'An old friend of mine died last night. I'll be needing a lift to the funeral. You'll do that for me?'

'Of course I will, Molly.'

'Then I'll get my coat and bag and I'll come with you.'

They waited in the hall while she went upstairs. Alec heard her moving about, first in her own room and then in the spare bedroom at the back of the house. There was a sound as though she'd dragged something across the floor and when she finally emerged, a navy blazer and pale blue scarf added to her attire, she was carrying not just her handbag but some kind of document case as well. He looked at it pointedly.

'Something I might want to read on the way,' she told him and then turned to DI Barnes. 'Are we ready, then? If we're going to be gone all day then we will have to stop for lunch somewhere. I'm not good at missing meals these days. I think I did far too much of that back in my youth and my body is now punishing me for it.'

'I'm sure we can manage lunch,' Barnes told her.

Molly led the way out of the front door and the two men exchanged puzzled glances. Alec shrugged. Molly was a mystery even under ordinary circumstances.

'So, who died?' Alec asked as he, quite unnecessarily, helped her into the front seat of the car.

'An old friend,' Molly said. 'He had cancer. The doctors did what they could but finally death was inevitable.'

'And does this old friend have a name?'

Molly fixed him with a cool grey gaze. 'His name was Joseph Bern,' she said. 'And I knew him for a very, very long time.'

Sitting in the detective's car, Molly turned her mind to Joseph. The news of his death, even though expected, had still hit her hard. Another one gone. Adam Carmodie had introduced them to Joseph, but she and Edward had quickly come to realize that he had been part of their disparate network for far longer. Another spider spinning an overlapping web.

Molly closed her eyes, remembering the night they had left Leopoldville. The streets had been filled with armed gangs of men and women, even children. Molly was still unsure of what had been happening or what the people were protesting against on that particular occasion. She had witnessed such street violence on several occasions in the previous weeks, but this time . . . this time there seemed more vehemence to it. A deeper level of resentment and anger.

It had all gone south so unexpectedly, she thought, and become so unutterably brutally. Rumour and counter rumour . . .

She had been at a birthday party, one of the interpreters' children. Adis, the interpreter, and little Adis – the birthday celebrant had been driving her back home. Edward had left earlier, called to yet another bloody strategy meeting, and Molly had stayed on, chatting with the other women, watching the children run and play in the tangle of a garden. It had been an almost idyllic afternoon, but those moments, Molly had long since learnt, are never destined to last. She had learnt to grasp them, hold on to them, like the jewels they were, bright treasures in a sea of utter darkness, but back then, she had been a mere novice; it had never occurred to her that such a perfect afternoon could be so utterly shattered.

Later, sitting in the front seat of Adis's rickety old truck, little Adis in the back, half asleep on a pile of sacks and blankets, driving through the almost empty streets towards their home, Molly could recall that sleepy, slightly tipsy sense of well-being that came from an afternoon of sunshine, laughter and good company.

They had turned a corner back onto the one of the main thoroughfares and the scene changed, utterly . . .

'My god,' Molly had said. 'Adis, what's going on?'

'Get out,' Adis said softly. 'Quickly, before they see you. Get Adis and hide.'

'What?'

'Now, Molly, please.' He turned to look at her and she was horrified by the fear in his eyes. 'Protect my son.'

She didn't argue after that. Silently, she slid out from the passenger seat and ran around to the back. Little Adis, puzzled as to why they had stopped, was trying to see over the top of the cab. 'Come quickly,' she told him. 'Come with me, now.'

To her relief, the boy asked no questions, but just scrambled down, into her arms. Molly backed away, looking around for a place to hide. She could hear the crowd, closer now, oddly silent, just the sound of feet and the chink of metal and, though afterwards she dismissed it as pure fancy, it seemed to her that she could feel them too, like a wave of heat and hate breaking over the truck and Adis and her.

'Hush,' she breathed. She backed into a shop doorway, praying it would be unlocked and praying harder that there would be no one inside. Pushed little Adis behind one of the wooden counters and hastily pulled boxes and crates to hide him. 'Stay there and don't make a sound.'

She could see the boy's eyes, wide and fearful, but he crouched low, kept silent. Molly wondered then and she wondered now at how this little boy came to be so well trained. Had his father drilled him for just such an occasion? Had he learnt how to hide and be quiet at the same time as he had learned to speak, to read, to run?

She could hear voices now, coming from outside. She crept to the window, peered fearfully outside. Her friend, Adis, was now out of the cab, the interpreter speaking to the crowd, his voice reasonable and calm even though he was surrounded by men armed with machetes and knives. They crowded in on him, backing him up against the side of the truck. Molly could see they were not interested in his words.

'Oh, God,' Molly breathed. 'Oh, my good God.'

She glanced towards the counter under which she had concealed the child and then at the rear of the shop, wondering if there was another way out. When she looked back at the street, she saw that a man had climbed into the back of the truck. He was throwing the sacks and blankets to the ground as though searching for something. She could hear Adis's voice, all sense of calm now abandoned. She knew that he was begging for his life. And she knew that he hadn't a hope in hell.

Even in the present moment, Molly could still see so clearly the way the blade caught the light, the way the man in the truck brought the machete down to cleave into the head of her friend. She saw

Adis fall, saw the men surrounding him raise their weapons, saw the first assailant leap down from the truck and knew if she was going to keep the boy safe then she would have to act now. To run before their attention turned on her hiding place.

She crossed to the counter, pulled the child out from behind the crates and boxes.

'We've got to find a way out of here. Come, now.'

'My father.'

She couldn't tell him. She couldn't find the words. His eyes widened, and Molly realized that on some level the boy already knew.

'I promised him I'd keep you safe,' she said. 'I promised him. We've got to go.'

She could hear the men outside, shouting now, yelling words she could not understand. It was as though the killing had broken the spell and turned up the volume on their rage. She led the boy away from the screams and into the back of the shop, finding a window they could climb out of and then landing in an alley. She turned away from the street and began to run, dragging the child with her, trying to put distance between them and the scene of Adis's death and taking little note of where they were going. Finally pausing to take stock only when she realized they were lost in streets she did not know.

'Do you know where we are?' she asked the child. He shook his head. 'Right, then, we'll have to guess.' Squaring her shoulders, Molly took his hand tightly in hers and they began to walk, keeping in the shadows, pacing softly, not daring to speak.

Three hours it took me to find my way home, Molly recalled and Joseph was there, waiting.

'Edward?'

'Safe, but he couldn't get back here. We've got to leave, now.' He looked at the boy who stood beside her.

'He's coming with us,' Molly said. 'I gave my word.'

'Then get him in the truck. We've got to go.'

Molly nodded. She had dived back into their little bungalow and grabbed a few of her possessions and a bag Edward insisted she always kept packed, a habit she maintained lifelong. Moments later and they were off, driving away at speed, the sound of the approaching mob carried on the wind.

TWENTY-FIVE

Naomi had an unexpected but rather welcome visit from Liz that morning. A little to her surprise, Liz suggested they go shopping.

'For anything in particular?' Naomi asked.

'Well, not really. I do this thing once a month. I take myself into town, have lunch and buy something nice. It might only be a new lipstick, but it makes me feel better.'

'Oh, I know what you mean and, actually, if you don't mind, that's not a bad idea. Alec is hopeless when it comes to that kind of shopping. My sister usually goes with me, but—'

'Well that's sorted then. I don't suppose you've seen that friend of yours again, have you? I don't suppose he mentioned me?'

'You mean Gregory? We saw him last night, as a matter of fact. But I don't know how long he'll be here. He moves around a great deal.'

Naomi wondered, again, if she should warn Liz off, but what should she say? Actually, he's a paid assassin and . . . well other things as well. The problem was she didn't actually think it would put Liz off.

'And did he?'

'Sorry, Liz, we didn't have long to talk and we were a bit involved in something,' Naomi told her. 'But I'm sure he liked you.'

'You think so?' Liz sounded hopeful and then Naomi felt her shrug. 'Oh, well, if it's meant to be, then something will come of it, I suppose. The problem is you reach a certain age and all the good men are taken. I suppose you met Alec when you were both very young?'

'Youngish. We went through our training together, parted for a bit and then ended up working in the same place. The rest, as they say. You never married?'

'No, I had my moments, but. Funny, a friend of mine died not long ago. He was older than me, but there was a time when, well, you know?'

His name wasn't Arthur Fields, or something, was it? Naomi thought. 'What did he die of?' she said.

'Oh, he had cancer. He went into remission for a while, but in the end, there was nothing anyone could do. It's a common enough story, I suppose, but it still hurts when it happens to someone you know. Right, off to town then,' Liz finished, brightly.

'I'll get my things,' Naomi said. 'And get Napoleon's harness on.'

They had touched on something, Naomi thought, that Liz did not want to talk about. Everyone, it seemed, had their secrets; their wounds. She wondered, briefly, what Gregory's were and then decided that she probably didn't want to know.

'You remember that first night,' Annie said. 'Down in the bunker beneath the railway station. I was so scared and you just seemed so calm. So –' she laughed – 'so you.'

'I remember,' Nathan told her. 'Bonnie had said I'd probably be getting some company. I didn't want company. I especially didn't want the company of a girl. I just wanted to play my game and be left alone.'

Annie reached for his hand and held it, briefly. Nathan didn't welcome physical contact, even now, but she could get away with it so long as she didn't overstep his boundaries. She wondered if Nathan would ever be able to deal with a normal relationship – whatever that might mean in Nathan's case. He seemed to rejoice when other people settled into some kind of steady pattern; it had pleased him, immensely, when she had found and fallen for Bob, but a Nathan relationship, well that would require a very unusual kind of person to maintain.

'I was so scared,' she said again. 'And cold.'

Nathan returned her touch, squeezing her fingers gently and she knew he remembered just as well as she did. Probably even better, in fact. Nathan remembered in almost photographic detail.

'You were shivering,' he said. 'But you didn't realize it. Then you went into the other room and·put on the clothes they had given you. When you came out, I took one of the blankets from the bunk and wrapped it round you and then I got another, but you were still cold.'

So he had put his game away, Annie recalled. Saving and switching off carefully and then he'd sat down on the bunk beside her and wrapped his long arms around both her and the blankets and he'd held her really tight. Eventually, they'd fallen asleep, curled up together on the narrow bunk and had woken only when, hours later, someone had brought them food. She'd not understood, at the time, just how hard that had been for him, of why Edward had been so surprised.

Nathan touched no one. He avoided even casual contact as a rule. But it had been the start of a bond that had lasted ever since that night and Annie figured that she and Nathan probably understood one another better than anyone else in the world. That he probably loved her more than anyone else too, with the possible exception of Bob.

She thought about her parents. Her father, it turned out, had been shot, though it had been a couple of years before she discovered the exact circumstances. And she had never been able to put him in a grave; his body lost among the rubble and debris. Her mother had died in a fire. Their home set alight by insurgents, along with half the other houses in the old town where they'd lived. Annie had always tried to believe her mother had been dead before the flames found her. Annie had been at school when the first of the rockets hit and the teacher had led them all into what shelter could be found. Half her classmates had died in the next blast. Annie had run. She could remember little after that until someone had found her, a man who worked with her father and then there had been Edward and Nathan and Clay. Clay, who had fed her need for revenge, though he had called it justice; Nathan who had shown her that none of that really mattered and Edward, steadfast and quiet, always in the background, always there, always reminding her to question the facts and challenge the opinions. Whoever it was that put them forward.

'We have to kill him, don't we?' She didn't have to say his name. Nathan knew she meant Clay.

'I think that's likely,' Nathan said. 'But it won't be easy, even now.'

TWENTY-SIX

Molly poked around in the storage locker, opening boxes and drawers and going through the motions of a thorough search but it was evident to Alec that she had decided within seconds that nothing was missing and her efforts were just for their benefit.

'Nothing,' she said finally. 'There is nothing missing. There wasn't a lot here to start with. Just things I couldn't be bothered with back at the house.'

'You're sure?' Barnes asked her.

'Of course I am. You think I don't know what I left here?'

'It's easy to forget,' Barnes persisted and Alec gave him full marks for nerve. 'Did you keep an inventory?'

Molly froze him with a look. 'Have we finished?'

Barnes shrugged. 'If you're sure.'

'I'm sure.'

'A man almost died because someone thought you had something of value here, Mrs Chambers. Perhaps you could look again.'

'I don't lie and I don't make mistakes,' Molly told him coldly. 'I spent my life travelling, ergo I spent my life keeping track of my possessions. Can we go now?'

'Yes, we can go now.'

Molly preceded them and waited impatiently outside beside the car. Alec could see that she was agitated about something.

'Where now?' he asked.

'Lunch,' Molly said. 'Old bones need regular feeding.'

Barnes bristled. 'How well did you know Joseph Bern?' he asked. 'And if you knew him, does that also mean you were acquainted with Messrs Hayes and Gilligan?'

Molly eyed him suspiciously. 'I met them,' she said. 'Why?'

Barnes seemed to be making up his mind about something. 'Look,' he said finally. 'It's not escaped my notice that the pair of you, you and Alec, have certain levels of experience, shall we say, that fall outside of what is normally in the remit of the average copper.'

'And?'

'And I could do with that expertise and experience. I'll buy you lunch, but first of all I want you and Alec to come with me.'

'Come with you, where?'

'To the offices of Gilligan and Hayes. I want you to take a look, see if anything strikes you as strange.'

Barnes would have missed that half-smile, but Alec did not. He was well used to monitoring those fleeting expressions. Molly wanted that, Alec thought. If Barnes had not suggested it then he was sure she would have done.

'I'll look,' she said. 'But I don't know what I'll be able to tell you that your experts couldn't.'

Barnes held the car door open and Molly packed herself inside, setting the bags she carried carefully on her lap.

'What do you have in there?' Alec asked her, indicating the document case.

'Oh, for goodness sake, Alec. Look. In case I got bored on the journey.' She half withdrew an arty magazine with a glossy cover. Apparently it featured an article of a restoration in Venice and something about a biennial.

'And there's this.' She let the magazine slip back and took out a complicated looking knitting pattern. 'I used to knit, if you remember.'

Alec winced at the memory of itchy, cable knit sweaters and his mother's insistence that he wear them at least once. 'I remember,' he confirmed.

'I thought I'd get my old patterns out, have a read through and see if I could still remember how. Some people appreciated my efforts, even when you didn't.'

Alec, put firmly in his place, closed her door and slid into the rear passenger seat.

The offices of Gilligan and Hayes were more impressive than Alec had anticipated. They took up two floors of a Victorian terrace beneath which was a small but expensive-looking antique shop.

Antiques, again, Alec thought. He wondered if they stocked Oriental porcelain.

Barnes led the way up the stairs and into a spacious external office. A modern, but quite expensive-looking desk faced the door, angled slightly so it was set at a diagonal against the corner of the room. Next to that was a wooden filing cabinet and three chairs had been set against the wall, alongside a surprisingly domestic-looking sideboard and a surprisingly cheap-looking coffee table. The sideboard was set out with cups and tall, brushed steel hot water flasks, the sort Alec associated with the worst kind of conference seminars. He glanced out of the window and looked down on to a street busy with cars and shoppers and he wondered how Naomi and Liz were doing with their shopping. He realized that, much as he hated that particular activity, he'd much rather have been selecting the right shade of lipstick with his wife – and, as usual, getting it wrong – than standing here, in this tidy room, with his pretend aunt and a increasingly desperate detective inspector, stuck in the middle of a murder case Alec knew instinctively Barnes was not going to solve.

That random and somewhat illogical thought took Alec by surprise and he wondered where it had come from. It wasn't that he doubted Barnes's competence or his persistence, Alec realized, it was more the sense that this was bigger, more complex and went higher up the pay scale than anything a mere DI was able to get to grips with. He glanced back down at the busy street, and feeling suddenly vertiginous, moved away from the window. The sudden feeling of dizzy disloca-tion, Alec knew, had nothing to do with the height of the building or the distance, not actually so great, from the street below. It was more to do with the sudden understanding that someone, or a group of someones, were just allowing the likes of Barnes and of Alec himself to go through the motions of an investigation. To satisfy the public and media demand that these things should be solved and dealt with, but that nothing they actually did would make a fractional difference to the shadow world that actually dealt with matters like this. The likes of Gilligan and Hayes and Gregory and even Molly inhabited what Alec was starting to think of as an almost parallel universe. One that occasionally impinged upon the consciousness of the rest; of what Alec thought of as the ordinary world, the normal population. When that happened, it was all a question of damage control. Alec wondered just who was pulling the strings this time, then decided that, unlike Gregory, he really, truly didn't give a damn.

'I want to start upstairs,' Molly said.

'Gilligan's office,' Barnes told her.

They all trooped up the final flight of stairs. No disabled access, Alec noted wryly.

'Toilets off to the right,' Barnes said, 'and Gilligan's office to the left.' He opened the door and stood back to let Alec and Molly inside. For a couple of minutes, Molly stood just inside the door and just looked. She had the attitude, Alec realized, of an officer first attending a crime scene. He could hear his old boss telling him, just stand and look, Alec. And don't forget the ground beneath your feet. Just because everyone else might have clod-hopped over it, doesn't mean there isn't something they might have missed.

Barnes stood uncomfortably in the doorway, watching as Molly eventually moved into the room.

'OK to touch things?' Alec asked, thinking he ought to check before she did.

'Yes, just watch out for the fingerprint powder, Mrs Chambers. It's a sod to wash out of clothes.'

Molly nodded. She was looking at Gilligan's desk. An ugly, heavy affair, with carved panels and a green leather top. There were a few papers in a wooden in-tray and a small, rather pretty art deco clock with an enamelled dial. A brass pen tray filled with very ordinary biro pens and a blotter that suggested Gilligan might have written with something a little less ordinary. Molly moved around the desk and opened the drawers. Alec came to stand beside her.

Molly removed the top drawer, felt beneath it and then riffled through the contents. Alec glanced at Barnes, who was watching her intently. Molly had that effect on people, Alec thought.

'Office stationery,' Molly said. 'Headed notepaper and compliment slips. Cheap, though, don't you think?'

Alec felt the texture of the paper. She was right, he thought, it was pretty ordinary. What had she been expecting? 'Expensive-looking envelopes, though.'

'True,' Molly said.

'Maybe they just want to make a good first impression. They reckoned no one would take notice of cheap notepaper if it came in a fancy envelope.'

She replaced the drawer and opened the next. Checked beneath it as she had done before. A cashbox containing two ten pound notes and a handful of coins. A stack of receipts for petrol and one for a cheap mobile phone. Alec leafed through them, found another two for mobile phones.

The third drawer was empty but for a woollen scarf and a pair of gloves, a scatter of coins and paperclips and the sort of debris that, in Alec's experience, was found at the bottom of any office drawer.

Molly moved on to the filing cabinet, riffling though but with little apparent focus.

'Anything of interest in the folders?' Alec asked.

'Not that I know about. They've been checked over, but left *in situ*. There's someone from the Home Office coming to take a look, and they stipulated we leave them where they are, which is why they are still here and not in some evidence box, gracing some poor PCs desk right now.'

Molly flicked through the folders, glancing now and then at the contents, but making no comment. Finally, she slid the drawer closed and stood back.

'Your man from the Home Office will find nothing,' she declared. 'He's being sent just to make it all look official. Anything important will already have gone.'

'What do you mean?' Barnes asked her.

'I mean this place will already have been cleaned out. That will have happened, at the latest, as soon as Gilligan and Hayes had been positively identified, but my guess would be it had already been given the once over by whoever put them in that van.'

Barnes shifted uncomfortably. 'You can't know that,' he said.

'Can't know it, but I can guess.' Molly sighed. 'Right, let's take a look downstairs.'

They returned to the reception area and then to the office previously occupied by Hayes. There, Molly repeated her search, but Alec could see that this was the same performance as she had given at the storage locker. 'There'll be nothing here of interest,' she said. 'I'll make a bet that half the files are missing and what's left is just fragments of what should be there. There'll be nothing left that's of any use to anyone; it will all be gone.'

'What exactly did Gilligan and Hayes do?' Alec asked.

Molly shrugged. 'Whatever paid best and for whatever master could offer them the most profit,' she said. 'Gilligan was an expert in international law and Hayes specialized in bringing cases of abuse against government bodies on behalf of individuals.'

'Some sort of human rights lawyer,' Barnes suggested.

'You could call him that.' Molly seemed amused. 'But the way he dealt was more like those adverts you see. You know the ones, have you had an accident, no win no fee . . . except that Hayes always took his fee, win or not. If not in cash then in some other way. Not that he ever lost.' She paused for a moment and then said, 'If you think of him as some sort of international ambulance chaser, you'd be closer to the mark.'

'And your friend, Joseph Bern, was he in the same business?'

Molly frowned. 'I like to think that Joseph also had a sense of honour,' she said. 'That he used Gilligan and Hayes as a front, as a means to an end, but—' She shrugged. 'Joseph was a survivor, and survivors tend to be pragmatic. He left the business maybe ten years ago, so I couldn't really say.'

'But you seem to be aware of what kind of operation Gilligan and Hayes ran,' Barnes persisted.

'Because sometimes even slime can be a good lubricant,' Molly said. 'They had contacts and expertise and though Edward and I regarded them with the same distaste most people reserve for said slime, they could, on occasion, be useful. We referred people to Joseph from time to time and after Joseph retired we made occasional use of Gilligan and Hayes.'

'For what kind of thing?' Barnes asked. 'And those files, are they still here?'

Molly smiled at him, her expression indulgent. 'What do you think?' she said. 'How do you think I can be so certain that the place has already been searched? Now, I'd like my lunch and before that I need to use the bathroom. I take it that's allowed?'

Barnes frowned, but then nodded and Molly headed back up the stairs. Alec heard the stairs creak and then the door open and close.

'Do you think she's right?' Barnes asked.

'I'd bet on it. I'll also bet you'll get nothing useful out of her about what cases she did refer. Molly is used to keeping secrets. If you push she'll just clam up even tighter.'

Barnes wandered over to the window and looked down at the street as Alec had done earlier. Alec took the opportunity to call Naomi on her mobile. She and Liz were also about to go and have lunch. She sounded relaxed and happy, Alec thought as he slipped the phone back into his pocket. At least one of them was having a decent day.

Molly returned a moment or two later and they left, locking up carefully. Molly watched, hawklike, as Barnes set the alarm, and something about the tension in her body set alarm bells ringing in Alec's mind. Then she took his arm and squeezed it tight.

'It's been nice seeing you, Alec, even if the circumstances are far from ideal,' Molly said.

'Something is wrong, here,' Alec said, but Molly's fingers, digging deep into his flesh warned him that now was not the time and neither was the company. Feeling foolish, but somehow still in the older woman's thrall, even as he had been in childhood, Alec held his peace.

Oh, Edward, Molly thought as they drove away. I hope you can forgive me, but it's been long enough and I wanted that thing gone.

She felt guilty. Horribly guilty. That slim little folder had not been out of their possession since 1961 and now she felt so guilty, it was all she could do not to cry out to Barnes to turn back so she could retrieve it, hold it close again and in that way also hold Edward close again. She felt that she had betrayed a trust, despite the fact that everyone she had ever made promises to were now long gone. She was almost the last man standing.

I'm doing my best here, Molly told Edward. That place has already been picked clean. It's the safest place I can think of leaving it. Our home will be attacked again. We both know that, my darling and the next time I will not be so lucky.

The big surprise, Molly thought, was that Clay had not tried again already. She wondered who had persuaded him to stay his hand and how long their influence might last. She felt so terribly alone.

She would not cry, Molly instructed herself. Tears always lead to questions and beside they would do no good. Tears didn't even relieve her grief. She wondered if anything, death aside, ever would or could again.

Adam Carmodie had been away from home all day and so was the last of their disparate little group to hear of Joseph's death. A message had been left on his answer phone, asking him to call the hospice and of course, Adam knew at once that Joseph had gone.

'Do we know when the funeral will be?' he asked, after the usual condolences had been exchanged.

'Joseph had invitations printed out,' she said, somewhat to Adam's surprise. 'He just left the date to be filled in. I think the vicar and he worked out all the arrangements a few weeks ago, so there'll be one in the post for you tomorrow.'

'That was extraordinarily organized of him.' Adam found he was laughing. Unable to help himself. Actually, he thought, it wasn't extraordinary, not for Joseph; it was exactly the kind of provision Adam would have expected him to make. He realized, abruptly, that perhaps laughter might have been an inappropriate response.

The nurse apparently didn't think so. She chuckled softly. 'Oh, it was, so typical,' she said. 'He was a lovely man. One we'll all miss.'

A lovely man, Adam thought as he lowered the receiver back on to its cradle. He supposed in many ways Joseph had been a lovely man. A good companion and, when it suited his purpose, a loyal friend. He had also been a fierce fighter and a ruthless decision maker and, perhaps, the bravest of them all. Brave or . . .

There had been many times when Adam, almost sick with fear, had wondered if Joseph was even capable of it.

He wandered through to his study and, guiltily, took the little red notebook from the desk drawer. He'd put it there the night he'd returned from the hospice and, quite deliberately, not looked at it since then. Slowly, he peeled off the elastic bands holding the notebook and its additional contents together and laid everything out on his desk. Leafing through the documents Joseph had given him was like taking a fragmentary but painful trip through Adam's own life; those parts of it that he had shared with Joseph Bern. Other faces looked back at him across the years. The faces of the lost and disappeared. Images of massacre and mass graves. Notes scribbled on scraps of paper, on the backs of photographs, recording scraps of intelligence that might lead to other scraps and fragments that might lead to . . .

Adams picked up the notebook and fed the photographs and notes back inside, rebound it with the elastic bands and slid it back into the drawer.

'I'll come to your funeral, Joseph. I'll come and say goodbye, but that's it. I have a life now.'

He flopped wearily down into the captain's chair set behind the desk. Before their meeting at the hospice, he had last set eyes on Joseph Bern some nine years before. Ironically, at the funeral of another friend.

Adam closed his eyes, recalling the winter day, snow piled on the neighbouring graves just so the ground could be broken and the coffin interred. It had occurred to him, then, to wonder at just how many of his erstwhile colleagues chose burial rather than cremation; though so many of them had bought their final resting place years before, in anticipation. He had mentioned this to Joseph. Typically, Joseph had taken time to think before making a response.

'I hear you've retired,' Joseph said.

'I have, yes.'

Joseph had been amused. 'Is that possible?' he wondered.

'I plan to find out. I'll let you know.'

'It's because we don't know if we'll ever make it back,' Joseph said. 'Most of us will finish in an unmarked grave in some godforsaken place. I think it is good to have a place in which to rest, even if all that remains of us is a headstone with just one date and perhaps a name.'

Adam remembered that he had laughed aloud, then, all eyes turned upon him, remembered where he was. 'Even that would be a lie, Joseph Bern. Do you even remember what date you were born on? Or the name your poor mother gave you?'

'Perhaps I never had a mother,' Joseph said. 'Maybe I sprang into existence in my sixteenth year, fully formed and out for blood.'

Adam could not recall his reply. He suspected he hadn't bothered with one. What could he have said?

'My name is Joseph Bern,' Adam said softly, recalling that bakingly hot day, just outside of Leopoldville, when Joseph had first stumbled into his life. Stumbled in and changed it utterly and, it had once seemed, forever.

Adam got up and poured himself a drink. He swallowed the whisky down without bothering to taste and then poured another. This he sipped slowly, sitting at his desk. It took a third before he finally opened his desk drawer again took out the file and, reluctantly, began to read.

It was 1992, and Adam had been setting up forward communications depots in advance of UN forces slowly moving up towards Sarajevo. He and a small team had worked their way through the mountains, and one day in mid-June were sitting in what was left of a shepherd's hut about three miles out from the city. Adam had a slightly confused memory of a mad, former RAF pilot flying them into Sarajevo airport under heavy fire but, at this distance in time, he could no longer be certain it was that particular trip he remembered or some other. It had almost become a standing joke that wherever you went in the world, you'd find a former RAF pilot.

The coms depots were a joke, Adam had decided. No sooner had they been placed than some other bugger blew them up, just in case the enemy could make use of them. The enemy on any given day being Serbs, Croats, Bosnian civilians, or local sheep, the fluid, ever shifting, daily uncertainties of this particular conflict making it hard to know even hour to hour where the lines were drawn.

Adam, technically a civilian, had also been in demand by the various journalists and news media personnel who were having a harder and harder time getting their stories out. Especially those that no side, at this stage of the conflict, really wanted to hear.

Adam and his team had stumbled upon several mass graves up in the mountains; had found many bodies unburied, too, still warm, on one occasion the rake of automatic fire clear across their bodies.

Adam hadn't stayed around to see if anyone came back to bury them.

Rumours were rife, as they were in any conflict, but one kept surfacing that struck Adam as more uncommon that most. An Englishman, with pale blue eyes, a mercenary, some said. A thief;

a black marketer. He could be hired as an assassin, could settle scores, could get where others could not.

He was a ghost, the rumours said.

He was responsible for some of the mass graves up in the lonely places, where no one went these days.

Adam had ignored these stories for a while, though he had wondered why, in a location rife with such people and where such acts were now commonplace, this man should have been singled out for especial notice.

Until that particular day sitting in the shepherd's hut, waiting for new orders, when Joseph Bern appeared, as mysteriously and unannounced as always.

Adam had not asked him what he was doing there. Joseph arrived with equipment that Adam's team had been requesting for weeks and orders that, with luck and a following wind, should see them out of there in a few days more. He also had a couple of bottles of slivovic, the local plum brandy and they had drunk to old friends and to not seeing one another for a goodly while and to the hope of not seeing one another again too soon.

'Clay is here,' Joseph had said.

'Clay? Why?'

'Oh, I don't know, running some dirty tricks, I expect. Finding profit where the rest of us find shit.'

'You've seen him?'

Joseph poured another glass and made no response. Adam had not pressed the point but that was when all the rumours and the stories coalesced into sense and when Adam decided that it was definitely time to be getting out.

And here it was, in Joseph's little red folder. Detail enough to sink the pair of them, Joseph and Clay. Congo, Bosnia, the First Gulf War History.

Adam closed the file and poured himself another drink. He'd bury Joseph Bern, say goodbye to his sometime friend and, meantime, do all he could to make sure none of this touched him. Contagion spreads, Adam thought. No one who was there would be immune.

TWENTY-SEVEN

A couple of days after their visit to Hayes and Gilligan, DI Barnes got a call from the investigating officer, the result of which was another visit to Alec and Naomi.

'The CSIs knew nothing could be taken away for investigation,' Barnes told them, 'so they took even more extensive photographs of everything *in situ* and two police officers were set to collate and inventory everything. When the man from the Home Office arrived, one of those officers was assigned to liaise with him. She took their inventory lists and all of the photographs along. Not that she needed it to notice that something was wrong.'

'Wrong?' Alec questioned, the small feeling of anxiety that had been growing in his stomach since Barnes arrived, now settling into a solid lump. 'Wrong like—?'

'Like a file that definitely wasn't there before.'

'Before?'

'Before Molly,' Barnes said.

'What kind of file?' Naomi asked.

'Apparently one which should not still exist. I don't know what's in it or why, but it's got a lot of people very flustered – I'm paraphrasing what my colleague told me, you understand.'

'So, you want to go and talk to Molly again?' Alec sighed. 'Look, I'm seeing her tomorrow. I'm taking her to a funeral.'

'Well, that's the thing. I've been told to say nothing. I've been told that the investigation into Hayes and Gilligan's unfortunate demise has now been upgraded. That we're out of the picture.'

'Surely, you should be relieved about that,' Naomi said. 'One less to solve.'

'Well, there is that, but, you know how it is, you have to be terminally nosy if you're going to make DI, so it's a bit hard to suddenly have that nose pushed out.'

'So, what are you going to do?'

'Nothing to be done. I've a desk piled high with other business, so I'll have to let it go. But I did manage to get hold of this. I thought maybe you should show it to Molly.'

He handed Alec a photograph. 'What is it?' Naomi asked.

'I don't know,' Alec said. 'Just a faded green file with a large red "W" stamped on it. Do you know what it is?' he asked Barnes.

'Not a clue. But someone thinks it's important.'

'And what's going to happen to Molly?'

'Well, that's the other thing. We've been warned off Mrs Chambers. She is, and I quote, "No longer to be considered relevant to our investigation."'

'Right,' Alec said. 'So why give me the photograph?'

'Because I think she needs to know that her message has been received. I just hope it's gone to the right people. I've no idea what she intended, but—'

'I'll see what she says,' Alec promised.

Barnes rose to leave and shook Naomi and Alec by the hand. 'Been nice meeting you,' he said. 'I hope the house hunting works out and you find out where you want to live.'

'Thank you,' Alec agreed. 'So do we.'

'So,' Naomi said as she heard Barnes's footsteps receding, 'that's that, then.'

'I suppose it is,' he agreed.

'What?'

'Well, it's like Barnes said. Terminal curiosity.'

'I do hope not. Terminal is, well a bit final.'

'So do I. And I know I've resented being dragged into all this, but now I'm told that it's none of my business, I think I'm going to find it hard to keep away.'

'So, do we show that photograph to Molly?'

'Damn right. At the very least she owes us an explanation.'

Naomi laughed. 'You know you don't stand a cat in hell's chance of getting one.'

'Well, I've got to try. Anyway, as Barnes said, she needs to know that her exploits have not gone unnoticed. So we'll show her the photograph and see what she has to say.'

'What she'll say is, Alec, you can at least stop and have a drink with an old woman. And she'll open that kitchen drawer and bring out the brandy and that will be that.' Naomi paused, a mischievous smile on her lips. 'It is rather good brandy, though. I wouldn't mind another glass.'

'That's all I need. The pair of you bonding over the brandy bottle.'

'Seriously, though. There's someone else that should get a look

at this photo. Someone who may actually be able to tell us a bit
more.'

'You're thinking Gregory, aren't you?'

Naomi nodded. 'Sorry,' she said, 'but apart from Molly, who's
tight as a clam, Gregory is the only sort of insider we've got.'

'And what makes you think he'll tell us anything? Even if he
knows anything.'

'Because, I think we've kind of proved ourselves,' Naomi said.
'Unlike Molly, who trusts no one to do anything except Molly,
Gregory at least thinks we're vaguely competent.'

Alec sagged back in his chair. 'I need a drink,' he said.

'Then you'll have to settle for coffee. It's only, what, eleven o clock?'

'Ten to,' Alec confirmed, 'so no way is the sun over the yardarm,
whatever a yardarm is. I'll text Gregory and get him to meet us later.'

Alec missed a beat. 'You've got his phone number,' he said flatly.

'Well, yes. How else are we going to keep in touch with him? It's
a bit hit and miss, him just turning up on spec like he did last time.'

'I don't think Gregory does anything on spec. But all right, then.
Text your hired killer. But that's it then. We finish and we walk
away. No more mess, no more Molly. If my parents want to check
up on her, they can phone. Or go and see her themselves. Agreed?'

'Agreed,' Naomi said. 'Except, of course, that you've promised
to take her to that funeral.'

Alec groaned. 'Naomi, I am liking this less and less. Joking apart,
I really do want out. I want a bit of peace and quiet and . . . well,
boring, I suppose.'

'Boring would be just fine,' Naomi agreed. 'So, you come back
here after the funeral, and the next morning, we go. Don't tell
anyone where we're going, we just go.'

'Any particular direction?'

'South,' Naomi said. 'Like the birds.'

When Bud had been in the army, he'd been trained as a sniper.
Laid up for hours at a time, breathing slow and steady, mind quiet
and largely empty of anything but random musings. Even his
body had become used to the periods of immobility; he'd learnt
to control the cramps and the discomforts, to block them out so
cleanly that they almost didn't register.

That had been long years ago and Bud had been a good deal
younger.

This job wasn't so bad, though. He had found a place to lay up from which he could see the house and most of the garden, but in which he was well screened. The girl knew he was there. Nathan would have told her, but even had he not, Bud recognized that sense of alertness she possessed; that almost uncanny way she had looked straight up at his hiding place. He figured that was because it was the one she would have chosen for herself had their roles been reversed.

The man, her husband, he was a different matter. He noticed things, Bud could see that, but they weren't security things. He supposed it had something to do with the man being an artist. Bud didn't know much about artists but they did seem like a breed apart.

Bud had been briefed on Bob's routines and so far the man had kept to them. Twice a day he walked the two dogs, spent a good deal of his time in the studio at the back of the house and, most days, wandered down to the village sometime in mid afternoon. Annie was usually with him then.

Bud knew there were other watchers. Nathan would have organized that. But he didn't look and he didn't ask, he just did his job, knowing that they would do the same. What you didn't know you couldn't reveal, even accidentally.

There'd been the odd random walker, but this wooded hillside was a little off the beaten track and somewhat too overgrown for even the most ardent of ramblers. Those few people Bud had seen he had heard long before they came into view. A father and two sons, rampaging through the woods, the boys, oddly, dressed as pirates. A courting couple, looking for a bit of privacy. An old woman looking for blackberries. None of them had noticed him.

It was, therefore, a surprise when a man got within fifty feet of Bud before he became aware of another presence.

The man was dressed in jeans, black T-shirt, an old padded jacket that had once had both colour and shape but was now a dull khaki, sagging at the shoulders and elbows. The man stood, waiting for Bud to acknowledge him, hands in his pockets, seemingly relaxed. Bud studied him for a moment longer, and decided there was nothing actually relaxed about him.

'Nice morning,' the stranger said.

'It is.'

'Rained in the night, though. Get you wet, did it?'

'Not so you'd notice.'

The man came closer, noting with interest Bud's shelter; a bender created from living saplings, pulled down towards the ground, roofed with polythene, camouflaged with leaf and branch. It was invisible even from a few feet away. The man had hazel eyes, Bud noted, and short, grey hair, and he was older than Bud first thought. Though he moved like a younger man, Bud reckoned the stranger had another twenty years under his belt compared to him.

'Mind if I sit?'

Bud shrugged and the stranger settled himself on the ground. The two men eyed one another.

'What can I do for you?' Bud asked.

'Probably nothing. Came here to speak to Annie, then I noticed she'd got company and I wondered why.'

Bud frowned and the other man shook his head. 'Oh, no. Not you. Took me a while to find you, which is why I thought you'd be the man to talk to. You've found the best position, of course. Dug in. Been here a few days, I reckon.'

Bud said nothing and it seemed the man expected nothing else.

'I'm guessing Nathan set you to watch. Clay wouldn't care about Bob and Annie can take care of herself, so I figure the target is that husband of hers and that got me thinking. Who would threaten Bob Taylor? And if you were the enemy, well it really would be a case of overkill. It wouldn't take all of you lot to take him out. One would do, when he walked those two dogs of his. Not a difficult target, Bob Taylor. An easy hit. Apart from the fact that Annie's here, of course. So I figured, not a hit squad, maybe a protection detail.'

Bud said nothing; again, he got the impression that this man expected nothing anyway.

'So I got to thinking again. Who would be such a threat that not even having Annie in the house could be enough? But also a threat she didn't want him to know was there? Annie likes her secrets as much as the next girl, and Bob Taylor is a good man, not a man to make enemies of his own. So—'

'So that got you thinking again,' Bud said, wondering where this was going. The other man might be a deal older, but Bud had been around long enough to know that should it come to a straight fight, he would not be at the advantage. He comforted himself with the thought that if this man had wanted him dead, he'd got close enough to have done the job before Bud had even been aware of him. Then he dismissed that as being any kind of comfort. Even a relative kind.

The man smiled. 'That got me thinking,' he confirmed. 'If Nathan put the protection in place, then he must be taking this very seriously, but at the same time, he's made no attempt to move Bob Taylor to a place of safety, which means he either can't or does not want to make use of his usual contacts and resources and, with the possible exception of yourself, he's had to draft in, shall we say, less experienced operatives than he'd like to use on a protection detail. So that makes me think he's protecting Bob Taylor from someone close. Close to Nathan and Annie, that is.'

Bud tensed as the stranger put his hand into the pocket of his jacket. He noted the flicker of amusement cross the other's face as he withdrew a tobacco tin, opened it and began to prepare a smoke.

'Want one?'

'I gave up,' Bud said.

'Wise.' Gregory lit the roll up and slid the tin back into his pocket. 'You ever meet a man called Edward Chambers?'

'Why should I tell you anything?'

'No reason. He and Clay went way back, then Edward crossed him and the two parted company. At the time, Clay let it go, or, more accurately, put the matter on ice. Edward could still be of occasional use and Clay knew exactly what pressure to apply. Then Edward died and Clay realized that some of the skeletons Edward had reason to keep in their closets, were making their way out. Edward was a gatekeeper, a collator, if you like. Such people hold a great many secrets in their care.'

'And you are telling me this, because?'

Gregory smoked in silence, then removed the tin from his pocket again, nipped out what was left of his roll up and replaced the stub in the tin.

'Tell Nathan that Gregory came here. That he is willing to help, should Nathan require it. That's all.'

Gregory rose and Bud watched as he moved off into the wood, within a few feet he had all but disappeared. Bud continued to watch until he was certain the other man had gone, the encounter leaving him with a deep feeling of unease. No, he acknowledged, as he realized that his breath was ragged and his heart rate fast enough to be almost normal. A feeling of fear.

TWENTY-EIGHT

ariq Nasir had worked in counterintelligence most of his adult life. Although no part of the intelligence service had ever advertised for a tea boy or general factotum, Tariq would be the first to admit that was where he had started out. As an assistant to the assistant of another very junior assistant. He'd never had a yen for field work; Tariq knew he just wasn't cut out for it. He was definitely not the athletic type, inclined to be clumsy – a doofus, his father called it – and beside, Tariq knew he didn't have that kind of nerve, but what he did have was a phenomenal memory and an eye for detail and a fascination with codes and patterns and the kind of random facts most people would dismiss.

Tariq's father drove a taxi. Tariq's mother had been a teacher, back . . . wherever. He had never known her. Back wherever, Tariq's father had been in service to a very important man and that man had secrets.

That, in fact, was about the depth and breadth of Tariq's knowledge of his family's past. He had been five when they came to London. To damp streets and tall buildings and traffic and such a mix of people.

Tariq had fallen in love at five years old and could not conceive of living anywhere else.

The only other thing he knew was that their being here was because of a man called Gustav Clay, who had, his father said, saved their lives. Clay had been a peripheral figure in Tariq's life all the way through his childhood, like some oft absent uncle, who turned up on birthdays and brought presents or sent him packets of foreign stamps for his burgeoning collection.

Tariq's father was a taxi driver, but he wanted more for his son. Not that either of them saw anything wrong with being a taxi driver; Ahmed had passed 'the knowledge' on his first attempt and was justifiably proud of that fact, but for Tariq . . .

Besides, they both recognized that Tariq, though he had managed to pass his test, was a pretty lousy driver. Too easily distracted and with no fellow feeling for the engine. He now drove an automatic, so he didn't have to remember when to change gear.

And so, his father had spoken to Clay. Clay had ensured that Tariq made the right university choices and then, equipped with a joint First in political science and mathematics, Tariq had come to work for him. And had learnt that there was more to Clay than stamps and birthday gifts.

Twenty years in the business, now, slowly working his way up, mentored and sponsored by a man who, though now retired, was seen as one of the Elder Statesmen of their closed little world, Tariq had prospered and he had thought that there were no more surprises possible that could make their way into his in tray. Until this one.

Tariq spread the crime scene photos out across his desk, looking for anything that he might have missed already. He knew a great deal about Gilligan and Hayes. The department had dealings with them from time to time; sometimes adversarially, sometimes because they could discreetly make a problem go away.

For the right fee.

He liked neither man, didn't know anyone that actually did, but it was still a shock to realize that someone had gone to a lot of trouble to kill them.

His office door opened and Tariq did not need to look up to know who it was. Clay never knocked and anyway, once you'd been around him for a while, you could sense his presence as soon as he entered a building. Or so Tariq thought – he'd never actually dared ask if anyone else felt it.

'Anything of interest?' Clay sat down and settled himself comfortably.

Tariq shook his head. 'Puzzles,' he said. 'And no picture on the box.'

Clay laughed softly and Tariq smiled at the older man. His eyes seemed blue, today. Not that pale steel grey that usually presaged a storm.

'I have the post-mortem report,' Tariq said. 'The police are chasing it, so we'll have to release something to them soon.'

Clay nodded. He took the folder that Tariq proffered to him and skimmed through. 'Cause of death. Asphyxia. Did they run out of air?'

'The back of the van was sealed, but no. It wasn't as simple as that. There was a valve going from the cab into the back. Forensic think that carbon dioxide must have been released into the rear. Just a trickle of it. They woke up from whatever drug they had been given, and they must have been drugged or someone would have heard them earlier and there are no reports, even though we have CCTV records of the van at junctions and lights and even in slow traffic. The best guess is that when the van was parked, the valve was switched on and from then on it was just a matter of time.'

'So, the rescuers had no chance of getting to them.'

'No, I don't think so.'

'And, assuming that they had previously been unconscious, do we know what knocked them out?'

'Best guess so far is Xenon. It's sometimes used as an anaesthetic, but it clears from the body pretty quickly.'

'Expensive,' Clay commented. He flicked through the rest of the report and Tariq could not shake the not unusual sensation that Clay knew all of this already and was just testing him.

'And the file Molly Chambers so kindly deposited in their office?' Clay sounded amused, but his eyes told Tariq something different. Clay was annoyed. Not angry, yet, but definitely vexed.

He shook his head. 'I've gone through it, but I'm still not sure where it came from or what it's supposed to tell us. I thought a visit to Mrs Chambers might—'

'No, that won't be necessary.'

'If she thinks she knows what it was about. It might help me to contextualize,' Tariq began, but he knew it was a profitless argument.

Clay rose. 'The chances are it's nothing,' he said. 'We are none of us getting any younger, sometimes things that have no real importance suddenly seem desperately so. Molly was widowed not long ago. I wouldn't want to, well you know—'

Tariq nodded. 'You knew the Chambers well,' he ventured. 'I'm puzzled. Why didn't she just hand it over to you?'

'Once, we were friends,' he said. 'Then we began to differ in our view of the world. Edward was an idealist; I am and have always been a pragmatist. We did not part on the best of terms and when he died and I sent my condolences, Molly made it plain that I would not be welcome at the funeral. It's sad when old friends fall out, but there it is. I won't have her upset, Tariq. As I said, we're none of us getting any younger and if Molly is making her final years more comfortable by rewriting her past, then who am I to interfere.'

He paused, patted his jacket pockets as though absent-minded. 'I almost forgot. I have something of yours.'

He laid a photograph down on the desk. 'It was in Herbert Norris's flat. I thought it best not to leave it there.'

Tariq looked at the picture. He remembered it being taken. The tall, white man standing next to Tariq in the picture had been a friend of Herbert's that Tariq had met only once or twice. Joseph something. Joseph Bern. They'd all had lunch together, by the river, had talked about everything and nothing and the sun had been shining.

'Where did you get this?'

'Didn't you hear me? It was in Norris's flat. You should be more careful.'

'Careful of what? Herb was my friend.'

Clay shook his head. 'I told you long ago, Tariq, and this business with the Chambers should just reinforce that. There's really no such thing as friends. Just people you might know for a while.'

Tariq watched him leave and then gathered up the crime scene photographs and slid them into a drawer. There would be nothing in them that would help with this particular puzzle, he knew that now. It was all about that file. The picture of himself and Joseph Bern he slipped into his pocket, suddenly aware that his hands were shaking. The question was did Clay know that he was lying when he said that he had found nothing in that file?

Tariq took a deep, uncertain breath. The answer to that one, he thought, was a definite yes. Clay always recognized a lie. The only real question was did Clay intend to do anything about it?

TWENTY-NINE

Joseph Bern's funeral took place in a little churchyard in a village called Ember. It was a peaceful place, the Church of St Anne and the Virgin was suitably ancient and venerable and the birds sang over Joseph's grave.

Adam could not help but think how inappropriate it all was. He remembered their last, proper conversation and felt that the likes of Joseph Bern *should* be buried in an unmarked grave somewhere in Africa, or be lost beneath the bones of other fallen in some unnamed, undiscovered scene of carnage high in the Balkans. A churchyard in a pretty, quintessentially English village was so not Joseph. But it seemed the man had settled here, drank at the local pub, worshipped – *worshipped*, for Christ's sake – in this church. Had made friends here.

The outstretched branches of a copper beech shaded the mourners, a surprising number, Adam noted, though he recognized only five and knew only three by their proper names. He was surprised that there were still new burials happening in this little churchyard, his own parish church – not that he actually went to it – was full to capacity and no one had been interred there for the past twenty-odd years. But he noticed several new graves here, slotted in carefully between the older burials, noticed too that some of the family names on the eighteenth century headstones were echoed in those newly buried.

The vicar had, in his service, spoken of a much travelled man who had finally found a place to settle and feel at home in. From some of his anecdotes, Adam gathered that the vicar had actually known Joseph quite well – or at least thought he had. Like the nurses in the hospice, he too referred to Joseph as Joe and it still sounded wrong in Adam's ears. He had seen Molly flinch at the sound of it and realized that she too found it aberrant.

He did not speak to Molly until they left the graveside. He'd exchanged a few words with the vicar and someone from the village had been round to all the strangers in their midst and invited them back to the wake at the local pub. Adam thought he might consider it, but he doubted anyone else would, with the possible exception of Molly and her carefully attendant escort. She came over and joined Adam beneath the copper beech, the younger man with her loitering where she had left him.

'Too many funerals for my liking,' she said.

Her words reminded him of the last conversation he'd had with Joseph.

'We're getting older, Molly.'

She harrumphed and Adam smiled. 'I see Jenkins came and that man, Masters or whatever his name was,' Adam commented.

'And three other damned spooks,' Molly agreed. 'They probably wanted to make sure he was really dead. A thorn in everyone's side was Joseph.' She paused for breath and then said indignantly, 'Did you hear what that man called him? Joe, for goodness sake. Joseph was never a Joe.'

They turned and began to walk back towards the lych gate. Jenkins, Masters and the rest had already disappeared. Adam wondered what they'd actually come for, but then, it was tradition wasn't it, that respects should be paid, even if those you'd actually known and worked with were mostly long gone. They were the last ones standing, Adam thought sadly. The legions of the lost trailing behind them back through all the years, back to when Molly and Adam and Joseph had been young. Young enough to still believe the world could be changed. 'Are you going to the pub?' he asked.

'Damned right. Adam, this is Alec. The honorary nephew.'

Adam shook his hand. 'I've heard a lot about you,' he said. 'You're a Detective Inspector, I believe.'

'Not any more,' Molly said fiercely. 'He went and quit his job, didn't he?'

Adam met Alec's resigned gaze and raised an eyebrow.

'Molly doesn't approve,' Alec said.

'Of course not,' Adam smiled. 'Molly never quit at anything. I don't think she knows how. Not even when she should.'

'Well, that's as maybe.' Molly linked arms with the pair of them and they sauntered slowly towards the pub.

The Green Man, Adam noted. Joseph would have liked that. 'It was a good turn out,' he said. 'I never expected Joseph to settle down somewhere like this.'

'It's a very lovely little village,' Alec said. 'I think we could live somewhere like this.'

'Alec and his wife are house hunting,' Molly said. 'Maybe you should bring her here, Alec. I mean there'll be at least one house up for sale, won't there?'

Adam noted the edge to Molly's voice and wondered what Alec had done to offend some Molly sensibility or other. 'What sort of thing are you looking for?' he asked.

'I think that's the trouble,' Alec said. 'I don't think we really know. We've accepted an offer on our place and we're living in a hotel at the moment.'

'Been a pair of gypsies the last couple of months,' Molly said. Adam got the impression she was almost envious of that.

Alec found them a table in the already crowded lounge bar and went to fetch drinks. Molly watched as he ordered and stood chatting to one of the locals. 'He's a good boy,' she said as though responding to Adam's unspoken reprimand. 'He knows me, knows I don't mean any of it.'

From Molly, that was quite an admission. Adam looked more closely at his old friend. Lines of strain showed around her mouth and eyes and her skin was pale, grey almost. She looked ill and tired. 'What is it, Molly?' he asked softly. 'What's wrong?'

She turned her gaze from Alec and full on Adam. The face might show her age, he thought, but the eyes, oh they were still the same, Fierce and blue and so very much alive. With a sense of shock he realized that he was still just a little bit in love with her even after all these years.

'A young man came to my home two weeks ago,' she said. 'He was carrying a gun an MSP SP-3 and he had a tattoo on his arm. *His* mark. He blew his brains out on my landing, made an almighty mess. Adam, do you know how many years I've waited for that moment, for my death to come? They think I knew him, something foolish I said, I'm afraid. But I didn't know him, not who he was, but I knew what he was, Adam, and who sent him. And now, what I can't understand is why I'm still here and that young man is not.'

Adam stared at her. 'Molly, you'd better go through all of that again,' he said. 'A little more slowly this time and in a bit more detail.'

Molly shrugged. 'Not much more to tell,' she said. 'Those are the bare facts of it.'

'Bare facts of what?' Alec asked as he set their drinks down on the table. He'd been clasping all three between his hands and slopped a little of his coke over his fingers.

'You're not drinking?'

'I'm driving,' Alec said.

'So is Adam.'

'Adam is staying over at the pub tonight,' Adam told her reprovingly.

'Oh? Fancy a change of scene do you?'

'No, I'm carrying out a charge Joseph left me with. He asked me to remove some papers from his safe and to check around for anything that might, well, you know.'

Molly snorted. 'Bit late for that,' she said. '*They'll* have been all over it by now.'

'I won't be checking for quite the same things,' Adam said. He glanced at Alec and Molly caught the look.

'Oh, you can say anything in front of Alec,' she said. 'He knows how to keep his mouth shut.'

'And what do I need to keep it shut about?' Alec asked irritably. 'Molly, if this has anything to do with—'

'Alec, I've already told you. I didn't know that young man and

I certainly didn't know the two men he supposedly shot before he came to call on me.'

'Two men? Molly, what is going on here? Alec, I'm sorry, I'm sure you realize that Molly is in the habit of riding roughshod . . . what young man and what murders?'

Alec took a deep breath and then a long drink, wishing he'd asked for ginger beer. Most soft drinks were far too sweet. Adam was watching him expectantly and Molly was just looking vaguely annoyed. He watched as she seized her own drink and swallowed half in a single gulp. She was drinking too much, he thought. Drinking a lot, even for Molly.

'Two weeks ago,' Alec began, 'a man came to Molly's house. He was carrying a gun. Molly spotted him in the garden and called the police but by the time they got there he had entered the house gone upstairs to where she was and he had shot himself in the head. We still don't know who he was and the only clues we . . . . the police have is that the gun was unusual, he had a tooth filled with an amalgam not used in the UK and he had a tattoo on his arm. The gun he used to shoot himself has been implicated in two murders, one a couple of months ago and the second a few weeks after that.'

He found he was watching Adam's face closely and that Adam's face was as enigmatic as Molly's often was. Though for utterly different reasons. Molly expressed everything she was feeling or thinking in a series of fleeting, almost indecipherable expressions. They flitted, but rarely settled for long enough for anyone to figure out what was actually going on in her head. Adam, on the other hand, was just about expressionless, a faint twitch of micro expression at the edge of his smile, but that was all. Why was he smiling anyway, Alec wondered and then realized that Adam was watching Molly and that Molly was having a very hard time controlling her temper. For some reason her old friend was finding that amusing.

'Herbert Norris and Arthur Fields,' Alec said, glancing from his aunt and back to her friend and suddenly irritated by the pair of them. 'Shot, both of them.'

'Of course they were,' Molly said tartly. 'Otherwise we wouldn't have known about the gun.' She swallowed down the remainder of her drink and began to rise. 'Come along then,' she said.

'Along where?' Alec asked.

'To Joseph's, of course. To help Adam find whatever it is Joseph wanted him to find.'

'Molly, I don't think—'

'What kind of tattoo?' Adam asked.

'What? Oh, some kind of Celtic knot. A . . . a triskele, I think it's called. Nothing unusual.'

'So, there you are, then. Are we going now?'

Alec frowned at her. 'Molly, I don't think this is any of our business.'

'Of course it is. Joseph was my friend too.'

'I know he was,' Adam soothed. 'And if Alec is in agreement, then I'd be happy for you both to come back with me. But just now, I'm hungry and I'm sure Alec is too and I'm equally sure that you should eat something. Liquid lunches might have got us both through when we were young, my dear, but the older I get, the more my stomach requires regular feeding.'

Molly sat down with a thump. 'Oh, all right,' she said. 'I suppose I could manage something; what do they have here anyway?'

'They have menus on the bar,' Adam told her. 'I'll go and fetch some, shall I?'

Molly watched him go and Alec shifted his chair a little closer to the table. The pub was crowded and, with his back to the room, Alec was very conscious of other people squeezing by. 'Maybe we could find a better table if we're going to eat,' he said. 'How long have you known Adam, anyway?'

'Adam Carmodie and I met in 1961,' she said. 'Before you were even thought about. Oh, but he was a handsome man, carried quite a torch for me back then.'

'You were just married,' Alec worked out.

'I was, but a ring on your finger doesn't stop others from looking. I'm sure you're well aware of that, with that pretty wife of yours. I'm sure she's not short of admirers even now you've claimed her.'

Alec laughed. 'True,' he admitted. Naomi certainly still had her admirers. He had seen pictures of Molly from back when she was young and knew she had been strikingly lovely with a mass of light blonde hair, usually bundled up into some kind of silver clip and, on the few colour snaps he had seen, that she'd had Wedgwood blue eyes. Her eyes, like her hair, were greyer now. Always, in photographs, she gazed straight out at the viewer. Looked them in the eye. Edward, in contrast, was usually looking at her, as if he could not quite believe his luck.

'Did Adam never marry, then?' he teased and at once realized he'd touched something tender.

Molly's eyes clouded. 'He married,' she said. 'They had a son. Both were killed, their car went off the road. She was such a pretty little thing, long dark hair and the deepest brown eyes. The little boy looked so much like her.' She looked up, smiled at Adam who had returned with menus tucked under his arm and another round of drinks on a tray.

'The girl at the bar suggests we go through to the other room if we want to eat,' he said. 'She says there's a bit more space.'

Relieved, even more people now crowding into the bar, Alec got up and followed Molly and Adam through to the dining area. It occurred to him, suddenly, that both Molly and Adam had seemed unusually interested in the tattoo. He frowned; just what was she keeping from him and was Adam Carmodie likely to be an ally in his questioning or a co-conspirator of Molly's?

Before stepping through into the dining room, Alec glanced back into the bar. Most of those who'd been at Joseph's funeral were still there – the vicar now sitting somewhat unsteadily on his stool. They'd been joined by others who were clearly local. The bar area itself was quite small – a second room led off this and Alec noted that the mourners were now decanting into this second room as the lunchtime locals drifted in. There were, he thought, some notable absences. The three military-looking men that Molly had glared at and then studiously avoided, for instance.

'Are you coming, Alec?' Molly called to him from where she and Adam had now seated themselves. Facing the door again, he noticed and smiled at the memory of Molly telling the boy, Alec, that you should always be certain of your exits whenever you entered a strange place. At nine years old, the advice had seemed profound and mysterious, later it had seemed a little pretentious. It was only much later that he realized Molly had been deadly serious.

He took his designated seat and picked up the menu realizing how hungry he was. He and Molly had made an early start that morning and the journey had been a complex if pretty one, drifting via narrow roads through countryside just displaying the first hints of autumn.

'We order at the bar, apparently,' Adam said 'and then they bring our meal to us.'

Molly nodded wisely. 'The trout,' she said. 'It's a while since I ate trout.'

Alec said he'd like the steak and kidney pudding. He felt he needed some proper sustenance for the afternoon of investigating Joseph's house and the interrogation of his aunt and her friend that he had determined was going to happen whether Molly liked it or not.

Adam took the menus and got up. 'My treat,' he said. 'It's a pleasure to meet with old friends and to find new, so let me get this.'

Molly nodded as though that was only to be expected and Alec, ready to argue, decided against.

'What are you hoping to discover at Joseph's house?' he asked.

'I'm not hoping to find anything,' she said.

'OK, so –' Alec thought how to rephrase the question – 'what are you afraid of finding?'

She fixed him with what, despite her age, was still a steely, youthful gaze. 'I'm not afraid of finding anything, Alec. I am simply concerned that our friend should not be remembered badly. I'd expect Adam, or you, to do the same for me.'

Alec hesitated, working again on his phrasing. 'And what do you want to lose, Molly? What would mean that you might be remembered badly?'

She smiled at him and he knew he'd got his questions right for once. 'If the gods are willing, Alec, I will have taken care of all of that myself.'

'And if they are not?'

'Then it probably won't matter,' she said. 'Alec, if I've not had time to dispose of my own bodies, then it probably means that I'm already one of them and the problem will no longer be yours.'

Adam had returned now and Molly turned to him, ready to strike up some other conversation. Alec sighed, but refused to be so readily distracted. 'What bodies, Molly? Frankly, my love, you are getting very annoying with all this effort to be mysterious. One of these days you'll really need someone's help. There really will be something you can't handle alone and we'll all have been driven away by your efforts to keep us at arm's length over the years and by all the times you've told the people who love you it's none of their concern.'

Adam looked quizzically at the pair of them and, to Alec's surprise, he smiled. 'I obviously missed the start of this,' he said, 'but he's right, Molly. Sometimes we have to pass the torch, you know. Even Joseph recognized that.'

Molly glared, but Alec could see that her friend had piqued her interest. 'In what sense?' she demanded.

Adam sipped his drink and then set it down, carefully centring it on the beer mat and for a moment Alec wondered if his presence would prevent him from answering.

'I saw Joseph about a week before he died,' he said finally. 'He entrusted some things to my care. Material he'd collected over the years. I've not looked at all of it yet—'

'Not looked? Why on earth not?'

'Because, Molly my dearest, some of us would rather leave the past where it is. Because some of the memories Joseph's notes have evoked are deeply painful. What I intend, this afternoon, is to go through Joseph's cottage, with your help and Alec's if that's being offered and remove anything I think Joseph may have wanted discarded and also anything that links my old friend to me. I'm getting old, too, Molly. I have a business and a life and friends that have nothing to do with what happened to any of us in our long and much too exciting past. I am happy with what I have and, frankly, my dear Molly, I don't want the bodies to be found or the skeletons to be dragged out of the cupboard or the boat to be rocked or any other overused proverb to impact upon my comfortable life.

'Think of this as a last act of friendship, after which, I will have buried Joseph properly. Buried him and all that was entailed with knowing him.'

'And does that include me?' Molly bristled.

Adam laughed softly, then their food arrived and Alec knew he was grateful to be saved from giving her an answer.

Naomi's phone rang. She'd been dozing on the bed, not so much because she was tired, but because she was both bored and feeling particularly apathetic. Once Alec returned from the funeral, they would be leaving here and getting on with their lives. She had promised that to herself and Alec had agreed, reiterating that agreement before he went to collect Molly. She felt that life was somehow on hold, waiting for his return and couldn't seem to summon much enthusiasm for anything in the interim.

Naomi groped on the bedside table for the phone, half expecting it to be Alec; but it was Gregory. It had been more than twenty-four hours since she had sent him the text and the attached image of the photograph Barnes had given to them. She had almost given up on getting a response. Had almost decided that he, too, had flown south like the birds content to let the mystery remain a mystery.

'Can we meet?' Gregory said.

'I suppose so. Alec isn't here.'

'No, I know, he's at Joseph Bern's funeral.'

Naomi laughed uneasily. 'Is there anything you don't know?'

'It would seem there is,' Gregory told her quietly. 'But I plan to remedy that.'

She waited with Napoleon in the hotel reception. Gregory arrived only a few minutes after she had come down. He took her arm.

'Where are we going?'

'For a drive, then a walk, I think. It's a lovely day. Don't worry, you'll be back before Alec is.'

Reluctantly, she allowed him to lead her to his car. He opened the back door for Napoleon and then helped Naomi into the passenger seat. 'Are you OK finding the seat belt?'

'I'm fine. Where are we going?'

'I thought we'd go back to that cemetery, where you and your friend, Liz went. It's a nice place to walk and I don't know of any decent parks round here.'

'And it's private,' Naomi said. 'Away from prying eyes.'

'That too.' He was suddenly curious. 'How do you know that, though?'

'I might not be able to see, but I can still hear perfectly well. No traffic noise, lots of birdsong, and that kind of, well, kind of dead sound you get when something is enclosed. You know what I mean?'

'Yes, I know. The cemetery is cut back into a hill side. I think they must have expanded it at some time. In front, the hill drops off quite steeply, so that would have been difficult for expansion, so they sliced the side off the hill. The rest of it is surrounded by a wall and mature trees. The main road is actually only about a half mile away but the lie of the land kills the sound of traffic.'

'And not many people go there.'

'True.'

'We could talk in the car,' she suggested.

She could hear the smile in Gregory's voice when he replied. 'Naomi Blake, are you afraid to be alone with me? We could talk in the car,' he agreed, 'but you look as though you need a walk. Some fresh air.'

'You could be right. We're going to leave in the morning. We agreed. Once Alec has done his duty and taken Molly to this funeral, we are out of here.'

'Probably wise,' Gregory said.

Naomi felt oddly deflated. She'd been expecting an argument, she realized, not this simple acceptance. 'You think that's what we should do?'

'I think you should do what feels right.'

What feels right, Naomi thought. What did feel right? 'Do you know what's going on?' she challenged him.

'I know a little more than I did.'

'Which is?'

Gregory laughed. She felt the car turn and the sound of the tyres change as they drove off the road and on to the gravel track. He pulled up, moments later and cut the engine. 'The sun is shining,' Gregory said. 'Shall we enjoy it while we can?'

'While we can?'

'Storm clouds coming,' Gregory said. 'It's going to rain.'

Joseph Bern's house was pretty and small. It stood alone, separated from a short terrace by a strip of garden and a picket fence. The garden surrounded the red brick cottage and a brick path led to the front door. Flowers had been planted in terracotta pots on either side of the porch and someone had obviously been watering them in Joseph's absence. Someone had also cut the lawn on either side of the path, but the narrow flower beds that ran beside it showed evidence of their owner's absence in the clumps of dandelions that poked between the summer bedding.

Inside a tiled hall led down to the kitchen and a flight of narrow stairs disappeared behind a railing that Alec assumed defined the landing. There was a room on either side of the hall. One seemed to have been designated as a living room, with a large red sofa dominating the space, two, smaller, fireside chairs and a rather decrepit looking television. The wall space was lined with shelves, some carried books, an assortment of African carvings, odds and ends of silver and strange little tourist souvenirs that advertised themselves as presents from Brighton and Cleethorpes.

On the other side of the hall, the room had been set out as a study. Here all the shelves were laden down with books, the desk, though bare of papers, had a businesslike air about it, Alec thought. Set with wire mesh trays and a pot of pens. A well-worn office chair had been set behind it and another stood in the corner next to a shelf upon which typed papers had been neatly stacked.

Both rooms, Alec noticed, had rather nice, tiled fireplaces with fire-baskets and all the other accoutrements of fire keeping: pokers and coal scuttles and the like. He'd like an open fire, Alec thought. There was something cheering about glowing coals and crackling wood. He glanced automatically into both grates, checking for recent burning. Molly went a stage further and shoved the poker up inside the chimney. A cascade of soot showered down into her sleeve and she swore, roundly.

'Needs his blasted chimneys sweeping,' she said.

Not knowing what to look for or what was required of him, Alec sat down behind the desk and watched as Molly and Adam cast about the room. Apart from Molly's attack on the chimney, they touched nothing, just looked and Alec was reminded again of the instructions his boss had given him at Alec's first serious crime scene.

'Stand and look. Then look again and don't forget the ground beneath your feet.'

He glanced at the desk and the contents of the in-trays. A diary, from the look of it, sat in one. Curious, he picked it up and flicked through, ignoring Molly's stern look. She obviously thought he was interfering. Apart from hospital appointments and the odd lunch, a note about the church bazaar and a reminder to pay his electric bill, the diary was disappointingly empty. Entries stopped altogether about a month before, Alec noted. Presumably when Joseph went into the hospice.

A handful of letters and bills occupied the other tray and Alec shuffled through. He was a little disappointed to find that they were mostly utilities – marked paid and the payment date noted down. A card from someone wishing him a speedy recovery and a letter from the vicar who had led the burial service telling Joseph that he would visit at the hospice on his – the vicar's – return. The letter was post-marked Brighton and Alec wondered if he had been the source of the seaside souvenirs. He wondered, if so, were they intended ironically or did he genuinely think that Joseph would like an egg timer with a picture of a beach on it, or a shell-encrusted box, topped off by a picture of Brighton Pier. He fought down the urge to go back to the pub and ask. He guessed the vicar would still be there, toasting Joseph's memory along with the rest of the locals. It seemed that Joseph – or Joe – had truly found his place in this little community.

The desk itself was modern and cheap, probably a flatpack from one of the big DIY chains, Alec thought. It looked out of place in the room. Too new and too stark. Three drawers, no locks, one deep enough to take files. He resisted the urge to look inside. It seemed rude to start a proper search before his companions (glancing through the contents of a wire tray really didn't count, Alec thought). But Molly and Adam seemed oddly reluctant to begin.

'What are you looking for?' he asked finally as Molly made her third, slow circuit of the room.

'Anything out of place.'

'And how would you know? You've neither of you been here before.'

'No, but I know Joseph. Knew, Joseph,' she corrected herself. 'You get a feeling for these things.'

Alec raised an eyebrow. 'Do you even know what you might be looking for? Anyway, you seem to think someone else will have searched here already, so I really don't quite see the point.'

Impatient, he tugged the drawers open and felt around inside, checking beneath them as well. They seemed oddly empty. Paper, envelopes, paperclips and other stationery supplies, all neatly placed, and the filing drawer held only old bills and the odd postcard. Receipts for a new fridge and DVD player, other random detritus the like of which would be found in any home office or, in Alec's case, kitchen drawer.

He got up and went to examine the nearest bookshelves. Volumes of poetry and travel, literature and science sat side by side. The company they kept seemed random; Keats beside an old Baedeker Guide to Berlin. A book on Middle Eastern spices next to an atlas that, judging by the binding, appeared to date from the mid-1900s. No rhyme nor reason that Alec could see.

'Don't touch anything else,' Molly warned. 'If Joseph left us a message, you could ruin the entire meaning by moving something you shouldn't.'

'A message? Molly, I think you're being deluded.' He sat back down behind the desk and closed his eyes, suddenly very weary with all this cloak and dagger stuff. 'Don't you lot ever retire?' he asked irritably. 'I mean, old spies, or whatever you all were, surely you eventually retire just like everyone else. Can't you just leave this to whoever . . . I don't know, whoever . . . the new spies are?'

'Some of us try to retire,' Adam said heavily. 'Some of us thought they had.'

Molly harrumphed and paced the room for a fourth time. Alec felt in his pocket for the photograph Barnes had given to him. He'd meant to show it to Molly that morning, but he'd been a little late getting to her house and she'd been cross and the moment hadn't seemed to be right. Another moment hadn't really come. Until now.

'Want to tell me what this means,' he said, lying the picture down on the desk. 'DI Barnes said it was found in the filing cabinet at Gilligan and Hayes. They know it wasn't there before our visit because the whole place had been photographed in microscopic detail. It mysteriously appeared after we let you off the leash for a few minutes.'

Adam glanced across, evidently puzzled. Alec saw Molly square her shoulders, stiffen her back, and prepare to go into denial mode.

Adam came over and picked the photograph up, frowning.

'Molly?' he said. 'Molly? You kept this?'

'What of it?' she said.

'What of it? Molly, these things should have been destroyed. You kept this?'

She shrugged again. 'Oh get off your high horse, Adam. We all did things we really should not have done. At first it was just an accident. There wasn't time when we left Leopoldville, so we just gathered what we could and took it with us. Later, well it seemed like, well, we didn't quite know what to do with it. Who to give it to.'

'Give it to? Molly, you could just have burned the damn thing.'

'No.' Molly shook her head. 'We thought so, and then we read it. We looked inside and we found . . . Well, it doesn't really matter what we found. You can guess. If not the exact details, you can guess what kind of thing we read. Edward realized it could be like an insurance policy. It could protect.'

'Protect you? You used this for blackmail, Molly?'

She shook her head. 'Not us. No. Others that had fewer resources, less help than we had. The vulnerable, the lost. Oh, Adam, you've travelled the same path as we did. You know what it's like. You have to be prepared to protect yourself and also, if you have any conscience at all, to protect those who have helped you, worked with you.'

'Which is exactly why files like that should have been destroyed, Molly. You know better than that. You know exactly how dangerous—'

'Files like what?' Alec demanded. 'Look, the two of you might get off on playing games. I can appreciate it might be hard to give up on all that mystery, all that sense of your own damned importance. It must get to be a habit, maybe even like some kind of drug. But some of us, most of us, just want a quiet bloody life. No dramas, no international crises, no skeletons in cupboards. Molly, for Christ's sake, will you just tell me what the hell is going on?'

'I can't,' Molly said. 'I can't, Alec, because I no longer know. I know what we all did and what the consequences were. Believe me, we did retire. We did hand over to the new, modern versions of ourselves. We did bury our pasts. But some things just won't stay bloody buried and it's no good pretending they will. Past isn't past until everyone involved in it or touched by it is dead and buried and everything that ever touched them is likewise. You can do nothing about that, Alec and neither can I and sometimes knowing more won't keep you safer or tell you what you should do. It will just make you a target. Just make you into one of those people who have touched those that were there and are, therefore, also a threat. So don't ask me. I can't tell and I won't.'

'I think it's a bit late for that,' Alec told her coldly. 'I'm already involved and so is my wife. Involved because we care about you and also because you've already pulled us in, Molly. You used me to lie to Barnes and you used me to help you plant this file, whatever it is, in Gilligan's office. Well, Molly, the upshot of that is that Barnes has been told to drop the case. That he's been told to leave you alone. Been told that this is now a Home Office affair and well above the pay grade of some simple little provincial DI. Is that what you wanted, Molly? Did you get the desired effect?'

The silence in the room deepened as Molly looked away from him, refusing to reply. Alec could see her lip quivering, the Molly equivalent of full scale emotional breakdown. Adam stood silent. Finally he said, 'It won't be the Home Office. That will just be a convenient label, a cover for whatever department is now dealing with the deep past. But Alec is right, my dear. We've been stupid and careless and the pair of us are far too old and far too tired to take all of this kind of thing in our stride these days.'

He held up a hand to stop her when Molly looked about to protest. 'Alec, this Inspector Barnes, is he the kind of man that is likely to just let things go?'

'I don't suppose so,' Alec said reluctantly. 'Being told to back off is a bit like waving a red rag at a bull. He'll wonder why. He may do as he's told, but, if he's anything like I would be, he'll just get hold of a big stick and poke at the problem from a distance.'

'Then you need to talk to him. Tell him to let it go.'

'Before I do that, you need to give me a reason,' Alec said. 'Like

I said, he's been in the job long enough to become an Inspector. You don't do that without being a tenacious bugger.'

Adam nodded. 'Look,' he said. 'I think even if Joseph left anything here for us then the chances are it's already gone. Molly, I think we should all practise what we preach and get out of this mess once and for all. Time to walk away.'

'You can't be serious!' Molly exploded.

'Oh, but I am.' He put a finger to his lips and took something from his pocket. To Alec it looked like an ordinary mobile phone. He held it up and showed it to Molly. Alec, watching, saw her nod.

'One quick look,' she said. 'In case we've missed something and, Adam, I'd like a souvenir. A book or a . . . I don't know, a something to remember him by. Joseph was a part of our lives for so long, I'm sure he wouldn't mind.'

Alec, not sure what was going on, said the first thing that came to mind. 'Who is the beneficiary of his estate, Adam? Molly, I'm not sure you should be—'

'Oh, Alec, don't fuss, so. Joseph wouldn't care what I took.'

Adam shrugged and Molly seemed to take that as permission. Once again she prowled the study, examining the bookshelves and occasionally removing something. To Alec's eyes her choices seemed random; as random as Joseph's shelving had been. He sighed, giving in to the moment and sat down again. Molly would take her own sweet time, he was sure of that. He took out his phone and thought about calling Naomi, then put it away, thinking he should wait until he had a sense of when he'd be taking Molly home. If Naomi was worried about anything she would call him.

Glancing up, he noticed that Adam had left the room and a moment later he heard footsteps on the stairs.

'Adam needed to use the facilities,' Molly said.

'So he could hide a file? Molly, what on earth did you think—'

Molly turned on him, her expression fierce. 'I thought it was time I did the right thing,' she said angrily. 'Sometimes, we just have to. All of us, no matter what.'

Alec held up his hands, signalling surrender and Molly turned away, taking another book from the shelf and flicking through the pages. As Alec watched, she paused, removed what looked like a postcard from between the pages and studied it for a moment before replacing it and closing the book.

'Right,' she said. 'Well I suppose we should be going. Whoever gets this place will be getting a cosy little home. Maybe you and Naomi should think about it if it comes on to the market.'

'Not enough garden,' Alec said automatically. He could hear Adam moving about upstairs and then descending, his footsteps slow and steady.

'I think we're ready to go, now,' Alec told him. 'Molly seems to have found her souvenir.'

Adam nodded. Alec could see he looked anxious about something, but Molly was hustling them out of the door and so he let it go.

'What were you showing to Molly? On your phone?' Alec asked when they were once more out on the narrow village street and heading back towards The Green Man.

Adam took the phone from his pocket and showed it to Alec. It looked like an ordinary smart phone, similar to the one Alec carried. 'As Molly may or may not have told you, my expertise is in electronics and communication. I made a few modifications to my phone. Added a few apps, as they say in modern parlance.'

He swiped through a few screens, then stopped at one which showed some kind of waveform pattern. It looked to Alec like the track he got on his graphic equalizer at home.

'And what does that mean?' he asked.

'It means that Joseph's place has been bugged,' Adam said. 'I don't know who by, but whoever it is, the bugs are still active. Whoever it is, they are still listening in.'

'You talked about saving a child,' Naomi said. It was warm for early October and she could feel the sun on her face and a light breeze carried the scent of flowers and damp earth. The small amount of light and dark visual perception left to her, suggested they were walking under trees, evenly spaced and grown tall and wide.

'A child. Yes. Adis. I have no idea where he ended up or even if he kept the same name, but I'm sure Edward ensured he was cared for. Did you meet Edward?'

'Once or twice. At Alec's family gatherings. He seemed like a nice man. Mild and quiet compared to Molly.'

'They do say that opposites attract. They were reputed to be the perfect team, though, professionally speaking. I understand they were also genuinely in love.'

'Oh, I think that's true, but what do you mean, professionally speaking and why was this child so important?'

Gregory considered for a moment and then responded to her second question. 'Adis was the first of many,' he said. 'Mostly children, but Molly was a stickler for loyalty. She believed that if someone put their life on the line to help you, then you were obliged to do the same in return.'

'I don't understand,' Naomi said. 'What people?'

'It's complicated,' Gregory told her. 'This is a lovely place, don't you think? Funny how full of life these cities of the dead can be.'

'Necropolis,' Naomi said. 'I always did like the word. But you're right; this place is filled with birds.'

'And rabbits and foxes. I suppose being right in the middle of nowhere, like this—'

'But you're dodging my question. What kind of people? You can't start on a story and then try and distract me.'

'It's more that I'm not much of a storyteller. I'm not sure where to begin, but I suppose the Adis incident is as good a place as any. That incident took place in 1961.'

'The Belgian Congo.'

'As it was, yes. As I told you before, there were many forces jockeying for position that summer and Edward was in the thick of it. You've got to remember, the UN was only about fifteen years old at that time. It was an organization still looking for its role in the world. Edward had acted as a liaison officer for the UN a couple of times before. I don't know if you knew, but he spoke about a dozen languages, had grown up in Africa and understood the situation on the ground far better than most Europeans ever could.'

'So . . . hadn't the president been assassinated or something?'

'The first elections had taken place, but there were so many conflicting interests moving in, all ready to stake their claim on the minerals, the resources . . . Anyway, Adis senior was a local interpreter, Edward had recruited him and the two of them had worked closely for, perhaps, six months. Then Adis was killed, violently killed. Molly witnessed his death. I understand, so did the boy. Edward and Molly fled and they took the boy with them. He had no close family and they knew, as the son of a collaborator who'd been killed for working with the wrong people, the kid's life would not have been worth a damn.'

'I'm not sure I understand,' Naomi said. 'Surely, it was just a job.'

Gregory sighed, paused for a moment and then said. 'OK, let's turn it around, take a more extreme example. In the Second World

War, in Vichy France, those who worked with the Nazis, even as interpreters, even if their lives were under threat if they did not, were at best shunned by many of their countrymen. At worst, some were tried for war crimes. Logic and quiet consideration of circumstance and consequence don't happen when you're stuck in a war zone. People react, people jump on whatever bandwagon happens to be passing, or they act according to what they genuinely believe is the justice of the moment.'

'But the Nazis were different. That was—'

'That was a time of crisis. Of invasion, of all out war. The disturbance in what had been the Belgian Congo might not have been on the same scale. It's most famous victim might have been Dag Hammarskjöld, but tens of thousands died or were displaced, or were forced into actions that might have seemed inconceivable just a year or so before. The only real difference is that the invading forces were not cohesive; they were a mix of big corporations and political factions. Ours, the Americans, the Russians, factions native to the country and factions from outside. Not some easily identifiable, single force, like Nazi Germany. Those that suffer most in the aftermath of such a process are those that were seen to take sides, to get involved, and then get left behind when whatever force they backed or employer they worked for moves out and moves on. People like Adis.'

'I heard something about the first Gulf War,' Naomi said. 'That there were journalists and interpreters who had helped the US forces. Or maybe not even helped them just did their job as interpreters or got involved in some way and they were executed. Is that true?'

'It's true of many places and many times. Naomi, you've probably seen film of when the US forces pulled out of Vietnam. The fall of Saigon. You've probably seen film of the evacuation of CIA personnel from the rooftop of the US Embassy. But how many civilian employees, friends, lovers, common law partners do you think got left behind?

'Pick any conflict, look at any moment in our history and I mean us as a species, not us as a particular race or a particular country or creed or place and the same patterns will be evident. Molly and Edward knew this, recognized this, but unlike most of us, they wanted to try and do something about it. Most of us, believe me, we are just grateful if we can walk away. Little Adis was the first child they rescued, but there were others. Children, adults, families. They hid them, they rehomed them, organized false identities.'

'Rehomed.' Naomi laughed. 'You make it sound like stray dogs.'

'I always did prefer dogs to people,' Gregory told her. 'As individuals, they always seemed so much more reliable. As a pack, they are loyal to their leaders in a way that humans rarely are.'

'Or should be,' Naomi said, suddenly angry, though she could not have said exactly why.

'Or should be,' Gregory agreed. 'Though I do admire loyalty, I suppose. To the right people.'

'The right people?'

'I don't think Molly and Edward would agree with my choices, but we all do what we do, according to our natures. My friendship with Arthur Fields, even though I didn't always like the man, means that I owe a certain loyalty to him. I would like to know who shot him and on whose orders.'

'You didn't like him? Arthur Fields?'

'Not always, no.'

'Then what makes you owe him anything? If it wasn't friendship—'

'Coincidence of place, of time, of action. Maybe also because I know it could have been me. It's self-preservation, if you prefer that as an explanation.'

'I'm not sure what I prefer, never mind believe.' Naomi frowned. What exactly did she know about Gregory? That he killed people, that he was full of contradictions, that, on occasion, he too had saved lives. That he did have an odd sense of loyalty, one which had led him to some particularly violent actions. 'These people Edward and Molly helped. How did they hide them? How did they help?'

'Why did the Victorians insist on putting up such damn great angels everywhere?' Gregory asked.

'I don't know. But I do kind of like them.' She looked up instinctively towards the sound of chittering squirrels overhead. 'Fighting?'

'Yes, two big males, both want the same tree. You still behave as though you're sighted. I've noticed it before.'

'I suppose I do. You can't change long ingrained habits overnight, I suppose.'

'Does it make you angry?'

'It did.' Naomi paused, well aware that Gregory was distracting her from the questions she had asked. He did this often, she thought, almost as if he needed thinking time. She decided to allow the distraction, just for the moment.

'For a while I couldn't get over the anger. I felt like life was over and it was, the life I knew, anyway. But I was lucky. I had family and friends who wouldn't let me give in. My sister Sam was the biggest help.'

'How?' Gregory asked.

Naomi laughed. 'Oh, stupid, simple ordinary things. When the doctors said I could be discharged in a couple of days, she bought my make-up bag into the hospital. I'd never been a big one for all the slap, you know, but, Sam and I, we'd always looked at it like war paint. You put it on if you were worried about a new situation and you prepared for battle. She knew how hard it was going to be, going outside, facing people again, so she brought me a new lipstick and she sat with me until I could put it on and do my eye shadow and all that stuff and not look like some five year old who's stolen her mum's cosmetics. Then after I'd only been out a few days, she took me shopping. Boy, was I scared. The world was so much louder than I could remember it being and I held on to her arm so hard I bruised it. But she was right; you can spend too long standing on the edge of the pool, trying to summon the courage to jump in. I'd lost so much weight in hospital that nothing fitted. Sam said that if I could see myself in a mirror, I'd have hated the way everything just hung on me. She said I'd get to thinking what I looked like to other people, and I'd be upset because I looked a mess, so she took me out and we bought new clothes, and when I got home I just sat and cried and she just sat with me and you know how people usually try to get you to stop crying? Well Sam never did. She just knew I had to cry it all out. That I couldn't start to get better until I stopped being angry and got on with the grieving, I suppose. In a weird way, I guess she used my vanity to get me through a really difficult time.'

'She sounds very wise.'

'Daft as a brush, she is. But yeah, I guess she is wise too. She's a great mother, devoted to her kids. Just a big kid herself in a lot of ways. We're very close. I miss them, moving around the way we have. I really miss them.'

'Then go home,' Gregory said. 'It's not a hard choice to make, is it?'

'We've sold the house.'

'Good. So buy another. Buy it close to the ones you love.'

It was apt advice, Naomi thought. And so obvious she wondered why she hadn't thought about it for herself. 'Do you have people to love?'

'Love? No. As I said, there are people I have loyalties to, but less and less as time goes by.'

'Who helped Molly and Edward? You said it must have been this Clay.'

'At first, yes. Later, I think they expanded their own network. But they continued to work with Clay. As I said, most of those they saved, they created a life for. False papers, a false past. It isn't so hard with children, I don't suppose. They can be persuaded to forget. New memories fill the old spaces.'

'If you think that, then you don't know children,' Naomi told him.

'Maybe so. Anyway, eventually it seems there was a falling out.'

'About?'

'I would be speculating,' Gregory said.

'Speculate away.'

'Shall we sit? The view from here is very pretty. I could describe it to you.'

'All right, but save the description and just get on with the story.'

They settled down on a bench. The sun was even hotter in this spot and Naomi breathed in the warm, scented air and allowed her body to relax. Somehow, she felt more at ease than she had felt in weeks. Gregory's simple analysis of their situation had focused her mind, clarified things. She now felt faintly ridiculous that they had made life so hard for themselves, but perhaps it was just that they had not been ready to accept it was as simple as that.

'You were speculating,' she reminded Gregory.

'I was. Yes. From time to time, Clay would . . . how can I put this? Choose to keep the children Edward saved. He trained them, educated them more often than not saw them through university and helped them into influential jobs. Sometimes they came back to join his organization.'

'Organization?'

'I think that was what caused the rift. Edward believed that these children deserved a second chance. That they should be, well, rehomed, as I put it before and left to be whatever they wanted to be. Clay believed that there were some who could never be rehabilitated. That life, childhood, as it should be, had ended for them and nothing could bring that back. So he channelled their anger and their hatred; their need for revenge or restitution and he trained them accordingly. Sent them out into the world to do his bidding and to build his empire.'

'Empire? That sounds rather grandiose.'

'It's this view,' Gregory told her. 'You really should let me describe it to you. It evokes the grandiose.'

Naomi laughed. 'You are a very strange man,' she said. 'So, these other children—'

'I think Clay may have sent one of them to kill Molly,' Gregory told her.

'Why would he do that?'

'Because, unlike Edward, who understood that although you may not like everything that happens, some things are beyond your remit; some secrets need to be kept. Molly Chambers, I believe, long ago shed those particular illusions or, if you prefer, dispensed with that particular safety net. Molly doesn't just know where the bodies are buried, she helped put quite a few of them in the ground and, now Edward is dead and gone, I don't think she cares who knows that or who else she might have implicated. Molly is what I suppose you could term a loose cannon. Frankly, she scares the hell out of me, and I'm not directly implicated in anything she may or may not have done. Clay is in it up to his neck and Molly knows that.

'What I still can't figure out is how the assassination failed. Why Molly is still here.'

'Because the would-be assassin shot himself,' Naomi said.

Gregory laughed softly. 'I don't believe that for a minute,' he said. 'I just have two questions. One is, how did Molly kill the man Clay sent to kill her and the second is, when will he try again?'

THIRTY

DI Barnes, as Alec had speculated, was not a man to take rejection easily. He felt that his nose had been well and truly put out of joint and, even if he couldn't hope to get to the bottom of things, felt he at least owed it to himself to try.

He had spent an hour ensconced with the young officer who had acted as liaison with Tariq Nasir, the home office representative, but learnt nothing new. Had spent a good deal of time looking over the crime scene photographs from the Gilligan and Hayes office and then even longer looking at the photographs from the warehouse where the security guard had been attacked, but after all that, was no further.

When the news came mid-afternoon that the security guard had finally regained consciousness, Barnes, having gained the assent of his opposite number, was on his way to the hospital even before he had ascertained whether or not the injured man was fit to talk. *En route*, he called Bill to check that he'd heard about his friend and made arrangements to come over and have another chat with him after. He wondered about Alec and if he'd come to any new conclusions; if he'd shown Molly Chambers that photograph.

He wondered about a lot of things and most particularly, why anyone should go to such elaborate lengths to kill two men and then steal nothing – that, of course, was if Molly was telling the truth about that, which, on balance, seemed a tad unlikely.

Barnes pulled into the hospital car park and tried to remember the directions he'd been given. He made his way up to the high dependency unit and gave his name to the nurse on reception, then showed her his ID. Behind her, a bank of monitors blinked and beeped and CCTV cameras filmed patients in their beds. Other staff moved across the screens. As she spoke to him, the nurse's gaze flicked back and forth from his face, to the cameras and the screens. Barnes wondered which one represented his security guard.

'I told the other gentleman, he really isn't in a fit state to talk,' she said.

'Other gentleman?' Not a police officer, then, he thought wryly.

'Said he was a lawyer, or something. I asked him if the storage company had sent him and he said it was about compensation, so I assumed—'

'What did he look like, this other man? Did he show you any ID?'

'He gave me a business card, said I should pass it on to Tony's wife when she visited him. He was a young man, dark hair, not as tall as you. Nice-looking.'

'OK, thanks. Mrs Clark isn't here?'

'No, she's been here most of the time and his brother's sat with him too, but once he'd woken up and the doctor told her they thought he was going to be all right, we managed to persuade her to go home for a bit and get some sleep. She was all in, poor thing.'

'Did you tell the other man that?'

'No, but he didn't ask any questions, anyway. Just gave me the card.'

'Can I see it?'

The nurse fished about in her desk. The card was unprinted on the reverse, but a mobile phone number had been written neatly across the centre. On the front was the name of a company and another phone number.

'Did he give his name? Only there's no name on the card, just the company.'

'Oh, yes. He said he was a new employee, that his personal cards hadn't come back from the printers yet. He said to call that number and ask for Nathan.'

She looked quizzically at him. 'Look, I didn't give out any personal information, you know. And I did a quick Internet search after he'd gone. It's a real company. I don't think it was just some journalist looking for a story. We've had a few of those, all right.'

'Good thinking,' Barnes said, also thinking just how easy it would be to set up a company webpage, then wondering just why he was so suspicious.

'Has he said anything?'

She shook her head. 'Nothing much. You can have a chat with the officer that's been sitting with him, if you like. There's been a police person here all the time.'

Barnes told her he'd appreciate that. He watched as she crossed from reception desk to ward and pressed a buzzer on a com unit. A moment later a uniformed officer came out from behind the glass doors. They hissed closed behind him.

Barnes introduced himself. The officer nodded. 'I was told you might be calling by,' he said. 'Not much to tell you, I'm afraid.'

'He's said nothing?'

'Rambled a bit. Something about an old woman and a girl, but it could be anything and nothing. He kept saying they came too early or something like that.'

Molly Chambers? Barnes thought. Was the man recalling when she had come to collect something from the locker? But who was the girl?

'And nothing about the attack?'

'Nothing useful. His wife asked him and he said he heard a noise, looked up, saw something crashing down and that was it.'

So, that was it, Barnes thought. He thanked the officer and watched as he crossed back towards the ward, pausing to clean his hands with gel before he was buzzed back through. He still had hold of the business card.

'I'm supposed to give that to the wife,' the nurse said.

'Right. Yes. I don't suppose you could take a photocopy for me?'

'This is a nurse's station in a high dependency unit, not office supplies,' she said. 'We don't have one here.'

'OK, no problem.' He wondered at the sudden change of tone and assumed he had just outstayed his welcome. Taking out his phone he photographed the card on both sides and then handed it back. 'Tell Mrs Clark that she should check this out with the local police before she acts on it,' he said. 'Could be a con.'

The nurse frowned. He glanced back as he left; she was staring at the card as though it might bite her. No doubt upset that the 'nice-looking' young man might not be all he seemed, Barnes thought and then wondered if he was just overreacting. Why wouldn't it just be an insurance company doing a bit of low key ambulance chasing? Or maybe even the storage company, doing a bit of damage limitation.

Because it felt wrong, that was why, Barnes thought and then wondered if there was anything about this case that didn't feel wrong.

'OK, leaving aside your stupid idea that Molly may have killed that young man,' Naomi said, 'what really doesn't make sense is if this Clay really wants Molly dead, why hasn't he done something about it? It's been getting on for three weeks, since—'

'At a guess, simply because another attack on her would draw more attention than he'd like. Presently, although there is the link of the same weapon being used in the Molly incident as in the two killings, Arthur Fields and this Norris character, there's not much else, so far as the police are concerned anyway—'

'You didn't know Herbert Norris, then?'

'No, can't help with that one, I'm afraid. It's possible he was a part of Clay's organization or that he had some contact with Molly, or even that he was something to do with Arthur.'

'You're talking about Clay's organization again,' Naomi accused. 'What sort of thing are we talking about here?'

They had arrived back at the car and Naomi heard the beep as he unlocked the doors. 'What kind of car is it?'

'A blue one.' Gregory sounded amused. 'In you go, big dog.' Napoleon deposited in the back, Gregory helped Naomi into her seat. 'Truthfully, Naomi, I don't know how large. Clay is a man I've avoided assiduously. I've never knowingly worked for him and I've never knowingly provoked him either. I'm not like Molly.'

'So, what do you think he'll do?'

'Wait a little while, then arrange for a heart attack or something similar.'

Naomi went cold. 'So, if he could do that, why send a man with a gun? It seems like grandstanding.'

'Exactly right,' Gregory said. 'Clay means to send a message, I think. The shooting of Arthur Fields was dramatic. It made the national papers and the international news. Arthur had friends, prominent enough that they didn't want to be seen at his funeral and who promptly erased all associations with his business. Herbert Norris's death does not seem to have created major waves, but Molly. Now that's another story. Molly and Edward are part of a lot of people's pasts.'

'You say people wanted to distance themselves from Arthur Fields, but I don't get why. Importing Chinese pots doesn't seem very dodgy.'

'Actually, that was the one element of Arthur's life that was totally genuine and totally above board. So far as I know, he didn't even use it as a cover for anything. You have to keep one part of your life clean. Pay your taxes, know your subject. Care about it. Do that with enough conviction and enough skill and you're halfway there. You have to live your legend; your cover story. Live it completely. There's no point going off half cocked; you'd be blown in a matter of days.'

'So, what else did he do?'

'Like I told you before, he was an economic hit man. A word here, a bit of pressure there. A promise made on behalf of . . . well, whoever.'

'And those who didn't attend his funeral. Were they afraid of connections being made?'

'Precisely. If they'd all turned up, Naomi, you'd have had a collection of the so called great and good and the politically influential, that even the local press would have started to wonder.'

'But why would Clay want him dead? And he wasn't exactly a young man; couldn't he have arranged one of those phoney heart attacks you were talking about?'

'I think . . . no, I'm guessing that Clay wants certain people to sit up and take notice. That he wants it to be obvious that he can get to anyone, any time. What puzzles me is the timing. What has changed that makes it so important to him to be making statements now? I think if I knew that, I could do something about it. About Clay, too.'

'I'm not sure I follow. What's stopping you?'

Gregory started the engine and reversed carefully. He was a very conscientious driver, Naomi thought. It seemed at odds with all she knew about him; then again, he was meticulous about everything else, too.

'So, what's stopping you?' she asked again.

'What's stopping me is that I don't know what booby traps Clay will have set, ready to explode in the event of his death. Think about it simply, in an ordinary way. You take one person out, Naomi, have someone die, even an ordinary, ordinarily blameless individual, it still causes ripples. You just think about it. A friend or relative dies, they leave a void, into that void other things will move, other people will shift. Friendships and associations that happened only because that person occupied a central position, they will fall apart and disappear. As the man said, *the centre cannot hold.*'

'Yeats.'

'Yes. I like his poems.'

Naomi laughed. 'You like poetry? I never would have figured—'

'I like *his* poems,' Gregory contradicted. 'I never said I liked poetry in general.'

'OK, so things fall apart. You're telling me that if Clay is taken out of the picture then there'll be some kind of power struggle or power vacuum?'

'That, too,' he said. 'What I'm saying is, when you take one of the gatekeepers out of the equation—'

'Someone like Edward. You said Edward was a gatekeeper.'

'I did, yes. When you take someone like Edward out of the equation, the secrets have a tendency to leak out and someone has to clean them up before any damage is done. Mostly, the secrets just die with the person, but there are always loose ends.'

'Like the file Molly kept. The one she dumped at Gilligan and Hayes.'

'Like that one. Yes.'

'And you don't know what else she might have.'

'No, but I suspect Clay does. Or at least Clay thinks he does. But that aside, if you take someone like Clay out of the equation, well it's a bit like taking the keystone out of an arch. Clay will have made sure that if he's assassinated, then a great deal of shit will hit a great many fans. It's in the interest of a lot of people that individuals like Clay live out their natural lives as peacefully as possible. Clay helped a lot of people to a lot of power over the years.'

'But you want him dead, now,' Naomi said flatly.

'And I'm not the only one,' Gregory confirmed. 'It's just going to be interesting to see who gets him in the end.'

'And who takes over from him?'

Gregory laughed. 'That too,' he said. 'Like I told your friend, Liz, I'm set to retire. But I could be persuaded otherwise, with the right incentive.'

Suddenly shocked by the implication, Naomi turned her head to face him.

Gregory chuckled. 'You're looking at me again, our Naomi,' he said. 'You've got your shocked face on. Well don't be. Better me than many of the others it could be.'

'What do you mean?'

'I mean, I'm a pussy cat compared to the likes of Clay. I do at least have a moral compass, though I'm not going to pretend I know which way it points most of the time.'

'And that's supposed to be a comfort?'

'Naomi, once this is over, or sooner if you and Alec decide to clear out in the morning, I'll be gone from your lives. Molly will, hopefully, have survived to be belligerent for another decade and the rest of the world will notice nothing different. It will be all change; all stay the same, just as it is on any given morning, any given year. No one will notice a damned thing.

'If we play this right, Clay will be buried with full honours and that will be that. Get it wrong—'

'Full honours?' Something in his tone suggested Gregory wasn't speaking metaphorically.

'Ah, didn't get to that bit, did I? Well just as Arthur Fields had a legitimate job, so does Clay. Moved from MI6 to MI5 back in the late nineties. He did a lot of work for the Thatcher government, I believe; was even posted at Menwith Hill for a while.'

'Menwith what?'

'Another place that doesn't exists. Or rather, that exists as an RAF base. The CIA are not permitted to spy on their own people from their own land, so they use a bit of ours. I understand its more NSA these days. Clay was there in the early days to smooth the path of communications, shall we say. I understand he's now an adviser for GCHQ. You've got to understand, he's older than me, so officially retired. Only people like Clay never retire.'

'I'm not sure I believe you, now,' Naomi told him, frankly.

'Oh? At what point did I cross your acceptance threshold? You can believe in all the unofficial cloak and dagger stuff, even believe that Molly might be mixed up in some dodgy dealings, but can't accept that one such dodgy dealer might also be employed by Her Maj's government.' Gregory chuckled to himself.

'I don't know what to believe,' Naomi said. 'I really don't.'

'Leave it at that, then. Just be careful, keep your distance as much as you can and if I think things are going to get rough, I'll do my best to warn you. My advice is the same. Go home, live quietly. Have lunch with your sister and take dog to paddle in the sea. Be conspicuously inconspicuous and, chances are, everyone will leave you alone.'

'Chances are? What kind of guarantee is that?'

'None,' Gregory told her. 'But it's the best I can do.'

THIRTY-ONE

'How is he? Did you see him?' Bill and the dog came to greet Barnes at the front door. 'Will he be able to have a visitor or two soon?'

'For goodness sake, love, let the man in. Come on through.'

Barnes followed the wife through to the living room and took the offered seat. 'You'll want tea? Of course you will. Sit down and I'll get some.'

Bill sat down and leaned eagerly across to Barnes. 'I heard on the news that those two men died,' he said. 'If we could only have got to them sooner. We all tried so hard to get into the back of that van. Who on earth would want to do something like that?'

'We still don't know,' Barnes admitted. 'But you and the officers did your best. You mustn't blame yourself in any way.'

'Hard not to, though, isn't it? And if he'd just come out to help us, then the office would have been empty and no one would have been hurt.'

Bill slumped back into his chair. 'What did they say at the hospital?'

'That he's woken up and talked a bit and they think he's going to be all right. I think it might be a few days before visitors are allowed, but you should be able to see him soon. Are you back at work yet? Has the scene been released?'

'The scene? Oh you mean the crime scene at the warehouse.

Funny thinking about it like that. I've been signed off sick for a week. They've got an agency in for a while. Four men, where there were just the two of us. Goes to show, doesn't it?'

Barnes nodded, though he wasn't sure what exactly it showed. 'Will you be going back?'

Bill looked meaningfully towards the kitchen door. 'She doesn't want me to,' he said. 'But like I said to her, I'm not far off retirement. Who's going to want me now? There's talk about the agency taking over completely. Boss says he'll see if they'll take me on, like, but—' Bill spread his hands wide. 'Who knows? If not, well we've talked about it and figure we might sell up and move closer to our daughter. Property is cheaper up there and we've no mortgage now, that's one big blessing, so we may do that.'

Bill's wife came through with tea and biscuits and the questions were repeated, the same answers given. 'His wife, Steph, she's been in a terrible state as you can imagine. She says this man came round to see her, wanting to talk about compensation or something. I'll bet the company are just covering their backs. They wanted to know if he'd seen anything, but Steph just told them poor bugger was still unconscious.'

'I'll bet it was just one of those no win no fee lot,' Bill said. 'They could do with the money, though. We don't get paid sick pay, you know. Just statutory and what use is that to anyone? She said I should apply for compensation too. On account of the stress, like. You think I'd get anything do you? Only it would help, wouldn't it love? Otherwise, I'm going to have to go back to work as soon as.'

Barnes felt he was being called upon to mediate here; that he'd walked into the middle of an ongoing debate. He really didn't feel qualified to make any kind of judgement. 'I don't know,' he said. 'It might be worth a go, but I imagine it would be a long process, anyway. I don't think these things happen over night.'

Bill nodded. 'That's what I thought,' he said. 'That's what I reckoned.'

Barnes left not long after. Bill could tell him nothing more and Barnes could offer very little in the way of reassurance.

As he left, Bill's wife suggested he take the dog out for his afternoon walk and, while Bill went to get himself organized for that, she followed Barnes out to the car.

'I didn't want to talk about this, not in front of him. He's been upset enough. But we had a visitor. Someone came round and

suggested that the press might offer us money for our story or
something. He said not to do it. That they'd make it worth our
while to say no. But I had to sign these papers and agree to say
nothing to anyone. Anyone not official, I mean.'

'When was this?'

'Two days ago. Bill had gone out with the dog.'

'And did you sign anything?'

She glanced anxiously towards the house. 'The man said he'd
make it look like a compensation claim. Say it was covered by the
company's insurance. Same as Steph. He said he'd make it look
right for Bill, so he didn't feel awkward about it. They said it was
some government scheme to help victims of violence?'

She turned this last into a question, as if hoping for confirmation
from Barnes.

'There are a lot of schemes around,' Barnes said cautiously.

'They said this was a new one. Anyway, I signed the papers and
filled in all the forms and showed them a copy of his sick note,
he'd not sent it off at that point. They reckoned it would all be
quick. That we'd get payment in about a week, ten days.'

He could see in her eyes that she didn't really believe in the legiti-
macy of any of this, but that she was hoping; the kind of hope that
comes from a situation edging on the desperate, Barnes thought.

'We've got bills, expenses. If he's off for any length of time—'

'Do you have a name or anything? A contact number?'

'He left a card. With a number. Told me if I had any problem,
to call and ask for Nathan.'

Barnes nodded. 'Let me know if you hear back,' he said. 'You
didn't give him any bank details or anything?'

'No, he said it would be a cheque.' She relaxed. 'So that's all
right, isn't it?'

Bill came out and the conversation ceased. Barnes left wondering
who the hell this Nathan was and what kind of game he was playing.
He called the local police and asked the CIO if he knew anything
and obtained a promise that someone would go round and ask some
discreet questions. That, Barnes considered, was about all he could
do. If Sheila wasn't even confiding in Bill, then it was unlikely she
would tell anyone else what was going on and Barnes could sort
of see her point. If the money turned up, that would be the time to
confide full details to her husband. If not, then she wouldn't have
to look a fool in front of him, on top of everything else.

Barnes drove away, feeling oddly depressed and no more enlightened than when he'd come.

'What have you got there?' Tom Flanders looked over Tariq's shoulder. 'A *watch file*? You don't see those too often. I've just made tea. Want some?'

'You make dreadful tea.'

'I know. I'll pour you one anyway. So what's in it? Is that the one that mysteriously appeared in that lawyers' office?'

'The very same,' Tariq said. He continued to turn the pages slowly as Tom disappeared and then returned, two red mugs in hand. He deposited one on the edge of Tariq's desk and then pulled up a chair. As Tariq finished with each page, he drew it across the desk and began to read.

'Where the hell did this come from?'

Tariq shook his head. 'I'm really not sure. It was acquired when the Chambers were in Leopoldville.'

'But that was never part of a British Colony.'

'True, but that doesn't mean we didn't have interests there, but it's not what you could term a Legacy File, I don't think.'

Tom nodded. He had made something of a study of the so called Migrated Archives; files documenting official deeds carried out under colonial rule and which had been repatriated – migrated when the civil servants who held them had returned to the UK. So called Legacy Files, documenting the colonial years, were supposed to remain in the archive of the country to which they belonged after it gained independence. Most had, but some had been brought back and placed in storage. Many were only coming to light now.

'And material that "*might embarrass Her Majesty's Government, that might embarrass the police, military forces or public servants*",' Tom intoned, '"*shall be reduced to ash and that ash broken up*".'

Tariq laughed at the impression. The words were those of the Secretary of State for the Colonies, Iain Macleod, as outlined in various memoranda from 1961, though the truth was neither man knew what Macleod had actually sounded like; the impression based on the Whitehall types that appeared in the old films they both enjoyed.

'This isn't a Legacy File,' Tariq said. 'It's hard to say what it is.' He flipped the cover closed again and studied the red 'W' stamped on the front. 'W' for watch, hence watch file. A file that should have been, as Tom suggested, burnt to ash and the ash ground to nothing. An alternative had been to put the unwanted folders into weighted crates and sink them in deep water, Tariq remembered, and if the file was likely to be missed, then a 'twin' could be created to put in its place.

'It could be a twin, of course,' he said, allowing his thoughts to surface. 'It could even be mischief-making. Look, a list of names and payments, by the look of it on this page. We'd have to cross reference with records for the time, always supposing we can figure out what colony it was created for, but it could represent payoffs. It could have been intended to replace something in the Legacy Files and at the same time implicate officials, or police or . . . well suggest someone was taking bribes.'

'In which case, why stamp it?' Tom indicated the red 'W'. 'That suggests it was destined for destruction.'

'A double bluff?'

'Maybe. We'd need to know the context to be able to cross reference the names. Then it would be an archive job. That could take weeks.'

'True. My question is, why did Mrs Chambers want to get rid of it now?'

'Why keep it in the first place?'

'I don't know,' Tariq admitted.

'You could ask her?'

'I could, but I've been told I can't.'

Tom laughed, disbelieving. 'And who told you that?'

'Who do you think?'

'Then go over his head. He's just a consultant these days.'

'Officially, he's just a consultant. Unofficially I can't go over his head because there is no one over his head. At least no one that would talk to the likes of me and thee.'

'So?'

'So we put the damn thing away and pack up for the night,' Tariq said. 'I like to think I have a life outside of work. Illusory as that idea might be.'

Tom was already on his feet and glancing at his watch. 'You mean we get to finish at the proper time?' he said. 'I'll go for that.'

Tariq laughed. 'Tom,' he said. 'Call me paranoid, but I think we should just keep quiet about this one for now. Until I know what to do with it.'

His assistant and friend raised an eyebrow. 'Who would I tell?' he asked. 'What would I tell? We don't know anything worth a damn.'

True, Tariq thought. But he had a feeling, one he'd had before and learnt not to ignore. One thing Clay had taught him was to take notice of his intuition. To trust it and just now it was telling him that this was not something he was going to like; that it meant trouble with a capital T.'

'You going to talk to him about it?'

Tariq shrugged. 'And tell him what?' he said. 'Nothing he doesn't already know.'

'How come?'

'Because, Tom, he will have seen it already, examined it before it ever got to me. You didn't read to the end of it. There's another list and I'll let you guess who's on it, not under his proper name, of course, but I'm familiar with several of his aliases.'

'Clay,' Tom said and suddenly, Tariq thought, he looked very pale.

THIRTY-TWO

Alec had called Naomi to let her know they were leaving just after four. It was a journey of about an hour and then Molly to drop off. 'Should be with you a little after six,' he said. 'It's been an interesting day.'

'Hmm,' she said. 'Mine too. We'll swap stories, later.'

Intrigued, Alec signed off and started the car. 'All set?'

'I am, yes.'

'What book did you choose in the end?'

'Oh, a volume of poetry, 'Molly said. 'W.B. Yeats, collected works. It doesn't have everything, of course, but it will do.'

'And the postcard inside?'

'Was just a book mark, Alec. You are so suspicious.'

'Can you blame me? Molly, why would someone bug Joseph's place?'

'As Adam suggested, so someone could hear what the likes of us might say about him. What we might find.'

'And do you think there was anything to find?'

She shrugged. 'How would I know?'

Alec gave up. 'We should report it to the police,' he said grumpily.

'Report what? That Joseph's house had been bugged? Joseph being a person of interest to more than one government department.'

'A fact you failed to tell me.'

'One I'd have thought you'd have worked out for yourself. Anyway, by the time the police did anything, the bugs would have been gone.'

'You can't know that.'

'Can't I? Alec, look, what will be will be. For me, probably for Adam, but you and Naomi can still walk away from this and I think you should.'

'And that little speech about contamination by association?'

'Maybe overstated the mark a little.'

'You really think that?'

'I really don't know. Alec, you'll have to forgive an old woman. I don't know what events have been set in motion and I don't actually know what I've precipitated either. I could, perhaps, have been guilty of a misjudgement.'

'You mean by dumping that file in Gilligan's cabinet. What is that thing anyway?'

Molly sighed. 'I suppose I thought I was still in the game,' she said. 'Truth is, the game, like life, has moved on and I've failed to realize that.'

Alec felt a twinge of sympathy. She sounded so melancholy. He crushed the twinge ruthlessly. That was the way Molly got to people; the way she manipulated those around her. 'The file, Molly? What was in the file?'

'Oh you are such a bore, sometimes, Alec.'

'It's been said before. But sometimes the world needs bores. Can you imagine a world made up of people like you?'

Molly laughed softly. 'Hideous thought,' she said. 'I don't think I could cope.'

'So, the file?'

She seemed to be gathering her thoughts, then she said, 'You know I grew up in Kenya?'

'I knew that, yes.'

'My father had a farm, but it was my mother and a farm manager who took care of the day to day operations. He worked for the government, the British Government as a local administrator. I like to think that he did a good job, that he was a fair man, but at that time, good and fair on either side didn't count for very much.'

'You mean the Mau Mau thing?'

'Thing!' Molly was outraged. 'I'll have you know—'

'OK, bad choice of words.' He slowed for a bend and frowned.

'What's the matter?'

'Brakes are a little spongy. Pads probably need changing or something. Anyway, you were saying?'

Molly looked long and hard at him and then, finally she said, 'I was about fourteen or fifteen, I suppose, when it all started to happen. At first it was just the Kikuyu, one of the biggest tribal groups in the region. They wanted independence and were no longer prepared to wait for it. There had always been underground movements, secret societies and the like, but this one felt different right from the get go. It was intense, organized and quite, quite brutal.'

'From what I've heard there was brutality on both sides.'

'Oh, there was. I heard reports of people being burned alive, of the wives of two missionaries being kidnapped and forcibly circumcised, of people being forced to make the oath to join the Mau Mau at knifepoint. Damned if you do, damned if you don't and once you'd joined, then you had to kill, prove your loyalty by killing a white farmer or a member of his family.

'Believe me, Alec, we were all afraid. Black and white. No one knew what would happen. The colonial old guard declared this was their land by right and wouldn't give it up without a fight and the Kikuyu and the rest said this land was their birthright and were equally immovable. It was not going to end well.'

'So, what did your family do?'

'Made sure we always had weapons to hand in case of attack. But the worst of it was, Alec, no one knew who to trust any more. People who'd lived and worked with us for years were suddenly people we were suspicious of. Would they suddenly turn on us? And my father, as the local bureaucrat, he was right at the forefront when orders came from London. Then the news came that the troops were being sent.'

'That must have been a terrible time.'

'Oh, it was. I've lived through worse, but that was the hardest in many ways because that place was my home. Home is a place where we hope to be safe, but nowhere was safe.'

'It's going to rain,' Alec said, glancing at the sky. Hoping it would hold off until they got back. The road ahead was full of bends and tight curves and for a second time now, he'd felt the brakes were spongy, slow to respond.

'The troops arrived that October and the arrests began. Schools were closed down, they arrested Jomo Kenyatta who was then President of the African Union. He disappeared for several weeks,

held incommunicado somewhere in the hills. Rumours spread that
the British had killed him. He lived, but many, many others were
killed by British patrols. It was a bloody time.'

'And what does this have to do with the file?'

'With that particular file, not a great deal. The chain of which that
file is a part was begun back then, though, in my father's study.

'I first met Edward when I was seventeen. And he was a young man
of twenty. He'd been sent to help my father, I didn't know what with
at the time only that suddenly the farm had become the centre of operations for the British administrators in the area. My mother and I were
told to leave, we'd be given an armed escort to the airfield and then
we'd be going to spend a little time with her sister in South Africa. In
the few days between Edward arriving and our departure, I got to know
him. Though it was another eight years before we married.' She smiled.
'He could have asked me right there and then and I'd have said yes.
He was such a handsome young man, so kind too.'

Alec laughed. 'And tolerant,' he said.

Molly smiled in return. 'That too. Boxes and boxes of files began
to arrive and be sorted. Some were sent out to the airfield and
eventually, I think, flown back to the UK. Many were burned and the
ones due for burning were stamped with a 'W'. They called them
watch files. Some others, not stamped, simply had their contents
burned and those files had other contents created to replace them.
I learnt later that these were put back into the records, taken back
to where they'd come from.'

'The authorities covering their tracks?'

'Yes.'

'And your file?'

'Ah, that was a strange one. One page did originate from that
time. I remember my father directing it to be stamped and Edward
questioning that decision. There was an almighty row. Edward,
young though he was, never worried about facing anyone down.
My father stood over him while he burned the file, except, of course,
that he didn't. Later, much later, I realized that the argument had
been staged, that my father agreed with Edward's decision, that the
little show was put on for the benefit of another.'

'Clay?' Alec guessed.

'Clay,' Molly confirmed.

'And what does Clay do now? He must have retired.'

'I expect so,' she said. 'I have lost touch with what he's doing.'

Alec glanced over at her. 'Is that true, Molly?'

'I've told you before, Alec. I do not lie.'

'Of course you don't.'

He returned his attention to the road ahead. Signs promised a series of bends, that he remembered from the journey that morning. Tight bends at the top of a steep incline. The view of the valley had been wonderful that morning but now the rain had begun and was growing heavier by the second. Alec slowed, easing his foot off the accelerator. He glanced at the dashboard clock and decided that they were going to be later that he had estimated. He'd have to call Naomi when they got to Molly's house.

He touched the brake again, aware that they were approaching the zig zag bends far too fast. Nothing happened. He tried again.

'Alec?'

'Hang on, Molly. I can't get the brakes to work.'

'Take your foot off the accelerator and then shift down through the gears,' she told him. She sounded oddly calm, Alec thought. He felt anything but. Panic rose and for a split second her words made no sense.

Then the sense of them broke through. 'I know,' Alec mumbled, doing what she said with alacrity. The engine braking slowed them down, a little. Alec wrestled with the steering. The bends were tight and the road slick with rain. He pumped the brake again, but to no effect. Molly grabbed for the handbrake and wrenched it on. The car skidded, turned, Alec struggled to bring it back on line, but knew immediately that it was hopeless. He turned the wheel sharply as the car began to tilt, realized in that second that he'd made the move too late and then the world began to spin and then explode as the airbags deployed. He heard Molly scream as the car turned and tumbled off the road and down the side of the steep fall. Then the world went black and Alec knew nothing more.

THIRTY-THREE

The landlord of The Green Man tapped on Adam's door. 'You've got someone downstairs looking for you,' he said. 'Young man, says his name is Nathan Crow.'

Nathan? Adam felt a stab of shock which almost immediately gave way to pure curiosity.

He followed the landlord down and went through to the bar. It had emptied of funeral guests now, though the vicar was still there, chatting in the corner with a man and woman Adam had noticed earlier. They had the look of old friends, relaxed in one another's company, Adam thought.

Nathan sat alone at the bar, drink in hand. Adam wandered over to a table close to the window and waited for the younger man to join him.

'Gustav Clay's blue-eyed boy,' he said.

'Except that my eyes aren't blue,' Nathan argued. He took a seat opposite Adam. 'Can I get you a drink?'

'No, I think I've had enough for one day.'

Nathan nodded. 'I asked the landlord to bring us some coffee,' he said. 'I thought that might be a good idea.'

'Because?'

'Because we've got a lot to talk about. What's the food like here? I could be hungry.'

Adam studied him thoughtfully. Nathan was twenty-six or twenty-seven, Adam remembered, depending on which version of events you believed. He looked both younger and older. The eyes were unreadable; experienced and a little cold – and definitely not blue, but there was something very youthful about Nathan. Something almost innocent-looking that made it very hard to pin his age. 'Did Clay send you?' he asked.

'Oh, most definitely not.'

'Then?'

The coffee arrived and Nathan smiled at the landlord. 'Are you still serving food?' he asked.

'Evening service starts in an hour. Last orders at nine,' he was told.

'Thank you.'

Landlord gone, he turned his attention back to Adam. 'You've got absolutely no reason to trust me or even to listen, but I talked to Annie.' He paused. 'You know about Annie, of course?'

Adam nodded. 'Another of Clay's protégées,' he said.

'We were.'

'And now?'

'And now I think we may well be on the same side, Adam Carmodie.'

Adam smiled and sipped his coffee. 'I always thought Clay inspired loyalty,' he said. 'Don't you owe him, Nathan?'

Nathan nodded slowly. 'I was thirteen or something around that when Clay found me, and he's had thirteen years of service and loyalty and, from Annie at least, something close to love. Don't you think there's a nice balance to that? He's had an equal part of my life. I don't think I owe him more.'

'I think you are just playing games,' Adam said.

'And, in your place, I'd think the same. The fact is, Adam, that Clay can no longer be trusted with something as precious as loyalty. Clay is on something of a campaign. And I don't think he'd extend that loyalty to any of us.'

Adam laughed. 'I'm not sure he ever would have done,' he said.

'Ah, now there you are wrong. Without Clay, Annie and I would have been lost. Annie because she had no one. Me, because I cared for no one. Clay may have trained us both, may have channelled what we felt; in my case simply honed what I already was, but he did a fine job. We wanted for nothing and we were never alone, never in need. I count that as loyalty. Not as affection, perhaps, I'm not certain Clay is capable of that, but he took care of us and we did what he needed us to.'

'So, what's changed?'

'What's changed is that Clay is no longer in control of what he does. At first, Annie and me, we assumed he was just settling old scores. Winding down to a peaceful retirement, if you like, but it's more than that. Clay might have been possessed of a cold kind of logic, but it was still logic of sorts. It took me a while to figure it out.'

'Clay is a megalomaniac,' Adam said. 'Surely it didn't take you all this time to work that one out?'

Nathan said nothing. He sipped at his coffee and waited for the silence to break. Adam half listened to the conversation in the opposite corner of the room. Snatches of it reached him; the woman slightly drunk and becoming overloud seemed to be recounting a comedy act she had seen on the television. Adam, who rarely watched television, couldn't get any of the references.

'Why have you come here?' he asked eventually.

'To ask for help in taking him down,' Nathan said simply.

'And why should I help you?'

'Because, if you don't, I think you'll be next on his list. He failed with Molly, I still don't know how. I do know he'd more or less written you off as harmless, but when you visited Joseph . . . well that attracted him. He scented blood.'

'And, if Clay has just sent you here to test me out? To see if I'm a threat?'

Nathan shrugged. 'No way to prove anything,' he said. 'You could ask him, of course.'

'I could.'

Nathan nodded thoughtfully. 'Clay is dying,' he said.

'Of?'

'Brain tumour. Inoperable.'

'Then our troubles will soon be over.'

'I doubt that. Adam, I think he wants to erase his past before he gets erased. He's a very angry man, right now, and I don't think he knows friend from foe any more.'

'Nathan, he never did. Clay was a bastard all his life. If occasionally he managed to do some good as a by-product to what he wanted, then that was pure coincidence and you know it. He got his pound of flesh from you and Annie and from others too. Then he cast them aside when they were no more use to him. He's always been the same and if you think any different then you are just plain delusional.'

'Annie said you wouldn't listen,' Nathan said. He smiled. 'OK, Adam, that's fine, but if you won't help out then just keep your head down. I can't predict what he'll do next or what collateral damage there might be.'

'And what makes you think I might not just warn him?'

Nathan got up and stretched himself. There was something catlike about the young man, Adam thought.

'Because you hate him,' Nathan said. 'Because although you've never been able to prove that Clay killed your wife and child, you've always known it. The only reason you've not taken him down yourself is you don't know what surprises he's left. What skeletons of yours might just rattle their way out.' He laughed softly. 'That's the amazing, crazy thing about this game. There are no innocents. We all have our guilty little secrets, don't we?'

Adam said nothing. He saw Nathan take out his mobile phone and then heard his own chime as a text was received. 'I've sent you my number,' Nathan said. 'In case you change your mind. I could use your help, Adam; there'll be a hell of a lot of damage limitation to do.'

THIRTY-FOUR

Tariq knew that he could do nothing at work. Any search he began would be flagged; Clay would note it. He knew, from work he'd done for him, that Gustav Clay had a number of alter egos – they were far more than simple aliases, and also that he was often paid through corporate tax schemes and into companies that, strictly speaking, did not exist.

Tariq went home, sat down with a cup of decent coffee and a sandwich, promising himself that he'd eat properly later on; he checked his firewalls and his security systems, examined the alerts and then went to work with the search. He used a beta version of his usual search engine and obfuscation, hiding his IP address. Anyone tracking the search would find that it originated in the Seychelles. Later, he'd change the IP again, be somewhere else.

Tariq had learnt a long time ago that often you could find unlikely links by examining the commonplace and that's where he began, looking for news reports on the deaths of Gilligan and Hayes and then, when that failed to produce many hits, looking at the break in at the warehouse. He moved to news of Molly Chambers, of the shooting at her house and then on to his friend Herbert Norris. He had known, when Clay handed him the photograph, that Gustav Clay had been responsible for Herb's death. Frankly, Tariq couldn't understand why. Herb had been one of Clay's fosterlings, as he called them. Kids he'd taken off the street somewhere and helped into a fresh life. He'd met a few of them along the way; Tariq supposed that in a way he was one of their number.

Herbert Norris had been a good kid, Clay had once said. 'But not our sort. Too straight, too simple.'

Tariq had been amused at the time, had been flattered by the idea that he, Tariq Nasir, was of the special kind that Clay approved. Now he was not so sure he wanted that accolade.

He deepened his search around Molly Chambers, finding the record of her husband's funeral and his obituary, using that as a jumping off point, searching his diplomatic record, his history and hers. Cross-referencing in his memory the things he knew about Clay and where he had worked. What he had done. Then he back-tracked, looking for information on Arthur Fields.

Tariq closed his eyes and allowed his mind to be still. A pattern was emerging, a spider's web of connections and pathways. So what was happening here? What was Clay trying to do?

Tariq opened his eyes, suddenly afraid. Suddenly understanding at least the look of the puzzle, even if he could not exactly see the picture. He picked up his phone and called his father, knowing he'd have just come in from work.

'Have dinner with me?'

'I would like that very much. Where shall we meet?'

Minutes later, Tariq had left the flat; he had money in his wallet and a spare card he kept only for emergencies. It might take a little persuasion to get his father to leave for a few days, but Tariq knew he'd manage it.

'Don't ask questions,' he would say, just as Clay had said all of those years before. 'Don't go home. We are leaving now. I have to keep you safe.'

Ironic, he thought, the way the world turned and life circled back again and again. The man you trusted will have you killed, Tariq thought. Maybe Clay was right, there really weren't such things as friends.

THIRTY-FIVE

When Alec hadn't arrived back by seven p.m., Naomi had called him on his mobile. She wasn't unduly worried not to get a response; if he was driving and didn't have his hands-free set up then he simply wouldn't answer the phone. Half an hour later and the mild anxiety had transformed to full scale worry If he'd been running late he'd have called her. At the latest, he'd have given her a ring when he dropped Molly home. In the unlikely event that he'd stayed with Molly for a while, then he'd definitely have let her know.

She phoned Molly's home number and then Molly's mobile, but there was no response from either. She could hear the rain, pelting against the window. Bad weather, bad road. Anything could have happened.

In the end she decided she would have to go down to the reception and ask for help. She didn't know the numbers for the local hospitals or even where the local hospitals were and she had no one she could call, except maybe Liz. Naomi thought about it for a moment and then realized she didn't have Liz's number in her phone. Who else?

DI Barnes had left a card with them, but as most of his dealings had been with Alec, Naomi hadn't put that number in her phone either. Groping around in the drawer of Alec's bedside table, she found what she hoped was the card and took it downstairs with her.

'Alec isn't back. He's really late. I don't know what to do?'

The receptionist took charge. She took the card from Naomi, dialled out, put the number into Naomi's phone. Listened to the one-sided conversation as Naomi explained to DI Barnes that: 'I'm probably worrying about nothing, but I can't reach him or Molly and—'

He promised to do what he could. That he would call her back. Made her promise to ring when Alec turned up as he was sure he would.

Naomi hung up, unable to shake the feeling of dread that settled upon her.

'I'll get you a drink,' someone said and she nodded dumbly.

She sat in the lobby, willing the phone to ring. Willing Alec to come through the door, her hands clasped tightly around the glass, though she could not have said what spirit she was drinking. His head on her knee, Napoleon whined softly, sensing her mood. She laid her hand on his back, seeking comfort from the warm fur and the soft snuffling as he nosed at her thigh.

The door opened and closed, a guest returning from a day out, chatting to someone. The door opened again and footsteps turned towards the bar. She waited, willing the phone to ring. Willing Alec to come home.

The door opened again and she recognized the footsteps this time. Her heart seemed to stop. Barnes took her hand.

'I'm sorry, Naomi, but there's been an accident. I'll take you to the hospital. It's drowning out there, you'll need a coat.'

'Give me your key, Mrs Friedman. I'll get it for you.'

Dumbly, she handed her key over to the receptionist. 'How bad?' she said. 'Please, don't lie to me.'

'It's bad,' he said. 'Molly has a fractured skull. Alec . . . is in surgery.'

He clasped her hand more tightly. 'It will be all right. I'm sure it will.'

'What happened?'

'Pouring rain, a tight bend. Maybe he took it too fast, we don't know. He went off the road and rolled the car. Thankfully there was another car following close enough to see it happen. They called the ambulance. The paramedics got there very fast.'

Naomi nodded. The receptionist had arrived with her coat and she slipped it on, heard Barnes asking if someone could look after Napoleon and then he led her to his car. Her hair was soaked by the time they got inside.

'It's a filthy night,' Barnes said. 'I'm guessing the road was slick, maybe mud, maybe an oil spill or something.'

'Alec wouldn't drive fast, not in this. The driver in the other car, did they say anything?'

'He was still on the straight when Alec entered the bend. He said he saw the car skid on the first bend, and then lost sight of it. By the time he got there, they'd gone off the road. The driver could see the lights still on and phoned the emergency services, then he went down the slope to see if there was anything he could do. They were both unconscious and trapped in the car, so all he could do was wait on the road, so the ambulance could find them easily. Naomi, he probably saved their lives.'

She nodded. If they live, she thought.

'It wasn't an accident. I know it wasn't.'

'Naomi, it's a bad road, these things—'

'It wasn't an accident!'

Barnes said nothing. Naomi tried hard not to cry but the tears rolled anyway. He reached out and clasped her hand. 'He'll be OK,' Barnes said. 'They got to him in time.'

Inside the hospital, the sound of doors and trolleys and footsteps. She had done this before, sat in a corridor waiting for news.

Barnes had spoken to the doctor. Molly was still unconscious and they were worried about fluid on the brain. Alec was still in surgery. He'd lost a great deal of blood, there were internal injuries . . . it was too early to tell.

Barnes had sat with her and then fetched coffee and then, when

Naomi had insisted, gone in search of someone who could tell her more.

'They've told you all they can,' Barnes had told her gently.

'I know, but . . .'

'It's OK, I'll go and ask again.'

She felt calm, now. Far too calm. It would break. But more than that she felt rage. There was no other word for it. It seemed to grow from some point deep in her belly and rise through her until her limbs shook with it and her mind was filled.

She found her mobile and searched, sound turned down so she could only just hear the electronic voice telling her the names in her phonebook. She found the number she wanted. Gregory answered on the second ring.

'I want him dead,' Naomi told him. 'I don't care how you do it and I don't care who you take down with him but I want him gone.'

'What happened?' Gregory asked.

She managed to tell him, choking on the words. 'It wasn't an accident. I know it wasn't an accident.'

'It's OK,' Gregory told her softly. 'Naomi, it's OK. Leave it with me. It's all in hand.'

'I just want him dead.'

She realized that Gregory had gone. That he'd hung up on her and for a moment the rage turned against him too.

And then she understood. Gregory had heard what she had to say and there was need for nothing more.

THIRTY-SIX

Gregory had kept on the move these last weeks, surfacing only to make contact with Alec, Naomi and a few others. He knew he was far from safe; a wanted man and not just by the authorities. Fortunately, he didn't believe he was top of anyone's list just now. More people assumed he was dead than knew he was alive and after a lifetime of being 'not there', Gregory was comfortable with anonymity.

Now things were shifting and he wasn't sure he liked it.

He believed Naomi; the coincidence of the 'accident' was just too great. Clay was accelerating, pushing the game on and from what Gregory knew about the man, that was unusual. The one thing Clay was truly comfortable with was time. He played the long con, not the quick return.

So what had changed, or was changing? He'd make a bet that whatever it was, it had to do with Molly's file.

Gregory hadn't quite figured out Molly's motivation in putting this back into Clay's hands – and she must have known that's where it would end up. Molly was neither stupid, nor naive so she must have had reason for doing this. Reason that seemed good at the time. Maybe she was hoping if Clay acquired this bit of information, he would leave her alone, assume he had it all. Gregory thought about it, putting himself in Clay's position. Would he believe that? No, not a bit of it.

He sent a text to Nathan on the safe number – *safer* number, Gregory corrected himself – that Nathan had given him. The call came back a few moments later.

'How bad?' Nathan asked.

'Molly Chambers is still unconscious. Alec Friedman is still in surgery. That's all I know. But she's convinced Clay is behind this and I wouldn't be at all surprised.'

'I'll call you,' Nathan said. 'Be ready.'

Always, Gregory thought. I was born that way.

Barnes had returned and taken up his station beside her. 'They can't tell me much more,' he said. 'But they've stopped the bleeding. That has to be a good start, doesn't it?'

She nodded, not trusting herself to speak.

'Is there someone I can contact for you? A friend, family?'

'No, they're all miles away. My sister . . . she's got the kids and her husband works shift, I don't know if—'

'She'd come to you. They'd arrange something.'

'I know. Look, I know this sounds stupid, paranoid, even, but I don't want anyone else here. Not anyone I love. I'm scared, for them. Scared someone else might get hurt.'

'I think you may be overreacting, just a little, don't you?'

'Maybe. I don't know.' She drew in a deep, quavering breath and thought of all the friends and the family who would come running to be with her. She only had to call them. She was lucky, Naomi thought and Gregory was right. She should be back there, just a phone call and a few minutes' drive away from those she loved and who loved her. What the hell were they doing, chasing around the country like a couple of sixties hippies, trying to find themselves?

'In the morning,' she said. 'I'll call Sam in the morning. Like you said before, it's a filthy wet night and it's a long drive. I don't want anyone rushing down here and risking an accident.'

'OK, if that's what you want.' Barnes's phone rang. He listened and then hung up. 'Naomi—'

'You have to go.'

'No, I don't have to. I can stay if you need me. The CSIs at the crash site have found something. They want me out there, but—'

'Go. Please. See what they've found. I'll be fine.'

'I'll get someone to come out to you. You'll be on your own for maybe an hour, I promise no more than that.'

'I'm fine. Wish I had Napoleon here though.'

'You want me to fetch him? They allow guide dogs here.'

'No,' she shook her head. 'Please, I'll be fine. Go and do your job.' She managed a smile. 'I know how this feels, remember. I hated the hospital shifts, the sitting around knowing there was nothing you could do or say that made it better and that feeling you could do so much more if you could just get out there.'

He leaned over and clasped her hands, 'I'll get someone out to you as soon as I can,' he said. She heard him talking, presumably to the woman at reception, and then his footsteps receding.

I know what it's like, she thought. Just sitting, just being there, feeling you are no damn use at all and it occurred to her, as she heard the door swing closed and she was left alone, that perhaps just being there had been the most valuable thing of all.

The rain hadn't eased since the accident. The ambulance crew and paramedics, the police officers, even the CSI themselves had churned up the sodden ground and reduced the grass on the steep bank to a mudslide. Barnes followed the designated path down, picking his way as carefully as he could, nearly ending up on his backside more than once. They'd had to stretcher the injured up this slope, he thought, the narrow valley into which the car had tumbled being far too narrow for the air ambulance to have landed, even if the weather had been clear enough to allow an approach.

It was fully dark now, the scene lit by powerful lamps that seemed only to illuminate the rain. A shelter had been thrown up over the car; it clung on to the slope, skewed at a precarious angle and the rain poured down from the road above and turned even the semi-protected scene to bog. One white clad figure knelt in the quagmire, another took photographs, a third had set up some kind of makeshift table and was attempting to protect its finds from the worst of the rain by rigging a plastic sheet over a box turned on its side.

'What do you have?' Barnes asked.

'We're trying to make sense of things *in situ*. Every time we move we're destroying evidence and if we try and move the car we'll just be mangling even more. But I've managed to get this off.'

'What is it?'

'Servo unit from the ABS. It's a vacuum pump. Essentially it's what makes the solenoid work that makes the ABS system apply the brakes in little pulses, rather than slamming them on, you know?'

Barnes nodded. He had a rough idea of how ABS brakes worked.

'OK, I'm not going to get too technical, but this one's been tampered with. A small hole has been made, weakening the servo unit, preventing the vacuum from operating properly.'

'Which means?'

'Well, I'm guessing here until we can test things properly, but he'd have still had brakes when he set out. Slowly, over the course of the journey, they'd have become less effective until eventually all he'd have had was the little bit of residual you get via the fluid left in the pipes. He seems to have tried to save the situation by using engine braking. Taking it out of gear and cutting the engine. And he applied the handbrake, but all that was probably too late. He hit the barrier right at the end, spun and tumbled down the slope, so far as we can tell.'

'Any idea how fast he was going?'

The CSI shook her head. 'No skid marks that we can make out. We'll see what's left after the rain. On a straight bit of road, he might have got away with it. The witness in the car behind says he was already into the bend—'

'But, from what you've said, there was no way of ensuring this was where the accident would happen.'

'No, but have you driven this road?'

'Not until tonight.' Barnes thought about the route he had taken. The road transected two valleys, taking the high ground. There were speed limits and cameras all along it, sweeping bends and tight, unexpected zig zags like this. He nodded, taking the point.

'No possibility that the hole was made during the crash?'

She shook her head. 'I'm pretty certain not. Someone made this happen. It's clever and simple and not foolproof. He might have pulled over earlier and called a mechanic when he felt something was not right, but most wouldn't, most people don't. They hang on, hoping it'll be OK. Human nature, I suppose. I'm guessing the brakes would just have felt a bit off, at first, and on a wet road he might have just thought it was, well, weather and stuff.'

Barnes nodded, knowing he would probably have done the same. Alec would have wanted to get back to Naomi. He would have taken a chance. Barnes hoped fervently he'd not taken too much of one.

Naomi listened to the ticking of the clock. It was just a quartz movement, she decided, the sound made by the hands shifting across its face. She held her third cup of unwanted coffee, sipping it at least gave her something to do and holding the cup at least stopped her hands from shaking.

People passed her. Voices regularly asked if she was OK, if she wanted anything. No one could tell her anything, no one wanted to commit. She'd been asked about Molly's next of kin; she'd not thought about it before, but assumed that Alec was probably it.

Someone had said that Molly and Alec would need things from home. Nightclothes, toiletries. Naomi knew this was just an attempt to make things sound normal and hopeful, but she clung to the idea. Tried to work out who she could send to Molly's house. Wondered who might have a spare key.

She should call Alec's parents again. They'd promised to come as quickly as possible, his mother distraught and horrified, but still concerned and even more horrified that Naomi was alone. But they were miles away. Maybe a four-hour drive. She wondered if she was putting them in danger by bringing them here but knew they would never forgive her if she'd not told them what had happened and then Alec—

She refused even to think about it; truth was she could think about nothing else.

Footsteps again, this time two pairs. One slow and measured and the other swift and light.

'Naomi! Oh my God, this is terrible.'

Someone sat down in the chair next to her and Naomi found herself swept into the woman's arms. It took a moment for her to realize that it was Liz.

'Gregory called me, said you were alone, said you might need a friend. So he brought me over.'

Gregory? 'Gregory's here?'

'I'm here. Don't worry, everything's under control. I just wanted to make sure Liz found you and see if there was anything you needed.'

'Thank you,' she said. Suddenly overwhelmed by it all. Mostly by relief that she was not alone. But maybe Liz shouldn't be here, either. Maybe . . .

Gregory seemed to sense her anxiety. 'It's all right,' he said. 'Nothing more is going to happen, it's going to stop, right here and now.'

She could feel Liz's curiosity, sense the frisson of excitement.

'Where's the inspector?' Gregory asked.

'Had to go. He's gone to the crash site. I told him I'd be all right. Someone's supposed to be coming, but—'

'Well you don't need them, now. I'm here,' Liz told her. 'I'm going nowhere.'

'Any news?'

Naomi shook her head. 'Not really. They've stopped the bleeding but Alec's still in surgery. Molly's showed signs of waking up, but that's all.'

'And that's all good,' Liz told her. Naomi nodded and tried to believe it was.

'The nurses said they'll need stuff. They'll be in here for a while. I know it's not immediate, but, I'm not sure what to do.'

'Let me,' Gregory said unexpectedly. 'I can go to Molly's place, bring back what she needs.'

Naomi frowned. 'I'm not sure I'd feel right—' she began.

'No, I mean, I don't think I'd want a strange man going through my underwear drawers,' Liz agreed, though Naomi got the distinct impression she might make an exception for Gregory.

'Naomi.' Gregory's voice was gently insistent. 'There may be other things that Molly needs taken care of, other than just fetching her toothbrush and dressing gown. I think we should make sure, don't you?'

Taken aback, Naomi found herself nodding. What other things? What did Molly have there that shouldn't be? Naomi wasn't sure she wanted to know. But Gregory was right, probably.

'I don't know if the house is alarmed and I don't know about keys or anything.'

'Don't worry. I think I can manage all of that,' he said. 'Now, what sort of things is Molly going to need?'

Liz took over, making him a list and Naomi was oddly relieved to be able to focus momentarily on the purely practical. Gregory left, taking Liz's list.

'Man of mystery,' Liz said. 'Where did you meet him, anyway?'

Naomi thought about it for a moment and managed a slight laugh. 'On a beach in Wales,' she said. 'But believe me, it wasn't nearly as romantic as it sounds.'

Word had spread. Soon everyone that mattered was in the loop. Nathan had sent a message to Adam, hoping he would respond; figuring he probably would. And to Annie, telling her that the time to act was now. Annie had been in touch with Tariq, only to find that he'd set his own wheels in motion. Clay, it seemed was already ahead of the game. Annie just hoped he'd be assured enough not to notice as they trailed behind.

She was about to leave when Bob came down the stairs. It was just after midnight.

'Annie?'

'I left you a note. I have to leave for a day or so.'

'A day or so. Annie, I thought. I hoped.'

She dropped her bag and came over to him, held him tight. 'I *will* be back for the opening night,' she said. 'I've not missed one yet.'

'And where are you going? I know I promised not to ask, but. Annie.'

'Listen, there are so many things you don't know. So many things I don't want you to know, but you've got to trust me this one last time. I'll be back for the exhibition and I'll wear my posh frock.' She smiled. 'I wouldn't miss it, Bob, and I'll tell you something else. This will be the last time I go. I promise that. I won't have to leave ever again after this.'

'Annie?'

'What?'

'Don't make promises you can't keep.'

She stood on tiptoe to kiss his cheek. 'I never have,' she said. 'And I promise, I never will.'

Adam was in a quandary. Finally he spoke to Nathan and then made up his mind. This was it, then; either they worked together and eliminated their collective past, or it reached out and destroyed them. There was nothing more to be said.

He drove home, collected a few things he wanted, then drove out to the shop and spent a half-hour putting together a kit he thought might be useful. After that, he called Billie.

'Billie, love, do me a favour and take yourself on holiday for a few days. Don't tell me where, just go.'

'Adam? I don't think I understand.'

'I think you do. Please, Billie. I don't have time to explain just now. Just go.'

She was silent for a moment and he thought she might be about to argue. 'The last time you told me to leave, was in Beirut in '87,' she said.

'I know. I remember. I'll see you soon, Billie. If you need cash, use the business Visa.'

He rang off. Beirut in 1987. The Druze militia had moved back into the city, and another round of bombings and kidnappings led to a final evacuation on non-essential personnel. Billie had stayed, right up until that moment when Adam knew he was to be reassigned. She had stayed for him.

He put the thought aside, knowing her well enough to trust that she would go, tonight, that she would hide herself away and all would be well.

If they did not succeed now, then none of it mattered anyway.

Gregory had no trouble with Molly's house. He moved slowly through the rooms, closing curtains and putting on only the smallest lights. He knew from experience that people took little notice of closed curtains and normal lights whereas shining a flashlight would always attract attention. The high hedges surrounding Molly's home also added security and he was not worried about being disturbed.

He stood on the landing and examined the floor and Molly's attempts to scrub and sand the floorboards. She'd made a right pig's ear of it, Gregory thought. He moved through into the front bedroom, obviously hers. A dressing gown hung behind the door and a blue nightdress lay on the pillow. He folded both and lay them on the bed, finding a pair of slippers tucked beneath the beside cabinet. Bending to pick them up, Gregory glanced beneath the bed. He reached under it and dragged Molly's travelling box out. It was an old tin box, Victorian probably, the sort of thing that would have contained all the worldly goods of some poor sod, back then, Gregory thought.

Not that he owned so very much more now.

He opened it, riffled carefully through the letters and photographs and cards she kept inside and he realized at once that he'd struck gold. Pictures of Molly and Edward and Clay, others too. Of his friend, Arthur Fields. Notebooks and memoranda, memos that by rights Molly should never have had, all layered with dance invitations and menus from Ambassadorial dinners, postcards and little notes from Edward that Gregory quickly set aside.

Some things were too obviously personal and did not need his great paws laid on them.

'Oh, Molly,' he said. 'You are one dangerous lady. But how did you dispose of Clay's boy, I wonder?'

He stood, looked back towards the landing. Molly would have had so very little time. Whatever she did, it had to be quick, easily accessible. He fumbled through the bedside table, found nothing but hand cream and tissues, a pen, notepad and a paperback book. Nothing beneath the pillow. Would she have kept whatever weapon she had used? Probably not. Molly was a professional after all. Yes, he argued with himself, but she's not going to find it easy to replace anything is she? The house had not been searched, would she willingly cast a weapon aside?

He looked again at the drawer and took out the pen, unscrewed the cap. Had his answer.

'Clever girl, Molly.' Gregory smiled.

A half-hour later, the house searched and a little hoard of finds stowed in the tin box, Gregory left the house with it and a bag containing the things on the list. He stowed the box in the boot of his car and drove back to the hospital. He arrived to the news that Molly was awake and Liz and Naomi were with her.

'She's tougher than she looks,' the nurse told him. 'Are you family?'

'A nephew,' Gregory told her, figuring if Alec could be an honorary family member, so could he. 'And yes, she most definitely is.'

Annie collected Tariq from a motorway services. He sat looking out of the window, drinking coffee. And looking thoroughly miserable. Annie's heart went out to him. Tariq was, in her opinion, a pure academic. He should have been ensconced in some safe research post somewhere, with nothing more challenging going on than a little professional jealousy, not stuck out on a limb like this.

She slid into the seat opposite. 'You OK?'

He nodded.

'Your dad all right?'

He nodded again. 'Upset, though. We all thought we'd stopped running a long time ago, didn't we?'

'Hopefully we have. Tariq, we'll get through this. We've just got to pull together.'

'I don't know what I can do. I'm just a geek.'

'There's no just about it. You can do what we can't. Tariq, have you heard of a man called Adam Carmodie?'

Tariq frowned, then nodded. Annie could almost see him accessing the memory. 'He worked with Clay in the Congo and in Bosnia, and Venezuela. He was a communications expert, electronics and surveillance, that sort of thing. What about him?'

'Think you and he can pool resources? I know it's a big ask, but you and Adam both have skills we need right now.'

Tariq hesitated and then nodded. 'You know we can't break into Clay's computer from the outside, don't you? We have to go in there. He'll have things in his private files that aren't on any server. He doesn't like to share. Not Clay.'

'I know,' Annie said. 'And I know we won't have much time. Tariq, are you all right with this? If we get you and Adam inside, can you take it from there?'

'Inside his house? Annie, I—'

'I'm scared too,' she said.

'You? You're scared of nothing.'

'I'm scared of not going home to my husband. I'm scared of not keeping a promise to him. I'm scared of a lot of things, Tariq. I always have been. I'm not so different.'

He stared at her and then nodded briefly. 'I worshipped him, you know that? We'd be dead if it wasn't for him. I feel like I'm a traitor. Like I'm—'

'I know,' Annie said 'But Tariq, he—'

'He killed my friend, or had him killed. Herbert didn't do anything to deserve that. He was just . . . he just . . . he . . .'

'He knew too much, Tariq. We all know too much and Clay isn't Clay any more. I'm not sure he ever was.'

Gregory had asked for a moment alone with Molly, and Liz had taken Naomi to get yet more coffee. 'Five minutes,' the nurse told him, 'and definitely no more.'

He wouldn't need any more, Gregory thought. He sat down in the seat Naomi had vacated and Molly turned her head painfully to look at him.

'She says you are a friend.'

'I try to be. I went to your house, Molly. I think I found everything, your box, the zip guns. The Taser. Molly, what do you want with a Taser?'

She almost laughed, but it was too painful. 'Edward thought it was a good idea,' she said. 'We can't keep guns in this blasted country. I've never been without a weapon. I felt naked.'

'Molly, I found three of the damn zip guns in your house. I don't know where you got them from, but they're beautifully made. Especially the pen. I can understand why you didn't get rid of it afterwards.'

'Single shot,' she said. 'I've never needed more than one. You need to take more than one shot you should find another occupation.'

Gregory chuckled softly. 'Clay underestimated you, didn't he?'

'Bloody did too.' She closed her eyes and looked set to drift off to sleep.

'Molly, I think I know what you did. Indulge me, stay awake long enough to tell me I'm right.'

She sighed. 'I almost died today,' she said. 'I want to sleep now.'

'Sleep can wait. I'm curious.'

'You're a pain in the nethers.' She shifted uncomfortably and then opened her eyes again. 'He almost killed Alec,' she said. 'He might not make it.'

'He'll pull though. I'm sure he will. And Clay will pay. I promise you.'

She studied him coldly for a moment. Then she said, 'Edward had them made for me. The pen, the cigarette lighter and the walking cane. It amused him, I think, but they had a practical use too for those times when we couldn't easily defend ourselves. The pen sat in the drawer beside my bed for years. Whichever bed I slept in. I never thought I'd use it. Then he came to my house. I recognized the tattoo on his arm and I recognized that blasted gun, a Soviet SP-3. And I knew *him* too. It shocked me a bit that Clay should send family after me but that was Clay all over. Thought it would shake me, I suppose.'

'It did, briefly, I'm guessing,' Gregory said.

'I knew there would be only seconds. I heard him come up the stairs. I took the chance that the woman taking my call would only hear the one shot. I dropped the phone and kicked it under the bed and I fired. I didn't know if it would kill him, but it didn't have to . . . I just needed a moment more. I shot upward. Up beneath the chin, through the soft palate, into the brain. I took his gun and I finished him. I used a pillow to muffle what little sound there was and I screamed like hell. I hoped the only shot they heard would be mine. You know the SP-3 it makes so little sound. Just the click of the firing pin.'

'Internally suppressed,' Gregory nodded. 'I've never owned one. Rare as rocking horse . . . as hen's teeth.'

'I did the best I could, under the circumstances, but I'd rather Alec didn't know.'

Gregory smiled. She was proud of what she'd done, he thought. It must have irked, on some level, not to be able to tell anyone, until now. 'You did a good job,' he said.

'My box. Did you find my box? It's under the bed.'

'I have it and I'll keep it safe, until you're home.'

The nurse came back into the room, indicating time and Gregory nodded.

'You rest up. I'm sure everything will be all right.'

Molly had already closed her eyes.

Gregory returned to the corridor. Liz and Naomi were talking to a doctor. Gregory stood a little apart until he had gone. He could see from Naomi's face that the news was good.

'He's out of surgery and Naomi can go and visit in about a half-hour, when they've got him settled,' Liz said. She beamed at Gregory. 'That's good news, isn't it?'

'Very good,' Gregory said. 'Naomi, I have to go now. You'll be all right?'

'I'll be staying,' Liz told him.

'I'll be fine. Thank you for all you've done. Alec's parents will be here in a couple of hours. Liz has booked them into the hotel for me.'

She looked so much well, he thought.

'And Gregory? When he's well, we're going to go back home. Find a place and just settle again.'

'Good,' he said. 'I'm pleased.'

He was aware of Liz's gaze on his back as he left.

THIRTY-SEVEN

The clock in the hall struck four. Tariq wasn't exactly sure what hall it was in, what house. It didn't seem to belong to any of the people present, but they all seemed very familiar with the place.

Annie was drawing sketch maps. Plans of the house in which Clay now lived.

Nathan outlining the security, the alarms, who might be there. Adam, the man asking the most questions. Running through radio protocol, mainly, Tariq knew, for his benefit.

Another man had arrived a few minutes before. He'd been introduced as Gregory. He now stood in the doorway, a steaming mug of tea in a very large fist. Tariq knew he had seen the man somewhere else. Or his picture at least. Probably in a security file.

The memory would solidify if he left it alone, so for now, he left it alone.

'We'll be on a very tight schedule,' Nathan said. 'Once we're in the house we'll have maybe seven minutes before the police arrive. There's a direct alarm, if any of the security is breached.'

'Seven minutes?' Tariq was horrified. 'I can't do anything in seven minutes.'

'We can do plenty in seven minutes,' Adam Carmodie said. 'Actually, it'll be closer to four, we need time to get out.'

'What!'

'Tariq, what we'll be doing is harm minimization, We take the hard drives, any backups we can find, any files, hard copies. The aim is to get as much clear as we can. That's our part in this. We can find out what we have later on, but Clay is a magpie. He'll have kept anything he ever had that might have been of value. We just have to make sure we get as much as possible.'

'There's a safe,' Nathan said. 'I've never seen anything in it apart from money, deeds to the house, that sort of thing. I don't think we can count on getting into that, not in the time we have.'

'You don't have any idea about the combination?' Adam asked.

'Electronic, changed at random intervals.'

Adam nodded. 'I've got equipment that could do it, but you're right about the time.'

'How many in the house?' Gregory asked.

'Could be four, could be more. Could be just Clay. The dogs will be there, but Clay is unpredictable, that's the thing. Annie and I, we come and go pretty much as we please, but he'll be on his guard. He may well not trust even us.'

'But he'll still let you in,' Gregory said. 'If only out of curiosity.'

Nathan nodded slowly. 'It could buy us more time,' he said.

'Dogs?' Tariq said. 'I'm not good with—'

'Pets.' Annie assured him. 'Two great lumps of Irish wolfhound. Soft as tripe.'

'He'll be wondering why you left your husband,' Gregory said to Annie. 'Nathan's watchers won't be the only ones around I don't reckon.'

He saw the look of panic cross Annie's face. Nathan took hold of her arms and turned her towards him. 'I've got men on the ground, Annie, enough to take care of him. I promise you.' He cast a look in Gregory's direction that was at once thoughtful and reproving.

'But Gregory is right. We walk up to the front door, just like normal. Once inside we assess the risk and Tariq and Adam make their way round to the rear. We'll get you in, one way or another right.'

'It's a little *ad hoc*,' Adam objected.

'And I think it'll have to be,' Nathan said. 'Adam, I don't like flying blind any more than you do, but sometimes you just have to improvise.

'We walk in through the front door. Maybe we owe him that.'

THIRTY-EIGHT

'Tell me about the boy who went to Molly's,' Gregory said. 'Who he was.'

Nathan shrugged. They were, for the moment, in the lead car; Adam, Annie and Tariq followed on behind.

'His name was Pavel,' Nathan said. 'At least, that was what we knew him by. He was seventeen when Clay brought him into the country. He was mad as hell, belligerent; everyone was the enemy.'

'His family?'

Nathan shrugged. 'His mother was dead. Annie and I, well we always figured he looked like Clay.'

'He sent his son after Molly?'

'I don't know for sure. Look, the thing you have to understand is that Clay took care of us all, trained us, taught us what to do and how to do it. Made sure we could live *in* society as well as outside it. He wanted us to blend, because being invisible was how we could be most useful. Pavel could never blend. It was beyond him.

'If Clay had brought him in before, when he was younger, he might have settled. But it's hard once you get them past a certain age. Everything gets frozen in place, somehow.'

'You sound like an authority,' Gregory commented. 'And very old.'

Nathan laughed at that. 'I feel very old,' he said.

Equipped with radios, courtesy of Adam, with radio monitoring equipment, RF jammers, all from the same source, they moved forward, Tariq and Adam now on foot, Nathan and Annie pulled in at the side of the road, now both in the first car. Gregory was to be rear guard, following in the second car when they moved forward, but remaining on the road.

'A one-man army,' Gregory joked.

It was still early, not much after dawn and the air was chill. Autumn was about to take hold, Adam thought. He led Tariq through the woods that backed the house. The grounds were high-walled

with cameras at intervals. Nathan had told them there was a central
control room, but also feeds to study and several other rooms. The
camera positions alternated, one pointed into the grounds, the next
out into the woods. All could be repositioned from the control room
inside. They approached the wall between two camera positions,
blindsiding the outward facing one. Adam was monitoring any radio
traffic that might be coming from the house, but there was nothing.
He had equipment with him that could have knocked out the cameras
and the control room equipment. A simple EM pulse generator,
crude, but powerful. It would knock out their radios as well, of
course, and could not be guaranteed to put paid to the alarm. Nathan
hadn't known if it was a make or break circuit, but logic dictated
it would probably be the latter. Any break in the system would
trigger a remote sensor and sound the alarm; it would not need the
intervention of anyone in the house. Shutting down the system with
the EM pulse would trigger that as effectively as cutting wires.

'You any good at climbing trees?' Adam asked Tariq. 'I'd like
to get a look over that wall without getting too close.'

'You do realize I'm physically inept,' Tariq reminded him. He
shrugged. 'I'll give it a go. Which tree do you have in mind?'

'Try that one. It should give you a clear view, and the foliage
should give you cover, if there's anyone looking out from the house.'

He gave Tariq a leg up to the first branch and then watched
anxiously as the younger man hauled and puffed his way into the
higher branches.

'Did you never climb trees when you were a kid?'

'I climbed on the climbing frame in the park. Where I lived there
weren't that many trees to climb.'

Adam nodded. Fair point, he supposed. 'Can you see anything
yet?'

'I need to be just a little higher.'

Adam's radio crackled. Nathan telling him that they were moving
forward.

Adam acknowledged. 'We're in position. I've got Tariq up a tree
so we can get the lie of the land.'

As Nathan responded, he heard Annie giggle.

'See anything?'

'Yes. But I can't quite . . . Adam, Annie said there were dogs.
Irish wolfhounds, right?'

'Yes, but she also said they wouldn't bother us too much.'

'Well this one won't. Adam, we've got a dead dog. Looks to me like someone blew its head half off.'

'You sure.'

'Of course I'm sure. It's dead and it's very bloody. Lying halfway between the wall and the house.'

'Come down,' Adam snapped. He got back on the radio. 'Something's wrong,' he said. 'Nathan, don't go inside.'

'I hear you,' Nathan said.

Tariq dropped down from the tree, his descent faster and even less elegant than the climb had been.

'What now?' he asked.

'We get the hell out of here, regroup and then figure out what to do next,' Adam said.

Together, they began to move back towards the road, less cautious now. Whatever was going on, Adam thought, keeping out of sight wasn't going to make a hell of a lot of difference.

'What?'

Tariq didn't get to finish the question. There was a flash. The ground beneath their feet shook and grumbled and then the roar exploded outward from the house behind the wall. Tariq didn't need telling to hit the ground. He dived and Adam followed him, waiting for the sound to stop and the shaking to cease.

'Nathan and Annie,' Tariq whispered.

THIRTY-NINE

For Bud, the past few days had been routine but not unpleasant. He liked being out of doors and Bob was an easy enough target to watch. It helped that Annie was in the house and that Bud knew there were three other watchers in the hills surrounding what had once been a small farm.

At night, he had kept watch using state-of-the-art night vision goggles that Nathan had provided. By day, Bob's routine was utterly predictable, walking the dogs, painting, the trip to the village. Annie accompanied her husband then and Bud had taken the opportunity to sleep for a couple of hours.

Since the night before, though, the mood had changed. Bud had been told to check in with Nathan every hour. Annie had left just past midnight and, though Bud didn't know what was going on, Nathan's increased state of anxiety had transmitted to Bud and he was now on full alert.

It was still very early. Dawn mist had begun to lift from the valley, but Bud knew it would be mid-morning before it completely burned away. He could fully understand why an artist would live in this place, in the rather plain, some would say ugly, whitewashed house, with it's funny little windows, none of which matched. It was a fabulous, almost mysterious location, tucked away, surrounded by trees and hills.

And it was a sod to defend, Bud added to himself.

Bob's studio was a large conservatory tagged on to and running the full length of the back of the house. It wasn't the prettiest of buildings, pent roof, UPVC, but it did the job, Bud supposed. He could see Bob working there, could see the work too, looking through his field glasses. It was all a bit mystical for Bud's taste, but each to his own. At least you could tell what it was.

Bob had walked the dogs at first light. Bud could tell there was something wrong with him just from the set of his shoulders and the fact he cut his walk short. He figured it was because Annie had gone. It must be nice, Bud thought, to love someone that much, though he supposed it hurt too and Bud wasn't too keen on emotional pain.

Bob was now in his studio, sifting through canvases, reinforcing the corners with card and wrapping them ready for transport to the gallery. He worked at a large table, laying stuff out carefully and methodically, but Bud, having watched the artist for a few days now, could see that he was distracted.

The car, a blue saloon, pulled into the drive and parked up. Bud watched, frowning. Usually visitors to the house drove right along the track and up to the front door. Bud would lose sight of them at the front of the house. A man got out and Bud studied him through the field glasses. The collar of his coat was turned up and Bud could not get a decent view. Alarm bells began to ring. Moving slowly, keeping the stranger in sight, Bud began to move off the hill.

Bob Taylor continued to work in his studio. Moments later, Bud saw him look up. The door to the conservatory opened. The man came through.

Bob turned and Bud, halfway down the hill, froze.

'Fuck and shit and buggery!' The stranger had a gun and it was pointed straight at the man Bud was supposed to protect.

A small sound caused Bob to look up from his work. Just for a moment he was hopeful. 'Annie?'

The door opened and the figure standing there was definitely not his wife.

'I've come to tell you something,' Clay said. 'It's about your wife. About someone needing to make funeral arrangements.'

'Annie,' Bob whispered. 'What the hell do you mean?'

'I mean, she's dead.'

Bob was numbed, utterly. So much so that he almost forgot about the gun this man who had invaded his home was pointing at him. He dropped down into the nearest chair, utterly stunned.

'I thought you might like to join her,' Clay said. He raised the gun, pointed it straight at Bob Taylor's head.

FORTY

From the road, Gregory had heard the blast, felt the ground shake him almost off his feet. A moment later and he was back in the car and heading up the drive. He could see the smoke rising from what was left of the house, debris still falling. Nathan's car standing in the middle of the drive, debris from the explosion all but covering it.

He skidded to a halt and saw, to his relief, Nathan and Annie emerge from what passed for cover behind the vehicle. Gregory glanced back as footsteps thundered on the gravel. Adam and Tariq running towards them.

'What the hell happened?' Gregory demanded.

'He wired the whole damned house,' Nathan said.

'Something's wrong,' Adam said. 'Nathan, don't go inside.'

'I hear you.' He looked at Annie and motioned her back behind the car, then picked up a stone and hurled it through the nearest window.

The flash, the noise. Nathan had already hurled himself behind

the car, crouched with Annie, clinging tight as the entire world
seemed to go up in smoke.

FORTY-ONE

B ud had no time to think, no time to contact Nathan, no time
for anything but to take the shot.

He saw Bob look up directly into the muzzle of the gun.
He saw the finger tighten on the trigger, he saw the burst of skull
and brain and blood and the man fall.

Bob was on his feet, staring in disbelief, first at the dead man
and then at the broken glass shattered on the floor. Then at Bud,
the man standing in his garden with yet another weapon.

Bud lowered his rifle, lying it on the ground and raising his hands.

'It's OK,' he shouted, 'I'm one of the good guys. It's all going
to be OK.'

Bob crossed to the broken window and stared out at Bud.

'He told me Annie had died. Annie!'

'Let me come in,' Bud said quietly. 'Let me make you some tea
and I'll get hold of Nathan and we'll clear up the mess. He'll know
all about Annie. You going to let me come inside?'

Bob nodded, dumbly. His face was white, Bud noted, even his
lips were blue.

'Sit down before you fall down,' Bud said. He made his way
round to the front of the house and went inside. Nathan responded
to his call a few moments later.

'I've just shot someone at Annie's place,' Bud said. 'There's a
bit of a mess. Just tell me she's all right? I've got a man here falling
to bits, thinking she's gone.'

FORTY-TWO

Alec opened his eyes. He still wasn't with it, Naomi realized, but the doctors said the prognosis was good. His parents had arrived and Liz had eventually gone. Naomi was deeply grateful to this woman she barely knew. There had been no word from Gregory, but she'd expected none.

'That friend of yours,' Molly said when Naomi, trying to divide herself between the two patients, sat beside her bed, 'he said he had my box. That he was looking after it.'

'Then he is,' Naomi said. She really couldn't raise the energy to ask, 'What box?' Naomi felt she didn't care any more.

Briefly, she sat down in the day room while the doctors fussed around Alec. She had relinquished her position to Alec's mother, figuring that a sighted woman would be able to make a better assessment of the professionals as they did whatever it was they had to do.

'You should go and get some sleep,' Alec's father said. He sat down beside her. 'You look all in.'

'I couldn't sleep yet. I'm just not ready, if you know what I mean.'

'I know what you mean. News is on, shall I turn it up?'

She nodded, willing to be distracted.

'An explosion at a house in Northamptonshire is believed to have been caused by a gas leak,' the announcer intoned.

'Bloody big house,' Alec's father commented. 'Bloody big explosion. The whole gas main go up?'

'There have been a number of dawn raids by police in three counties. It is understood that one home in London and two in the Midlands were targeted. Police say this is part of their ongoing anti-terrorist campaign. One business premises specializing in electronics was also searched. No arrests have been made.'

'In other news—'

Naomi tuned out. She closed her eyes, wondering what was going on with Gregory.

'At least have a nap in the chair; we'll hold the fort.'

She nodded, suddenly overwhelmed by exhaustion. Almost asleep, she did not hear her father-in-law leave, or someone else come in through the door. Gregory stood for a moment, wondering if he should wake her. Decided he should.

'Naomi?'

She dragged her mind back to full consciousness. 'Gregory. You're here.'

'I won't stay long. I understand he's going to be all right.'

Naomi nodded, tears beginning to fall again. 'I'm sorry,' she said.

'For what? Being able to grieve is part of what makes us human.'

'Is it? What's happening, Gregory?'

'News, in brief,' Gregory said. 'Clay is dead. Not quite in the way I expected him to be, but dead, nonetheless. Molly's box is at the hotel. I left it with the receptionist, she said she'd put it in your room.'

'Is it over?'

'Mostly. Clay is still reaching out in a way, even though he's now dead. You heard the news? Well, he's set the police on Adam Carmodie and a couple of others he had a grudge against. Adam will have some questions to answer, and so will others, but we can sort it out. A minor inconvenience.'

'Are you sure?'

Gregory laughed. 'Oh yes. We've got enough material to be able to blacken Clay's name, make any decision he made seem suspect. Thanks to Joseph Bern and our friend Molly. It'll all come out in the wash, as they say.'

'I'm glad. And you?'

'Have things to do. I'll come and say hello when you're settled again. That's if I'm welcome.'

'You're welcome,' Naomi said. 'Always will be.'

She heard him leave and then a nurse returning. 'He's asking for you,' she said. 'Here, take my arm.'

EPILOGUE

*B*ob Taylor has long defied categorization. His detractors may speak of him as a mere illustrator, or a fantasy artist, while others speak of him in the same breath as the Brotherhood of Ruralists, but Bob himself declares that he never set out to be categorized.

Figures run through the Birchwood. Men and women and wolves, chasing and playing as though involved in some bizarre game of hide and seek. For all the movement in the figures, there is a sense of the scene being frozen. A single moment, captured and held. Deliberately so. It is a Bob Taylor trademark, this quality of stillness, like a slice through time.

Annie looked up at him. 'Good review, Bob. Another one. You must be really pleased.'

He nodded. 'I'm trying to be,' he said. 'Annie, I'm just feeling a bit overwhelmed right now.'

She reached across the table. 'I know you are,' she said. 'But it's all right. It's all going to be fine.'

He smiled across at her. 'You looked lovely in your posh frock,' he said. 'There are more pictures of you than there are of me. *Wife and photographer, Annie Raven,*' he quoted.

Annie laughed. 'Well that's my cover blown,' she said. She saw the shadow cross her husband's face, but Annie knew she couldn't let him retreat from this. He had to face it head on. If he didn't it would haunt his work and seep into his dreams and destroy the man she had fallen in love with.

'You're alive,' she said. 'So am I. We can figure the rest out as we go along.'

It was three weeks before Alec and Naomi travelled north again. A friend came to collect them and Sam, Naomi's sister, drove their car back. It was three weeks too, before Tariq returned to work. Tom brought him a mug of his awful tea.

'Thought we'd seen the last of you. Glad you're back. Who'd have thought it though. Old Gustav Clay?'

Anyone who knew him, Tariq thought.

Three weeks before Carmodie electronics reopened its doors, Billie piled the stack of new catalogue requests on to Adam's desk.

'Our little hiatus has led to a backlog,' she said. 'It's not done us any lasting harm, that's for sure.'

'That's good,' Adam said. 'Billie, I've got something to ask you before we make a start. Billie, how about the two of us get married. Like we should have done back in Beirut?'

Billie grinned at him. 'Thought you'd never ask,' she said.